THE TAPE

Also by Marilyn Dungan

SNAKEBIRD

THE TAPE

Marilyn Dungan

Arcane Books
Paris, Kentucky

Published by Arcane Books
P.O. Box 5102
Paris, Kentucky 40362

ISBN 0-9666478-6-6

Library of Congress Catalog Card Number 99-94562

First Edition 2000

Printed in the United States of America

For Julie, Hardy & Kenny

Acknowledgments

Many people helped in some way in the writing of this novel. But no matter how small the contribution—perhaps a bit of conversation that I scribbled on a scrap of paper or just a gesture or smile that caught my eye—most observations played a part in the writing of *The Tape*.

However, a number of people deserve special thanks; to John King for his tireless copy-editing and Patty Adams for her swift and knowledgeable desk-top publishing services.

Thanks to Deputy Sheriff Kay Fryman of the Bourbon County Sheriff's Department for information about police procedure and to Attorney Jimmy Brannon for interpreting several of the *Kentucky State Statutes*.

My appreciation to Hardy Dungan, D.V.M., for once more allowing his mom to badger him about veterinary procedures.

I'll be forever grateful to Linda Hertz for again creating an exceptional cover design. Thank you, Doris Hamilton, for sharing your knowledge of Scottish customs. I am fortunate to have such remarkable sisters.

For the rest of my family and dear friends who continue to prod and encourage me along this uncertain road, my unending gratitude.

Prologue

Peter jiggled the key until it caught and slipped to the right. Hearing the familiar soft click, he shouldered the swollen cabin door and it rasped open for the final time. He dropped his duffel bag and slapped the wall switch, wincing as the glare of an octave of bulbs on the wagon wheel chandelier shot through his eyes. Shrugging off his London Fog, Peter hung it in the recessed cubicle beside the door, adjusting the padded shoulders to the wooden coat hanger.

In the horse hame mirror to his right, bulbous eyes stared back at him through bubble-wrap spectacles. He grimaced and twitched away. Never again would he have to view his pale, slight body. Enough, that for a bit longer he must feel its tight musculature, his stiff neck and face, his pursed lips frozen in a sour pucker. His fingers curried his clipped brown hair that molded his skull with precision cutouts for ears. He cleared his throat.

Lifting his bag, Peter crossed to the knotty pine bookcase that covered the north wall of the log room. The state-of-the-art high-fidelity system filled four shelves of the unit.

"Ah, yes," he said, as he ran his hand over the components. Ever since his father had introduced him to electronics when he was a teen, he had always owned the best. An unaccustomed quietude and pride suffused his body. He punched the power button on the control panel and unzipped the navy canvas bag. Retrieving the audio tape, he inserted it into the cassette player.

Instantly, the sounds filled the room. So familiar now. The confusion. The cries. His own voice protesting. He knew every inflection by heart.

Reaching again into the bag, he extracted the coil of rope. He threw it high and it swooped cleanly over a crosspiece rafter in the ceiling.

Meticulously, Peter's slender fingers formed a slipknot and his delicate white hands drew it snug against the timber. A fitting gallows, he thought. Here it began. Appropriate that here it would end. The injustice. The guilt. "Time for punishment," he sighed wearily, his shaky exhale deep and despairing.

Stumbling to the oaken desk with scars of a hundred years, he peered over its marred surface and through the frosted window. The leaden sky discharged a flutter of snowflakes that whirled and settled on his black BMW in the driveway. He visualized the blacktop drive writhing away between hemlocks that choked the cabin. In his mind, he saw it buckling and looping its way for half a mile through the forest of evergreens.

Sitting on the edge of the ladder-back desk chair, he withdrew a pen and a sheet of stationery from the center drawer and began to write. A few sentences and he was done. Clearing his throat, he replaced the pen and stood.

The second running knot was perfect—tied high on the rope while he stood on the desk chair. At least his scout training hadn't failed him, he thought. He stepped down and watched while the stout cord of fibers spun a bit, the enticing loop settling directly above the chair.

The action on the audio tape concluded. The sounds diminished. Only when silence filled the room, did Peter rewind the cassette. He checked his watch—impatient to be done with it. Ejecting the cartridge, he placed it on the note, lining the edges of the cassette precisely with the top of the paper. He folded his spectacles and placed them on the tape.

After climbing the chair, he lowered the noose. The coils around his throat were comforting, lulling. His eyes closed. He envisioned his gleaming shoes, the keen creases in his woolen slacks. A sob of relief escaped his lips. He patted his hair and cleared his throat one last time.

1

"Good Lord, woman, we're not driving to Keeneland in this piece of crap, are we?" Shar asked, her pointed dimpled jaw dropping in disbelief.

Laney McVey unlocked the trunk of her white 1989 Nissan Sentra and swung one of Shar's bulging pieces of luggage inside. "Watch what you say in front of the Whooptie, gal. She's one reliable piece of transportation." She stuffed two more bags and a long leather covered case inside and bounced the lid until the latch caught. "You planning to stay a while?"

"Just a week, but I'm having second thoughts. I have my standards, you know." Shar tugged on the passenger door a couple of times before it crunched open. "Lordy, you've sunk to a new low, woman," she said, folding her twiggy frame into the front seat.

Laney started the Whooptie and cracked the stick shift against Shar's bony knee. "Damn, you have the longest legs. Wish you were running at Keeneland today. I'd put all my money on you."

Shar threw back her head and let loose with a whinny that set Laney to laughing so spiritedly, she braked too quickly for the red light at the Bluegrass Airport exit and stalled the Whooptie. The driver behind sounded his horn.

Laney turned left, shot two lanes and pulled into the racetrack entrance. "Damn, I've missed you, Shar Hamilton. We're going to have a blast this week."

"I don't know how you'll find the time, with running your bed and breakfast and writing your novel. By the way, how's the book coming along?"

"Book's good. I'm about through my first draft."

"When you told me this was the time to visit, I was surprised. I thought you'd be swamped with visitors."

"You've hit it at just the right time. I have about two weeks before things start gearing up for the Derby."

"What? This isn't the Derby we're going to?"

"Shar, the big race today is the Bluegrass Stakes. It's the last derby prep race before the big one on the first Saturday in May. Anyway, the Derby is run in Louisville."

"But woman, I bought this outfit especially to humble your horsy confederates at the big event."

"Shar, believe me, the South will never be the same. You look terrific." And indeed she did, Laney thought. Shar's jumpsuit slithered over her slim body like a hot pink glaze and her fitted white woolen jacket, piped in the same shocking pink, pulled the outfit together and also provided warmth on the cool spring day.

"When do I get to pet the vet?" Shar's smoky eyes fluttered playfully.

"Gray? He's meeting us in the clubhouse dining room."

Laney rolled down the window and slipped an attendant a few dollars to park the car.

Grimacing at the sorry Nissan, the fellow shuddered. Shar shrank a few inches in her seat.

A fine drizzle began as they left the Whooptie. The two of them ran for the stone clubhouse entrance where Laney gave another attendant in a dark green jacket and beige cap, her clubhouse tickets and he stamped the backs of their hands. An elevator zipped them to the third floor.

As they entered the main dining room, Gray waved to them from a table in front of a bank of large windows that were framed with beige draperies blooming orange poppies. The window wall overlooked the box seats and race track. They maneuvered their way through the beamed dining room that was fast filling up with the fashionably dressed horsy crowd—conspicuous hats taking center stage. Laney felt a little underdressed without a chapeau, but she had figured her wild red pepper hair would cause enough attention. Anyway, Shar sported a straw boater with a brim wide enough for the both of them. The hat band matched her jumpsuit and Laney saw heads turn as Shar passed through the dining room ahead of her.

When they reached the table, Gray was already standing and he grabbed Laney's arms in his broad hands, pulled her close and kissed her full on the lips. She tasted bourbon and a flick of his tongue chaser before he released her mouth. She felt her face flush. Gray smiled and quickly held out his hand to Shar. After introductions, Laney smoothed her sea foam green pleated skirt under her, unbuttoned the green and brown plaid tunic jacket and slipped into a chair across from Gray. Shar compressed her six foot body into a captain's chair next to Laney. A waiter dressed in a white tuxedo shirt and black bow tie and vest materialized like magic and Laney ordered Bloodies for the two of them.

As usual, Shar was in high spirits. She had never met a stranger, so by midway through their lunches, Shar was talking, eating, laughing, and drinking—all simultaneously. Laney caught Gray's you-told-me-so glance several times. He seemed tickled by Shar's vitality and grinned and nodded a lot. Under the table, Laney's stockinged foot slipped its pump, found Gray's pant cuff and crept up his ankle. She enjoyed watching his face redden and his eyes fumble around the dining room in flustered distraction.

"Excuse me, Dr. Prescott?" said a short chubby man dressed in a creamy beige silk jacket who had mysteriously appeared at Gray's side. Gray's leg snapped back, carrying Laney's foot with it and she struggled to wiggle her toes free. "I'm Barry Hogarth. May I speak with you a moment?" The man's mirrored sunglasses reflected Laney's bright, crimped hair as double coronas as he bent over Gray's shoulder.

Laney recognized the name immediately. She had read in Sunday's *Lexington Post* about Sunburst Productions filming a movie in the Bluegrass Region starring actress Karen Crosswood. Hogarth was the director of the thriller about a murder in the thoroughbred industry.

Evidently, Gray was also familiar with the filming, as he stood and shook the man's hand and introduced him to Shar and Laney. He excused himself and stepped a short distance away from the table. Laney's curiosity was peaked and she strained to eavesdrop on their conversation without ignoring her friend. All she caught was Gray's firm answer to a question posed by Mr. Hogarth:

"Mr. Hogarth, I realize you'd like to meet your time schedule, but I can't induce a mare just so you can catch the birth of a foal on film. Could result in the death of both mare and foal. Won't do it. Sorry."

As Gray turned back toward his table, he was roughly jolted aside by a handsome man who had just scrambled to his feet from the table near theirs. The gentleman's florid face accentuated his thick crop of blond hair. His bloodshot eyes bulged alarmingly. Laney whispered into Shar's ear that the man was her neighbor, Dr. Derek Beale, a veterinarian who worked for Jason, Carroll and Robinson—a mixed animal practice in Lexington.

"I overheard your conversation, Mr. Hogarth," Beale said, giving Gray a supercilious look as he passed, "and I'd like to offer my services to induce the mare for your film." Derek's arm readily encircled Hogarth's shoulders and he led him out of the restaurant into the rock walled entranceway where the two men stood in avid conversation next to a gigantic tub of white hydrangeas.

"Damn it. He knows better," Gray said, as he seated himself, obviously upset by Derek's maneuver.

"What happens if you induce a mare?" asked Laney, while returning a wave from an attractive woman at the same table that Derek had vacated. A couple, their backs to Laney, sat across from her and the woman turned and also waved at Laney. The gentleman with her didn't move.

"Good Lord, woman, do you know everyone here?" Shar remarked, "Or are all these people somehow related to you? A bit of inbreeding, perhaps? However, their eyes don't seem to be too close together." She nudged Laney with her elbow.

Laney, tilting her head at Shar, crossed her eyes. "The couple with their backs to us are Chris and Amanda Taylor," she explained. "Chris is a chemistry professor over a large research group at the University of Kentucky. He's authored a slew of papers and three books on nuclear magnetic resonance. I understand he's up for the chairmanship of the department. Absolutely brilliant—graduate of Harvard, member of Mensa and all that. They're good friends of ours. Amanda has invited us for lunch at the country club on Tuesday."

Gray turned his turquoise eyes on hers and Laney's tummy did a hop. "To answer your question, Laney, when a mare is induced with Oxytocin, she has a harder labor that accelerates her through the stages too quickly. Sometimes it results in a placenta previa or a hip lock on the foal. Foal can asphyxiate and the mare can hemorrhage."

"Yuck. Lovely lunch conversation. I'd much rather nibble on that gorgeous morsel that offered to do it. He resembles my second husband, Simon. Never really got over him," Shar said, licking her red lips.

"Hands off that one, Shar. The Robert Redford look-alike who just blew off Gray is married to that voluptuous brunette sitting with Chris and Amanda," Laney said. "Her name's Dory."

"A curse on the woman!" Shar said, wiggling her fingers in Dory's direction. "Gray, why would Derek offer to induce a mare if it's so potentially harmful?"

Gray squirmed slightly in his seat and he took a sip of his bourbon and water before he spoke, "Derek seems to thrive on new experiences, even if there's risk. In fact, the greater the risk, the more I think he goes for it. Know he got his flying license just for the thrill of it. I, for one, wouldn't fly with him. Heard from Chris that Derek performed some rolls and loops the one time he went up with him. Scared the hell out of him. Derek's latest craze is rappelling down cliffs."

Laney watched while Derek shook hands with Hogarth, then rejoined his wife and the Taylors. He avoided looking at Gray as he passed, but smiled and nodded at Shar and Laney.

"I remember that even as a kid, he was impulsive, tired easily of things," Laney said. "With his lack of concentration, I don't know how he completed vet school."

"I do. I'd give him an 'A' on looks alone," piped Shar.

Their waiter removed their luncheon plates.

"Enough about Derek. The first race is in about ten minutes. Going to place a bet, you two?" Gray asked.

"I am," Shar said, and opened the Keeneland racing program to the first race. She placed the booklet flat on the table. With her eyes tightly closed, she extended a cadaverous forefinger that circled over the program and lowered slowly until its long, blood red glossy nail settled on the number two horse, Money Clip. He won by a length.

The rain ended in time for the running of the Grade II stakes race and Pulpit, a Bourbon County horse, won by three and a half lengths in the unexpected Kentucky sunshine. As the Whooptie inched its way out of Keeneland in bumper to bumper traffic, Shar kicked off her shoes and stretched out her size ten narrow feet.

"Now *that* was fun," she announced, wiggling her painted toes.

"Well . . . I guess so," Laney said. "You won over three hundred dollars with your eyes shut and only that obscene blood tipped finger of yours."

"You won the Bluegrass Stakes."

"Well, whoopee. All eighty cents."

"You could have bet more than two bucks, woman. Speaking of big bets, gorgeous Derek was at the five-hundred dollar window every time I placed a bet. Guess I should have been a vet instead of an assistant editor at *Three Rivers Magazine*." Shar paused. "Do you miss Pittsburgh?"

"Sometimes. But I think my Kentucky roots were deeper than I thought. And Mother and Gray are here. I miss my sister though." Laney's eyes brimmed with the thought of Cara.

Shar reached over and patted her leg. "You sure challenged fate on that one. But I guess if I had lost a sister, I would have hunted down the son of a bitch who did it too."

Shar was referring to the year before when Laney's sister, Cara, had died in what at first was thought to be a canoeing accident.

"I'm not suited for detective work," Laney said. "But finally my life has settled into a peaceful day to day schedule." She crossed her fingers. "However, any week with you is sure to be a heady experience." She grinned at Shar who had propped her bare feet on the dash—a considerable feat, considering the length of her legs. "I only have one other guest this week, and Mother and Jesse have promised to help out," Laney went on. "But don't worry, I'll squeeze in my writing."

"No time set aside for Gray? He's mad about you, you know. His eyes reflect X's every time he looks at you."

With just the mention of Gray, Laney's insides warmed like she had just drunk a snifter of brandy. "We touch base sometime every day. He's my worst—or should I say— best critic when it comes to my writing. I can always count on him to give me a frank point of view when I get into a rut. And to be perfectly honest, I need that more times than I care to admit. After my sister died, I had a hard time getting motivated. Gray encouraged me to start my writing even before I thought I was ready. It's been therapeutic." Laney sighed as she thought of how close the two of them had become. "He understands more than anyone how tough it is to get over losing a sibling. Remember me telling you that Gray's twin brother died in a car accident the night of their high school graduation?"

Shar nodded.

"It not only left its mark on Gray, the tragedy helped destroy his parents' marriage."

"Does Gray's mother still live in Hickory?"

"No, Patty lives in Florida with her sister now. Gray just returned last week from visiting her. He goes every spring."

As they drove through Hickory, Laney noticed that many of the shop windows were already decorated in derby silks and horse paraphernalia. In a few days, colorful Kentucky Derby banners would be strung on every light pole in town. Laney waved at an enormous woman in a jungle print caftan who filled the doorway of her shop on Main Street. Even though it was almost seven o'clock, Second Hand Rose was still open. Rose waved, setting the flabby flesh of her upper arm waggling.

"Woman, this is so different from Pittsburgh. I've lived in my apartment for three years and don't even know the name of my neighbor next door," Shar said, as they drove by the granite and Bedford stone courthouse across the street from Rose's.

"I bet you know the name of the hunk across the hall, though."

"Steve Steiner," Shar giggled.

Laney turned right onto Hickory Pike and a few rolling green hills later, she slowed.

"Say, Robert Redford and his lucky lady are behind us," Shar commented, craning her neck toward the back window.

Laney glanced at the rear view mirror, rolled down the window and did a backward wave. "They live at the next farm. I'm sure glad Dory's driving."

As Laney turned right onto her lane, Derek and Dory sped on past in an old red Porsche that needed a paint job.

The Stoney Creek Bed & Breakfast sign, swinging gently on its black post, welcomed them.

"Lordy, woman, no wonder you left *Three River's*. This place is breathtaking!" Shar said, leaning forward in her seat, her head pivoting a hundred eighty degrees to take it all in.

Laney drove down the blacktop lane to the accompaniment of Shar's oohs and ahs. Unreasonable, heavily in foal to Captain Jim, stood by the fence cutting another scallop with her teeth. "She's due this week, Shar. You may be lucky enough to see her foal while you're here." The twenty year old gray mare lifted her head and glanced at the Whooptie as they passed, then resumed her cribbing.

The car escaped the alley of scarlet maples that appeared to Laney to have sprouted leaves just since that morning, and swooped through the stone pilaster entrance.

Shar gasped. "I think I'm in love. This has to be the most magnificent Victorian house I've ever seen."

The limestone house rose two majestic stories and the quintuple of double sash windows over the white wooden porch glowed orange in the reflection of the evening sun.

When Laney braked to a stop in the circle drive, Shar shouldered her door open, unfolded her bones, and jumped to the blacktop in her stockinged feet. With a squeal, she opened her arms to Blackberry's barking welcome. The exuberant Border collie, sensing instantly that she had found a playmate, leaped high and almost toppled her, knocking her straw hat askew and leaving two strategically placed muddy paw prints on Shar's slight bosom.

Laney convulsed in laughter at the sight and promised to take the jump suit to the cleaners.

As they walked the curved brick path to the porch, Laney scanned across the velvet lawn to the hundreds of blooming jonquils—slashes of gold along the black fence lines and blazing yellow circles around the wild cherry and maple trees. The redbud and dogwood buds nearer the stone house were beginning to swell, and beneath their branches, tips of tulip leaves, like tiny rabbit ears, poked through the earth. All promised to bloom in time for the Derby in three weeks.

Laney gave Shar the fifty cent tour of the house. The moment they stepped into the darkened hall, the old stone house's rich Persian rugs, glowing woodwork, and woody furniture polish scent seemed to momentarily quell Shar's exuberance. As they passed into each room, her exclamations became more subdued until they were almost reverent. When they entered the parlor and Laney wound the polyphon—the tinkling sounds of Victoriana filling the room— the expression on Shar's face evoked fears that her friend might drop to her knee and genuflect. Laney should have known better. Instead, Shar reached out and took Laney in a stiff-arm stance. As the tin record played the ragtime tune, "Hello, My Baby," Shar initiated a syncopated strut around the parlor with strides that took two of Laney's to every one of hers. By the time the polyphon wound down, they were two red faced, out of control zanies, collapsing onto the oriental carpet.

It was some time before Laney could stop the giggles long enough to settle Shar and her mounds of luggage into a cozy bedroom just above her own room near the back stairs.

"I'm giving you this room for a particular reason," Laney said, trying to keep a serious face, "to keep you away from my other guest who is arriving tomorrow—a single gentleman from Florida looking for property in St. Clair County. I thought it might discourage you from gamboling about if you thought I could hear any antics overhead."

"Why woman, you cut me to the quick. After divorcing my last husband, I swore off all bipedal primates . . . unless I happen to discover one with a capacity for articulate speech, abstract reasoning, and a hefty bank account. No more rapturous liaisons for me." With that, Shar tested the canopied double bed with several well placed rump bounces and announced with a lascivious wink, "This will do nicely."

While Shar freshened up, Laney dashed to her own room and changed into her jeans. When her head burst through the neck of her Kentucky Wildcat sweatshirt and she felt her crimped hair explode about her head, she grimaced. "A cinnamon colored thunderhead," Gray called it. She coaxed the better part of it behind her ears and snapped a giant barrette around the bulk. Desperate strokes with a makeup brush won't confine the freckles, she brooded, so she didn't bother. Hearing the doorbell, she jerked her sneakers from under her bed and dashed through the kitchen and down the hall. When the front door swung open, Gray stood on the porch, his hands tucked under his armpits in his familiar shy gesture.

Gray still wore his Keeneland attire—navy sport coat and khaki dress trousers, but his untied paisley tie hung crookedly down his blue oxford cloth shirt. Penny loafers were the only thing between the wooden porch and his naked feet. God, he's gorgeous, Laney thought, taking in his twinkling eyes and tanned face with strong smile lines cutting his cheeks. His slightly overlapping lower teeth didn't take away from his magical grin.

"What's going on?" he asked.

"I haven't seen you for a whole hour and a half," Laney said, throwing her arms around his neck. Her sneakers bopped his ear.

"Have an emergency call. Thought maybe you and Shar would like to see me in action."

"I would," a voice called from the top of the front staircase.

Laney spun about in time to see Shar straddle the cherry wood balustrade and launch herself, fanny first, down the banister. She landed with a "oof" at the knoll post and bounced down the last two steps. Her infinite legs were compressed into a pair of Hamilton tartan blue and red leggings and an oversized red sweatshirt hung to mid thigh. Tall man's store, Laney thought, but couldn't for the life of her imagine a guy wearing the blue exclamation printed across the front: "I CAN'T STAND IT ANYMORE!"

"Well, are you coming? Gotta go," Gray said, chuckling and shaking his head at Shar's antics while moving off the porch toward his

Jeep Grand Cherokee.

"Let me check our dinner," Laney said on the run down the hall to the kitchen. She lifted the lid on the crock pot lamb stew she had put together before leaving for the airport that morning and her jaws drew pleasantly as the savory aroma hit her nostrils. "You'd think I never had that Reuben, slaw and derby pie for lunch," she groaned to herself. Turning the dial to warm, she dashed out to the Jeep, locking the front door behind her.

Blackberry sulked on the porch as Laney clambered into the front seat of the Jeep.

"Where's Puccini?" Laney asked, immediately missing Gray's tabby cat sleeping on the dash of his vehicle.

"Brought him but he didn't come when I called him just now. He's been doing that a lot lately when I go on calls. Think he's catting around. Will have to collect him when we get back. Jeff Irwin brought him home when he disappeared on his farm last week. He found him up in the rafters of his tobacco barn where his boxer, Morgana, had chased him. He's terrified of the old bat . . . with good reason." Gray dropped in a tape of the opera, *Norma*, and turned the volume down to low when Joan Sutherland threatened their hearing.

Shar, whose music tastes ran more to Yanni and John Tesh, winced in the back seat. Her narrow hips were scrunched against Gray's ultrasound. She held a stainless steel bucket in her lap and straddled a wooden-handled twitch. "What's this emergency call?" she called over the music.

"It's at the farm next door. A foal with a stomach ulcer," Gray answered.

"Next door? You mean at Derek's?" Laney exclaimed, looking up while she tied the laces on her sneakers. Gray turned right at the end of the lane.

"Oh boy. I get to see that vet again," Shar purred.

"Afraid not, Shar. The call came from a tenant on the back of his farm. Woody Wakefield. I'm uneasy because Derek treated the foal yesterday and Woody thinks that the foal is worse and wants *me* to look at it. It's the children's pet."

"Why doesn't he call Derek back?" Laney asked.

"He did, but Derek wouldn't come to the phone. Dory said he'd gone to bed . . . didn't feel well."

"No wonder. He's sloshed. You saw him at Keeneland," Laney said.

Gray didn't comment and turned right into the entrance of Hickory Pike Farm, named for the road that ran by the farm and led to the town of Hickory. The name blazed from shiny new bronze plaques set into the red brick pilasters. When Gray reached a Y in the lane, he bore to the right and Laney caught a glimpse of the brick main house as they passed the left fork that swung through a dense grove of trees. They passed a white frame house where two small children—a boy about ten and a younger girl with tousled blond curls—jumped off a porch swing and ran behind the Jeep. Gray slowed and came to a halt in front of a black tobacco barn about fifty yards from the house. Woody, a man with deep furrows between his eyes and puffy bags below, stood in the gaping entrance with his hands tucked into the bib of his worn overalls.

Gray was the first to climb out. He shook hands with the man and introduced Shar.

Woody tipped his John Deere cap, exposing thinning red hair. He grinned as he read Shar's sweatshirt—his forehead grooves smoothing, the bags beneath his blue eyes menacing his lower lids. "I sometimes feel the same way, Miss Hamilton," he said. Laney smiled at the man she had known since he had worked for her father at Hickory Dock on weekends and during the summers while he had been in high school and she still in elementary.

"Let's see that foal, Woody," Gray said. They all followed Woody into the shadowy barn to a makeshift stall at the end of the last bent. Terry and Melinda were already inside the stall, the girl with her arms around the bay foal's neck, her mouth covering the colt's velvet nose with kisses. Terry held on to the oversized leather halter that threatened to slip off the foal's head.

"Stand aside, Melinda. Let Doc Gray see the foal," Woody said, and Melinda moved away obediently.

"How did Derek treat her?" Gray asked, a frown appearing between his eyes when he saw the colt.

"Oiled her. He said it was clear it was a stomach ulcer."

"His mommy died when he was born," Melinda said, a tear washing a track down a grimy cheek. "He won't die too, will he?"

"Hope not, Melinda," Gray said.

Gray placed his stethoscope on the colt's thin chest. The foal's breath came in rapid gasps and he looked about anxiously. Gray stepped back and the foal took a step or two forward. He was so weak, he stumbled. Gray slipped his hand under his chin and the foal ground his teeth.

"See . . . that's what he did when Dr. Beale saw him. He said they grind their teeth when it's an ulcer," Woody said.

"Or in pain," Gray said, moving out of the stall and going to his truck. The children were back loving on the foal the instant he left. Shar leaned on the metal farm gate that served as one side of the stall.

"Sure is puny, isn't he? The children have bottle fed him from the time he was born, but he stopped eating two days ago," Woody said.

Gray returned with two syringes. He squirted one into the foal's mouth and gave him a shot in the neck with the other. The foal stretched out his legs, then collapsed into the straw. His sunken eyes stared vacantly.

"Gave him some penicillin and a shot of Zantac," Gray said, as they moved out of the barn. The children remained behind with their pet. "Listen Woody," Gray said, in a voice low enough that the children couldn't hear. "I don't think the foal's going to make it. Think you'd better prepare the kids and please call me if the foal dies. Okay?" Woody nodded, thanked Gray, and shuffled back into the barn.

The ride back to Laney's was punctuated with silence.

When they arrived at the bed and breakfast, Puccini was asleep on the hood of the Whooptie, high enough to be safe from Blackberry's drooling jaws, although which pet truly had superiority had never been determined.

The visit to Woody's cast a blanket of gloom over the rest of the evening. Gray, Shar and Laney all picked around on the lamb stew, fruit salad, and crusty fresh bread baked by Laney's mother, Maddy. Shar, finally pleading exhaustion, excused herself and climbed the back stairs to her room.

"Gray, I can understand Shar being upset over that poor foal, but you're used to this. Why the gloom?" Laney asked.

Gray stood and carried his dinner across the kitchen to the butler's pantry and scraped the leftover stew into Blackberry's bowl on the floor. Nothing wrong with her appetite, Laney thought wryly, as the dog dug in.

"Can't get over the neglectful way Derek doctored that foal. No follow-up. Sticking a tube down his stomach and oiling a foal without giving it Zantac and an antibiotic is no treatment for an ulcer . . . if indeed it is an ulcer," Gray added under his breath.

"Are you saying that it could be something else?" Laney asked.

"Can't say."

"Can't or won't?"

"Both. Listen, think I'd better go. Sorry about dinner. Know I didn't do it justice. Bet it was good. Talk at you tomorrow." He brushed his lips quickly over hers and was out the front door before Laney could even get out of her chair.

Later, as she filled Blackberry's water dish, she noticed a tiny mound of green in the bottom of her bowl. Laney had forgotten that the dog hated peas. She had spit out every single one.

2

Gray slept sporadically. Every time he awakened, he thought of Frisky and those two children. Something kept nagging at him. By daybreak, he was already dressed and Puccini was bugging him for an early breakfast. The gray and black striped cat scratched open his cabinet door with a white paw and meowed and rubbed against the dwindling stack of canned cat food until he toppled one out onto the floor. Gray filled his water bowl and popped the ring on a can of sliced beef and gravy. The tabby settled in for breakfast, his pink tongue delicately working the gravy off the surface. Gray gathered up three other empty cans on the cracked linoleum and tossed them into the already full trash can. He overloaded the dishwasher with two day's dishes, glancing at his watch every few minutes.

At six-thirty, he called Woody. His wife answered the phone.

"Mary, this is Dr. Prescott. How's the foal this morning?"

"Oh Gray, Frisky died during the night," she said, her voice catching.

"Damn . . . where's Woody?"

"He just left to take the foal to the back of the farm before the children discover him."

"I need to talk to him. I'll be right there." Gray hung up the phone, grabbed Puccini in mid-bite and ran down the apartment stairs, through the clinic waiting room door to his Jeep in the parking lot. Puccini stretched out on the dash and promptly fell into a morning nap.

He made the drive from Hickory in about twelve minutes. Woody was just driving back to the barn when Gray arrived and he pulled his battered truck up to Gray's with a screech. They each opened their windows.

"Where's the foal," Gray asked.

"I took him to the sinkhole. I was on my way to the house to call you."

"Show me the way," Gray demanded. Woody seemed startled by Gray's firm tone but backed up, circled round and drove toward Stoney Creek, which formed the back boundary of Hickory Pike Farm. At the point where the blacktop ended, Gray followed Woody onto a gravel road that traveled up a gradual ridge until it ended abruptly, overlooking a deep depression in the landscape. Beyond, Gray saw a line of trees marking the edge of a cliff that dropped steeply to the creek. Gray stopped behind Woody's pickup and jumped out of the Jeep. Below, he saw mounds of straw muck from the horse stalls and a dark withered form lying on top of the latest deposit.

"There he is," Woody said, pointing to the foal. "The turkey vultures will clean him up."

Gray grabbed his surgical kit, stuffed rubber gloves into his pocket and bounced and slid down the sides of the muck covered sinkhole until he reached the mound where the foal rested. He put on the gloves and handed a pair to Woody who had followed him down.

"Put these on and do only as I say," Gray commanded. When Woody was ready, Gray directed him to turn the foal belly up and keep him stationary by holding up the front legs. He removed a scalpel from the kit and made a quick deep incision from the sternum to the pelvis. Woody gasped as Gray reached into the cavity, pushed aside the intestines and found the stomach.

Damn, Gray thought. Looks normal. A ruptured ulcer would have jumped out at him. He incised the stomach and inspected the walls. No shallow ulcers or erosions. "Damn!"

"Whatcha looking for?" Woody asked.

As though he hadn't heard, Gray dropped the stomach and with slippery gloves reached above the bloody incision. Ten minutes later, he dropped the severed head into a plastic bag and twist tied it. Gray's and Woody's gloves and the scalpel were sealed in another plastic bag. With orders for Woody to wash up thoroughly after he buried the foal deep into the muck, Gray sped down the road with his gruesome package. He called the emergency number of the health department in Hickory on his mobile phone and a rotund man with curly black hair was waiting for him at the door when he pulled up.

"Sorry, Randy, these things always seem to happen on a weekend or holiday. But this is urgent."

"I already called your buddy, Vic, from the diagnostic lab in Lexington and he'll be waiting for you," Randy said, as he let Gray into the clinic with his key.

The next few minutes were devoted to preparing the specimen for its one hour ride to Lexington. Gray dropped the head, enclosed in its plastic coffin, into a rectangular metal can and packed it with ice. After sealing the can with a tight lid, Gray sped on to Lexington. Only then did he miss Puccini.

Laney knocked on Shar's door three times with the toe of her foot. A stony silence from within told Laney what she already knew from when she lived in Pittsburgh—that Shar was dead to the world. Balancing the wicker tray against her left hip, she opened the door a crack. The opaque blinds shrouded the room in a colorless gloom. Laney balanced the tray on the mantle and hurried to the window. She heard the clicking of Blackberry's unclipped toenails on the back stairs and knew what was in store for Shar. Sure enough, as Laney drew the blinds, the dog scratched off around the doorway, took a leaping dive toward the mound under the comforter and commenced to gnaw with tiny munching bites at the form under the coverlet. Light exploded from the window while muffled curses under the coverlet let Laney know in no uncertain terms that Shar was alive and well—furious!

"What in the . . . quit!" A wild strawberry blond haystack

popped out of the covers preceded by two frenzied gray eyes that promised to pop right out of her pixie face. "Laney McVey, get this Tasmanian devil off me immediately!"

"Blackberry, enough." Laney laughed, pulling the Border collie off the bed. Shar slid from beneath the covers and stood buck naked shaking that long scarlet tipped forefinger at her.

"Don't *ever* do that again," Shar said with narrowed eyes that commenced to crinkle at the corners. She bent and petted Blackberry. "I was dreaming about my last husband, Paulie, and thought maybe he was finally into some kinky stuff." Swinging her hips audaciously, Shar sashayed into the bathroom. Laney spotted a purple thistle tattoo on her left buttock as she sauntered by.

After Shar showered and donned a skimpy, fiery silk robe, the two of them languished at a small skirted table beneath a sunny window. They sipped steamy coffee and relished Maddy's warm butter pecan biscuits smothered in orange marmalade.

"Do you treat all your guests this way—breakfast on a tray in their rooms?" Shar asked, licking marmalade off the tips of two fingers.

"I leave a wicker basket with a carafe of hot coffee, fruit and warm homemade bread of some kind at their door. They can still eat in the dining room downstairs until nine-thirty, if they prefer. Most opt for the room service at no extra charge," Laney said, scratching Blackberry's belly with her foot as she spoke. The collie lay spread eagle on her back, her left hind foot thudding against the oriental carpet in an involuntary cadence.

Their Sunday interlude was interrupted by the phone. Laney reached into the deep pocket in her apron, extracted her portable and clicked it on.

"Gray, you're in a wad. What's wrong?"

Shar jumped to her feet, dug around in a suitcase, and came up with some wild colored garment. She motioned toward the bathroom as Laney listened with growing alarm to Gray's conversation.

"Gray . . . please . . . calm down," Laney was saying as Shar exited the bathroom several minutes later dressed in denim tights and a patchwork tunic in bright primary colors. Laney suddenly pulled the phone away from her ear and just stared at it. "He hung up."

"Good Lord, woman, you look like you just swallowed a hair

ball," Shar said, looking at Laney's reflection in the mirror hanging over the bureau while brushing her pixie into a shining cap.

"That was Gray, calling from the diagnostic lab in Lexington. Frisky died last night and—"

"Aw . . . what a heartbreak . . . those poor sprouts." Shar's eyes watered up and she wiped her nose with the side of her hand. "But Gray thought he wouldn't survive. Maybe Woody prepared them—"

"Shar," Laney interrupted, her voice shrill. "That's not the half of it. Gray got a pal of his who works at the lab do a preliminary on the foal's brain . . . something about doing a positive fluorescent antibody test. It's rabies!"

Shar's eyes expanded and she lowered herself into the chair across from her friend.

"Melinda, Terry and Woody will have to have a series of rabies shots immediately," Laney went on. "They've been bottle feeding that foal since he was born. They could have been exposed to the virus with just a little cut on the hand or through mucus membranes." The recollection of Melinda's mouth kissing all over the foal's nose sickened her.

Laney related Gray's conversation and why he had suspected that it might not be an ulcer from the start. "A paresis in the foal's left foot gave him the first clue, along with the foal's apprehension and empty eyes. Then the foal died during the night. When Gray autopsied the stomach this morning and didn't find an ulcer, he was pretty sure it was rabies."

"What's a paresis?" Shar asked.

"Gray said it's a neurological weakness. Remember how the foal stumbled and his foot kind of knuckled over? I just thought it was because Frisky was sick and weak."

"Gray!" Shar suddenly yelped, looking alarmed. "He had his fingers in Frisky's mouth yesterday."

"I asked him about that. He said that he had had the rabies vaccine while he was in vet school at Auburn. All the students had to have it. He'll only need a couple booster shots."

Shar was unusually quiet for a moment or two. When she spoke, she echoed Laney's thoughts exactly. "What if Woody hadn't called Gray last evening? Woody would have just disposed of the foal and he and those sprouts could have died." Shar shivered.

"If humans get infected with the rabies virus, symptoms usually appear in twenty to sixty days. Once you have symptoms, it's always fatal."

"Derek Beale will have to be called, won't he?"

"He treated the foal too . . . if you want to call it that," Laney growled, throwing her napkin onto the tray and jumping to her feet.

"Woman, you're really hot over this."

"If you think I'm hot, you should've heard Gray. He's boiling."

"At least Gray caught it in time. Speaking of time, when is your guest due to arrive?" Shar began making her bed.

Laney realized Shar was trying to divert her attention away from the serious circumstances. Reluctantly, she helped by smoothing the quilt from the opposite side of the bed.

"Not until late this evening." Laney took a deep breath, trying to put a lid on her anger. "I thought I'd show you around the farm this morning. This afternoon, we're meeting Gray at the Finish Line for lunch. You remember me telling you about that restaurant in Hickory. Food's yummy."

"Food? . . . did you say food? . . . after that breakfast? I hope this guest of yours likes fat women." Shar seized one of the pillows off the bed and stuffed it under her tunic and waddled about the room singing at the top of her voice:

> *"I'm the fat lady of the circus.*
> *He doesn't care if I'm as big as a school bus.*
> *It was love at first sight*
> *When he saw my cellulite.*
> *Oh, ain't love simply fabulous?*
> *Oh, ain't love simply fabulous?"*

The two of them dropped onto the bed in a puddle of laughter. Blackberry pounced and made it a threesome. With her arms around the pet that she had inherited from her sister along with the farm and the cranky "whoop-de-do" mode of transportation, Laney felt her anger dissolving like sugar in a cup of hot coffee. She only wished that Gray were there. If anyone needed a teaspoon of laughter in his cup of fury, it would be Gray.

Laney sat on the steps of the office next to the foaling stall. Their bikes rested on their stands next to the door. Shar and Blackberry were lying side by side in the grass, Blackberry getting in a quick nap before continuing with the herding of the two-wheeled "sheep."

"I'm done in," Shar gasped, on her side gulping water from the cup Laney had filled from the office sink. "You say you do this every day? I'd say you have an inherent tendency toward masochism."

"You must admit it's invigorating," Laney said.

"So is sticking your finger in a light socket," Shar moaned. "Say, Gray must be here. Isn't that his furry dash ornament?"

Laney's eyes followed Shar's finger to a bedraggled striped cat approaching from the direction of the house. "Sure looks like him." Laney stood and looked about. "Gray must be at the house and Puccini is catting around again." Holding out her hand, she approached the cat and lifted him into her arms. His wet, muddy fur left a large smudge on her white sweatshirt. "I wonder why Gray is here. The plan was to meet him at the restaurant. Guess we'd better get back. We have about an hour to get ready."

Afraid that if she put Puccini in the basket, he would leap out when Blackberry began worrying him with barks and ugly looks, Laney held him under her left arm and steered the bike with her right.

There was no sign of Gray at the house.

"Strange," Laney said under her breath. Once inside, Laney rubbed Puccini down with an old terry cloth towel. She put the cat in the pantry, gave him water and closed the door so Blackberry wouldn't torment him. She phoned Gray from the kitchen. It rang for the longest time, the answering machine never cutting on. "Odd," Laney said, "I don't remember Gray not switching on the machine before."

"Have we another mystery, Sherlock?" Shar remarked, as she wiped her red face with a wet paper towel next to the kitchen sink.

"Don't even think it!" Laney said, a little too vehemently. But she definitely felt unsettled as she followed Shar into the back hall to get dressed.

3

Laney nibbled at her salad. She and Shar had decided to begin their lunch without Gray. When they had arrived at the Finish Line, a few minutes late themselves, Jesse Mills, the assistant manager and good friend of Laney's, seated them next to a window overlooking Main Street. Gray had reserved his favorite table a week in advance when he'd learned that Laney's Pittsburgh friend was coming for a visit.

Laney introduced Jesse to Shar, watching in amusement how Shar sized up Jesse's uniform—a turquoise and black jockey silk tucked into black slacks.

It was inevitable. "Did your horse win?" Shar asked, her face expressionless.

Jesse laughed out loud and tiny fans formed on the outside corners of her pretty gray eyes. Her shiny nut-brown bob bounced below her jockey cap.

Shar ordered coffee and Laney, iced tea. Laney kept glancing out the window at the Whooptie parked across the street from the restaurant. She could see Puccini asleep on the dash. She had stopped at Gray's on the way into town to drop the tabby off, but being Sunday, the place was locked up and Gray hadn't answered her knock. The weather was cool and she had left all the windows open a crack so that the cat wouldn't get overheated.

"He's okay, Laney," Shar said, talking through a bite of juicy cantaloupe.

"I know. Maury gave me a bowl of milk for him."

"I didn't mean Puccini, woman. I was referring to Gray." Shar's dangling gold thistle earrings swiveled as she chewed.

"I can't imagine what's keeping him, Shar. He's never late for anything." Laney looked at her watch again. It was two o'clock. "He should have been here forty-five minutes ago."

As though reading her mind, the owner of the restaurant, Maury Morrow, appeared at her elbow with a portable phone in his hand.

"There's a call for you, Miss McVey."

"Thank God," Laney said, reaching quickly for the phone. She thanked him and he hobbled back toward the kitchen, his bent arthritic knees obviously paining him. Laney put the phone to her ear.

"Gray, where are . . . oh . . . Mother . . . it's you," Laney said, a sinking feeling in her gut. Her mother wouldn't call her here unless it was something serious. She listened to her mother, the thumb of her left hand wiping furiously at the condensation on her glass of iced tea. "All right, we'll stop on the way home."

"Mummy, right?" Shar said, when Laney clicked off the phone. "You look as sour as a pickle. What did she say to upset you?"

"It's not what she said. All she said was that she wants us to stop on the way home, but I know it's something more than that. Her voice always skitters around like a bead of water in a hot frying pan when something is on her mind."

"Then let's get noshing, woman."

When Laney and Shar drove through the stone gateway to Hickory Dock, her mother was squirting mud off the concrete boat ramp with the pressure washer. The water hadn't seeped more than a foot up the ramp from the recent rains, but Maddy was a stickler for neat and clean. The two of them stepped out of the Nissan. Laney scooped up Puccini from the dashboard. Maddy glanced their way, shut off the washer and hurried over.

"Maddy, look at you. You two look like sisters," Shar gushed, bending down and almost lifting Maddy off her booted feet with a powerful squeeze.

Shar wasn't far off the mark, Laney thought, admiring her mother's girlish figure and barely lined freckled face. Maddy's brown eyes dappled with amber peered from under her favorite floppy-brimmed knit hat that she would replace with a white sailor one when the weather turned hot. Beneath the brim, a sparkling mist from the power washer had settled on her crimped, redwood colored hair.

During the past year, it seemed to Laney that her mother had grown happier by the day. Laney knew that the sheriff of St. Clair County had been a major factor in Maddy's contentment. Maddy had been seeing Gordon Powell ever since her divorce from Laney's stepfather had become final.

"I can't believe it's been almost a year since I helped Laney move from Pittsburgh. Bet you two have a lot of catchin up to do," Maddy said, as they walked toward the small frame house with the large deck set back from the creek.

"We're doing that, along with stuffing our faces and bicycle training for the next *Tour de France*," Shar said, her long legs taking the steps to the deck three at a time. A pair of red panties flashed from beneath her short Hamilton tartan skirt.

As soon as they were inside, Laney dropped Puccini to the floor, hoping he wouldn't make a mess somewhere in the house.

"What are you doin with Puccini?" Maddy asked, when they were seated at Maddy's kitchen table and sipping her strong hot coffee.

"Good question. We found him at the farm about noon . . . but without a trace of Gray. We were to meet him at the Finish Line at one-fifteen, but he never showed," Laney said.

Maddy studied her cup that she kept turning in its saucer. Laney caught her mother's nervous mannerism out of the corner of her eye.

"Out with it, Mother," Laney said, in a loud voice. "Why did you want me to stop by?"

"Why Laney, I just wanted to see Sharlene again." She rubbed her right eye.

"Like hell—"

"I'll go see what Puccini's up to," Shar said, bouncing out of her chair.

"Sit down, Shar. The cat is fine. Mother?" Laney demanded.

"I don't want to spoil your visit with Shar . . . but I guess you'll find out sooner or later. Gray may have been arrested."

"What? . . . when?" Laney sputtered. Shar grabbed Laney's arm and hung on.

"Seems there was a fuss out on the country club golf course this mornin between Derek Beale and Gray. I think a few punches were exchanged and Charlie Breathitt, the golf pro, called the sheriff's office. Deputy Rudd took the call and decided to check with Gordon before going over there, Gray bein a friend and all. Gordon was here and he decided to go instead."

Laney and Shar shared an intuitive look. At that moment, they heard a vehicle pull up to the house and soon they heard a soft knock at the door. Before Maddy could get out of her chair, a wiry middle-aged man with a blond crewcut peeked in the door.

"Gordon." Maddy beamed when she saw him.

"When I saw the Whooptie, I knew that Maddy had called you," Gordon said, addressing Laney. He winked at Maddy.

Laney introduced Shar to Gordon.

"So you're Hickory's Sheriff Taylor," quipped Shar. "You're better looking than Andy Griffith by a long shot. Where's Barney?"

"Locking up Otis for the night. Gotta get drunks off the streets of Mayberry," Gordon said, grinning big at Shar, his smile lines digging in around his mouth. "Okay, you all. Know you're dying to know . . . so . . . no, I didn't arrest anyone. When I got out to the club, the fight was over and both of them had gone their separate ways. No one has pressed any charges, so I guess, other than perhaps a couple bruised egos, no one got hurt."

"Who started it?" Maddy asked. Again, Shar shot Laney a knowing look.

"Seems Gray came storming across the golf course in a golf cart and found Derek on the second green. Chris Taylor, Derek's golf partner, said Gray started in on Derek about some foal he had treated. Evidently, Derek had had a few snorts early in the clubhouse and he accused Gray of stealing his client. That Derek had shot five over on the first hole hadn't helped matters."

"Where's Gray?" Laney asked, her recent lunch doing a rock 'n' roll.

"I don't know. After that call, I had two others that kept me busy on this beautiful Sunday when I had better things to do." He kept glancing over at Maddy with his gray-green eyes. His arms were folded across his well-built chest and Laney noticed the bulge of his gun through his red and white windbreaker.

Observing the vibes passing between Gordon and her mother, Laney announced, "We'll be going. I have a guest checking in this evening." Shar scrambled to get Puccini, who was beginning to sniff around the kitchen. With a quick kiss on her mother's cheek, Laney led the way out the door. Puccini got a quick pit stop by the creek but Shar grabbed him up again before he could take off on one of his jaunts.

Puccini, belly up with paws curled into tiny mittens, purred in contentment in Shar's arms as they pulled out of the dock entrance.

"Can't you just see Gray careening across that golf course in one of those carts? What if there had been a golf tournament going on?" Shar said, lifting one of Puccini's paws to her mouth and like a golf announcer, speaking quietly into the furry microphone: "Ladies and gentlemen, on the fairway to your left . . . fast approaching the second hole at breakneck speed, is an out-of-control golf cart on a suicide mission. It seems the kamikaze pilot is madcap Doc Gray and he has skillfully avoided the rough and is now screaming expletives at one of our tipsy golfers who is waving his putter on the second green."

Laney did her best to keep her sober demeanor, but Shar's vivid parody gradually penetrated until she cracked up so thoroughly, she had to pull the Whooptie over.

"Damn, you can see humor in anything," Laney said, wiping her eyes while driving away from the curb.

They stopped at Gray's before leaving town. Laney could see both of his vehicles parked in the lot. "He's here," Laney announced unnecessarily, snatching Puccini out of Shar's hands.

"I think I'll stay here," Shar said, tilting her head back and shutting her eyes. Laney didn't argue with her, thinking that both Gray and Shar might be embarrassed over what happened.

Gray answered the door to the clinic with his head turned unnaturally to the left. Laney grabbed his jaw and looked straight into his eyes. "How bad is Derek?" she asked.

"Not a scratch, damn it."

"I know you only eat fast food so no chance for a steak treatment on that shiner. Try an ice pack. It'll help the swelling."

"Thanks, Doc. Who told you?"

"Mother."

"Where'd you find Puccini?" Gray had already claimed his tabby. Laney could hear the cat's strong motor the instant Gray took him out of her arms.

"At the farm," Laney said.

"You were at Woody's?" Gray's good eye narrowed to match the other one that was in a squint.

"No, at my farm. Did you stop there around noon?"

"Huh-uh. Drove straight to the health department. Didn't miss him until I was on the way to the diagnostic lab with the foal's head around seven forty-five, and I've just been too upset to run him down. He must have jumped out of my truck at Woody's this morning."

"Then he must have made his way to my farm. As the crow flies, it's not too far."

"You mad at me?"

"Not exactly. Just concerned . . . that you got so out of control, I guess."

"I . . . I never . . . I can't remember being so angry." Gray shook his head in frustration.

"Those kids. Woody. They have time to get the shots. That's the important thing."

"I'm sorry about today. Shar must think I'm a real jerk."

"Actually, I think she was rather amused by the golf course incident. I'll have her relate her version to you some time." She smiled at him. "I do, though."

"What? Think I'm a jerk?"

Laney nodded. "But I love my jerk," Laney said, then kissed him softly on the mouth.

4

Laney couldn't believe how tired she was. It took every bit of her strength to roll out of bed at seven to prepare Malcolm Lamont's basket. She decided to wait on Shar's, knowing that she would probably sleep in after staying up late talking with her new guest.

Laney had excused herself about seven-thirty the night before and had sequestered herself in the library to work on her novel. At first, the day's excitement caused a lack of concentration, but a writing tip—reading the last two chapters of her manuscript—got her going and she had completed six pages by the time she'd hung it up.

Laney wasn't sure what time Shar had turned in, since she and Malcolm had hit it off and didn't even seem to realize when she'd said goodnight. When Laney left the library about midnight, the two of them were still at it in the parlor.

Malcolm had told them that he'd been born in Scotland forty-two years ago. Both his mother and father had been from Edinburgh. Even though his parents had immigrated to the States after his birth, Malcolm evidently was very proud of his heritage since he visited Scotland frequently. His current farm was near Ocala, Florida and he had traveled to Kentucky to purchase a farm for his outstanding herd of purebred Angus cattle. Some of his prize bulls actually came from Scotland.

Laney thought the attraction between the two was probably

because of their Scottish heritage. Shar had retained her Hamilton name through all three of her marriages and wore the Hamilton tartan often. Her fascination with things Scottish went as far as acquiring a feisty Westie she named Nessie, after the Loch Ness monster.

"Yoo-hoo," a voice called from the front hall and Laney turned from pulling a large round pan of hot cinnamon rolls out of the oven to see Malcolm striding into the kitchen. "May I bother you for a spot of coffee, Miss McVey?"

"You may, Malcolm, if you call me Laney."

"Done . . . Laney, it is. I know I chose your room service option, but with such a glorious day urging me to arise, I couldn't stay in my room a moment longer." He chuckled. "The last time I visited your fair state, the sun shone warmly one morning but by afternoon, the temperature dropped twelve degrees and it began snowing." Malcolm stared out the French doors onto the screened porch, his hands deep in the pockets of his brown tweed trousers. A pale beige sweater vest covered a chocolate-colored cotton turtleneck.

"You know what they say about Kentucky weather—if you don't like it, wait five minutes," Laney said, grinning at the little fellow. He couldn't have been over five foot seven or eight inches tall. Two lively brown eyes peered through tortoise shell eyeglasses above a neatly trimmed mustache and goatee. His perfectly oval head was topped by an enviable crop of curly brown hair.

Laney poured two cups of freshly brewed coffee into a couple of mugs and placed them on Malcolm's wicker tray along with a large bowl of fresh strawberries and a tiny clear glass pitcher of dairy cream. Opening the French doors, she carried everything out to the iron table on the porch overlooking Stoney Creek.

"Ah . . . delightful," he said, as he followed her out into the screened area.

"Wait for me," a voice in the kitchen called and presently Shar joined them with her own cup of coffee. "How could anyone sleep with such aromas drifting up the back stairs."

Shar's eyes shimmered like silver lame in the morning sun that mottled off the creek. A lightweight jumpsuit that matched her eyes was tied at the waist with a braided Hamilton plaid belt fashioned into a jaunty bow over her left hip. Mentally comparing herself to Shar, Laney felt absolutely frumpy in another one of her blue and white Kentucky Wildcat sweatshirts and jeans. I'd have to be up for at least an hour to even come even close to how together she looks, she thought. Actually, Laney was astonished at Shar's early appearance when she recalled that it had taken a full Blackberry assault to arouse her the morning before.

At the moment, Shar and Malcolm were devouring the cinnamon rolls and fresh strawberries like there was no tomorrow and their eyes twinkled like four bright buttons in the sun.

Laney was about to sit down with her company, when the front doorbell rang and she excused herself.

"Sally," Laney exclaimed, when she saw the wife of her farm manager, Aaron Sloan, through the screen door. "I haven't seen you forever. Too busy racking in those real estate commissions, I bet. Come on in. I believe Malcolm is raring to go."

Sally followed Laney through the house to the screen porch. As they stepped through the threshold, Laney caught Malcolm withdrawing his hand quickly from Shar's. Laney introduced Sally to Malcolm and Shar, learning that Malcolm had talked with Sally over the phone several times from Florida.

"I have three or four farms for you to see in the area today, depending on how much time we spend at each place," Sally said, squinting her heavily lashed eyes against the bright sunshine flooding the porch. "We'll start with Taylor Ridge on the other side of Hickory."

"Taylor Ridge? *The* Taylor Ridge? Chris Taylor's farm?" Laney exclaimed.

"A new listing as of Friday," Sally said. "Chris said they want to move to a smaller place, perhaps to one of those townhouses in Lexington."

"I can't believe it," Laney said. "The farm has been in that family since the Civil War. Amanda never mentioned it to me . . . wanting to sell, I mean. She loves that place," Laney said, scowling.

"Well, don't quote me, but I understand it's heavily mortgaged. Sometimes keeping up a family home place can bleed you dry," Sally said, the sun highlighting her black hair with streaks of bronze.

Laney thought about Sally's comment. She couldn't imagine the Taylors going into debt so soon after Chris had inherited the place just five years before. But on second thought, who really knows other people's financial woes except the people themselves.

"Laney, would you mind terribly if Sharlene accompanied me on my farm hunting outing? I promise I'll have her back in time for dinner," Malcolm said.

"Not if you will join us for dinner," Laney said. "I'll ask Gray, too."

"Done," said Malcolm, and the three of them waved and departed through the French doors.

Laney poured a second cup of coffee and looked out at the new carriage house where the buggy house had stood just a year ago. The beautiful frame building complimented the limestone house perfectly. It was similar to the old structure—up to the cedar shake roof that Laney knew would weather in time. The iron weathervane had been salvaged from the rubble and now perched upon the cupola that was painted a pristine white that matched the rest of the structure. Working black shutters hung at the six foot long windows and matching window boxes were overflowing with bright yellow pansies. There was one original feature that Laney had insisted upon being changed. The icehouse below. The fifteen foot deep pit beneath the floor in the original building had been filled in completely and the new carriage house now rested on a stone foundation. Just a thought of her terror-filled experience there could still trigger nightmares.

"Bet I know what you're thinking about," Gray's soft voice said from her left. "I can't forget that night, either."

Laney turned to see Gray standing on the flagstone path behind the porch. She unlatched the screen door and he stepped upon the glazed red tiles and gathered her into his arms. When she raised her lips to his, she knocked his sunglasses askew. The swelling in his injured eye had subsided somewhat, but it squinted in the sudden glare. Laney replaced the frames on his nose.

"I met Shar and her latest acquisition. They're absolutely consumed by each other. Seems like a pleasant fellow, though a bit too formal for my taste."

Laney giggled. "Shar will loosen him up. Wait until he sees her banister routine."

Gray snorted in laughter while nuzzling her neck, this time knocking his glasses to the floor. "Listen, I've taken the day off. I owe you for yesterday. How about a canoe ride?" Gray said, picking up his glasses.

"What about your calls?"

"Only had a herd to work at Johnson's. Natine postponed it until tomorrow. Got my beeper for emergencies." He patted the little black accessory on his belt.

"You're on," Laney said eagerly.

Gray's paddle sliced through the clear water with hardly a sound. Sitting at the bow, Laney rested her paddle across her lap. In the center of the canoe, Blackberry sat straight and still, her periscopic ears perking with every sound from the creek. For a change, they had decided to travel upstream instead of the usual route toward the dam.

"Look at those little guys," Laney said pointing to a wood duck and six downy ducklings heading for some weeds along the bank. "I see some kind of wildlife every time I get on the creek."

After traveling about a quarter mile through Laney's farm, they passed between some of Stoney Creek's steepest banks as they paddled through Hickory Pike farm. Laney felt a drop of temperature caused by the looming palisades of limestone that obscured the sun. Overhead, three turkey vultures circled.

They turned the canoe when they reached Irwin's cattle farm and rested a bit where the steep cliffs diminished, allowing the sun to warm them.

"Can't be, Laney. Chris would never sell Taylor Ridge," Gray said.

Laney had just told Gray about Hartman Real Estate's new listing.

"Sally said the place is heavily mortgaged . . . that they plan to move to Lex," Laney said.

"Didn't tell m—" Angry waves appeared above Gray's sunglasses. Gray picked up his paddle again, savagely attacking the water. Laney knew how close he and Chris were, at least used to be. Lately though, they hadn't seemed as thick and she suspected that their weekly chess game had stopped. Maybe Gray was hurt that Chris hadn't told him about his plan to list the farm. After all, Taylor Ridge was one of Gray's important cattle clients. She began to paddle also, although Gray's thrusting was what was really carrying them along.

"Gray," Laney called to him. "You're paddling like you're killing snakes. Slow down." The plan was to stop for lunch somewhere on the way back. She had packed a cooler with beer, peanut butter and jelly sandwiches, apples, and three cinnamon rolls left over from breakfast.

Once again, they were passing back through the cliff area and Laney's eyes searched the banks ahead for a sunny grassy area to picnic.

"Gray, look! Isn't that Puccini?" Laney pointed toward the right wall of rock with her paddle.

Gray's head jerked upward, his paddle stopping in mid-stroke. He pocketed his sunglasses in his shirt and scrutinized the sheer cliff. He drew in his breath when he saw the animal slinking along a low ledge.

"Looks like him. Damn it, anyhow! Left the Jeep window open, just in case he needed to take a leak. On the prowl again. Puccini!" he yelled.

Gray closed the distance to the bank with several thrashing strokes, splashing Laney in the process. Her wet hair hanging below her straw hat began to frizz immediately.

Gray maneuvered between two rocks and tied the short tow rope to a flimsy branch that seemed to be growing out of the water. He climbed out of the boat and Laney scrambled out behind him, almost tipping Blackberry and the cooler into the water. The Border collie scrambled to her feet, ready to bolt over the side of the canoe.

"Stay," Laney commanded, and the dog sat. Laney grinned at Gray's wry look in response to Blackberry's obedient behavior.

"I'll fix him," he said, "And I really mean, fix. A simple surgery and Puccini's libido will be no . . . more."

Gray grabbed hold of Laney's hand and pulled her along the shale and rocks. Ahead of them, Puccini suddenly disappeared behind a group of scrubby trees in front of an outcropping of limestone. Laney felt like a rock climber as they worked the narrow path that intersected the lower facade of the cliff. Suddenly, Puccini darted back. Gray's hand flew outwards and grabbed air. Laney instinctively swiped at the gray blur and miraculously came up with a hind foot as the cat flew by her. She grappled, then clutched Puccini to her chest—the tabby yowling and flailing with his sharp claws.

"Got him," she announced, the cat slowly calming in her arms, although she could still feel his panicky heartbeat.

Gray turned and looked at his errant cat. His eyes—the turquoise and the black—both opened wide with alarm and his lips parted.

"Laney, there's blood. He's hurt."

Laney looked down. Sure enough, all four paws were covered with blood. As Gray searched each paw for an injury, the sticky redness transferred to Gray's large hands. Puccini didn't wince with the probing.

"Can't find anything," Gray announced, looking back over his shoulder in the direction from which Puccini had come. "Hold on to him."

Laney readjusted the cat in her arms while Gray followed the slightly ascending ledge that widened and curved behind the group of undersized cedars growing out of a crevice filled with earth. For a second, Gray disappeared from sight. Then Laney heard an outcry—like he had been struck hard in the gut.

"Ahhhh!"

A moment passed, then two, three. Just as Laney was about to follow after him, Gray reappeared, staggering back toward her, his face white, his hands beating the air to keep his balance while he careened along the narrowing rock shelf.

"Gray . . . what . . . ?" Laney reached out with her left hand to help stabilize Gray's scrambling descent. The move almost caused both of them to topple into the creek. Her hat made the trip alone and bobbed next to the canoe. Gray skidded to a stop and wrapped his arms about her and Puccini, breathing great whining gulps of air. Laney felt his body convulse violently. Terrified that perhaps he had been bitten by a poisonous snake, Laney pulled backwards in fear and searched his face. "What is it, Gray?"

It was a moment before he could speak. Then the words came tumbling like an avalanche of stones, "Derek . . . he must have fallen . . . on the path . . . his skull is crushed."

Laney felt her heart suspend beating for an eternity, then begin catch-up with a hammering that pounded all the way to her brain.

"Dead? . . . he can't be . . . Gray!" And she thrust Puccini into his chest and shoved by him, while all the death of just a year ago crashed down on her. "Can't be," she cried.

She almost stepped upon Derek's contorted body as she lurched around the trees.

No sound came from her open mouth—although she heard the scream in her mind.

Derek lay on his back, his head misshapen and resting in a pool of congealed blood. Tiny bloody cat tracks faded away on the rocky trail at her sneakers. A black harness wound tightly about his groin and waist, and his leather-gloved left hand still grasped the slack rope. His right hand was hidden by his twisted body. Laney thought she might be sick as she visualized Derek's braking hand desperately gripping the rope ever harder to stop his fall.

"Don't Laney," Gray's shaky voice said behind her, his free arm wrapping around her neck and pulling her face into his shoulder. They stood that way for several minutes until he spoke again. "He was rappelling down the cliff and the rope must have worked loose from its anchor—most likely a tree." His eyes traveled up the facade of the cliff. "Must be at least a hundred feet."

Laney pulled her face from Gray's shoulder and forced herself to look at Derek, her eyes pulling in every detail—his frozen eyes staring upward as though looking at the sky, his golden hair clotted black and red against his skull.

The rope lay haphazardly about the ledge and over Derek's body—the anchor end protruding from the puddle of blood about his head like a snake rising from a crimson pool. Laney's insides twisted, then kinked in a spasm of pain as she gasped, "Gray . . . the rope! It's been cut."

5

"Well . . . what do you think?" Deputy Freddie Rudd asked with a gulping breath. He had just washed down a bite of a Chocomart cupcake with his soft drink.

"How can you eat those mummified things?" Gordon answered, disgust in his voice.

Freddie shoved the last of the pink coconut covered chocolate and marshmallow morsel into his mouth with a flourish. He patted his ample belly and stretched out in the passenger seat to give his snack room to digest.

"I think this county is fast becoming a high crime area. That's what I think," the sheriff said. He and his deputy had just stopped at Four Corners Shell Station to give Freddie time to replenish his junk food supply after leaving the scene of Derek Beale's murder. The body was now on the way to the coroner's office in Frankfort and all evidence had been collected and bagged.

"I bet I could count the homicides on one hand during all the years I've been on the force and now there have been three in the last year."

"At least the first two were solved in fast order, thanks in part to Laney McVey and Doc Prescott," Freddie said. "I hate that they are involved in this one."

"Involved? Discovering a body doesn't mean that they are

involved," Gordon said, but he knew what Freddie was driving at. He didn't have to wait long for the inevitable question.

"What about Doc's fight with Derek yesterday morning?" Freddie asked, slurping at the ice in the bottom of his cup.

"He'll be questioned tomorrow, along with anyone else who saw Derek in the last day or so." Gordon was pensive. "Not much to go on at the crime scene, other than the severed end of the rope. For a moment there, I thought perhaps that the rope had been cut by a sharp edge of the rock at the top of the cliff where Derek went over. I think that's what the murderer wanted us to think. But it appears that Derek had rappelled in this spot before, since the rock edge had been rounded off with a hammer."

"It was clear as hell what happened after we inspected the end of the rope still attached to the anchor above. The cut was made too far back from the edge. Three inches too far back and clean as a whistle. Whatever cut the rope was one sharp instrument," Freddie said.

"The knots around the trunk of the tree were good and tight. He seemed to have known what he was doing."

"Except . . . he didn't wear a helmet . . . and it was right in the back of his pickup at the top of the cliff along with other rappelling equipment."

"When you fall that far, I don't think a helmet could save you. I think the coroner will find multiple injuries."

"When do you think it happened?" Freddie asked.

"Could be that the last time anyone saw him alive was Sunday morning about ten forty-five at the country club when he had that altercation with Doc. He must have planned to go rappelling after his golf game because Chris said yesterday after the fight that Derek had driven his Isusu pickup to the club. Apparently, he carries his rappelling equipment in the bed of the truck next to his vet bed. When Dory called the station this morning, she said Derek hadn't been home since he had left for the club yesterday morning."

"I wonder why she didn't call earlier," Freddie pondered.

"Who knows. Maybe he'd stayed out all night before. Ironic that we were on our way out to the farm to talk with Dory when the call came in from Doc that they had discovered his body. He said he and Laney found him about eleven o'clock. The coroner will be able to tell us more about the time of death after the autopsy."

"Gray sure was shook up when he showed us the body. I was glad he hadn't brought Laney back to the scene. She's been through enough in the last year," Freddie said, ending his sentence with a belch. "And now another murder."

"Quit reminding me."

Laney, Gray, Malcolm and Shar sat at the table in the crimson dining room. Gray replenished Malcolm's and Shar's goblets from the bottle of French burgundy.

"Malcolm, thank you for the outstanding wine," Laney said, waving the bottle away as Gray prepared to freshen her glass. "Please Gray, I'm afraid I've already had too much."

"Drink up, woman. We all need to put on a toot after today," Shar said.

"It's just been too ghastly for words," said Malcolm. "And to think all of you knew the deceased."

"Well, I never met him although I saw him at the races on Saturday," Shar said.

"Malcolm, we all attended the same high school here in St. Clair County. Anytime you grow up in a small community, you can't help but feel upset when something happens to one of your classmates," Laney said. "In fact, this is the second person in our graduating class that has died in the last year," Laney added.

"Really?" Malcolm said.

"Pete Sands committed suicide in November. It was a terrible shock. He hanged himself," Laney said.

"Good grief!" Malcolm exclaimed.

"Well I may not have known Derek Beale, but from what I've gathered in just a couple days here, you two weren't crazy about the guy," Shar said. Gray sliced at his steak nervously.

"You would have had a hard time getting to know him, Shar, because he was always in motion. Connecting with him was like trying to hit a moving target. He always seemed dissatisfied with life . . . frustrated, may be a better word," Laney said and pushed aside her plate, her grilled steak and baked potato untouched. The wine was giving her a buzz and Gray's quietness was bothering her.

"His poor wife, Dory. Derek always treated her like she wasn't there," Laney rattled on. "But she's been a good friend to me since Cara died."

"She's a stunning woman," Shar said. "I should have knockers like that."

"Sharlene," Malcolm said, his face turning pink. "Your bosom is quite adequate, my dear."

Laney suppressed a laugh.

"Let's change the subject," Gray said, finally breaking his silence.

"Malcolm, did you see Taylor Ridge Farm today?" Laney asked, realizing instantly that it was another sore subject with Gray.

"I did, indeed. It's an absolutely splendid farm with perfect cattle facilities. I may make an offer, but I can't match their asking price. I'm sure it is worth it but I have my limit."

Gray had the same pained expression that Laney had seen on his face earlier when she told him about Chris's decision to list the farm.

"Did you get to meet Chris Taylor while you were there?" Gray suddenly asked.

"No, however Mrs. Taylor and I spoke briefly before she excused herself and drove out the gateway. She seemed quite distressed. Perhaps she had just heard the news about Mr. Beale."

"What time was this, Malcolm?" Laney asked, as she stacked the plates onto a heavy silver tray.

"Let's see, Taylor Ridge was the first farm we looked at. About ten o'clock, I'd say."

"Amanda was probably upset to meet someone that was interested in the farm. We didn't find Derek until eleven. She couldn't have known," Laney said, again calling to mind Derek's blue eyes staring vacantly at the sky. A wave of nausea hit her. She swallowed and carried the tray to the kitchen.

In a minute, Gray followed her there. "I'm leaving. I've said my goodnights to Malcolm and Shar. Going to neuter Puccini first thing in the morning and I need a good night's sleep."

"You didn't get dessert. Take it with you." She removed a pan of gingerbread from the pie safe, cut a large square and placed it in a container. Before sealing the lid, she spooned a giant dollop of whipped cream on the top.

Gray accepted the container absently, his eyes tired and troubled. His black eye was beginning to turn a yellowish green. She kissed him lightly on the lips.

"You said you have to talk to Gordon tomorrow. Is that why you're so troubled?" she asked.

"There are several things eating at me."

Laney knew he would tell her when he was ready. She walked him to the screen door. Holding it ajar, she took a couple of deep breaths and the cool night air and the sweet fragrance of jonquils growing in the yard seemed to clear her head. Blackberry nudged by her into the dark hallway. Gray left Laney there and climbed into his Jeep. She watched him toss the gingerbread container on the dash where Puccini usually lay and he stared straight ahead as he stepped on the gas. No familiar strains of opera escaped through his open window as he rolled out the entrance.

It was no use. She just couldn't concentrate on writing this evening. Maybe if she tried an early morning session at the computer, she would do better. As she deleted the page she had just typed, the phone rang. Lifting the receiver on the library phone, she wasn't surprised to hear Amanda Taylor's voice on the line.

"Laney, I hope it's not too late. Tomorrow . . . I'm . . . I'm looking forward to tomorrow but I have a favor to ask," Amanda said in a soft faltering voice.

Her comment stunned Laney. She assumed, because of Derek's death, Amanda was calling to cancel their luncheon date at the country club. She and Chris had been really thick with Derek and Dory lately.

"Sure, if I can," Laney said, pressing the phone closer to her ear so she could better hear Amanda's voice fading in and out.

"It's about the twentieth class reunion in July. I . . . I was coerced into writing the program. I don't know why I agreed . . . you know how badly I write. It must have been in a weak moment during that committee meeting at Joyce's . . . you know how strong her mimosas are. Anyway—"

"You want me to write the program," Laney interrupted.

"Would you?" Amanda's sigh of relief came from a great depth. "With selling the farm and now Derek's mur . . . death, I just can't handle anymore." Laney heard a sob, then a long quivering breath. "I guess we really shouldn't go to lunch tomorrow," Amanda went on. "In respect for Derek."

"I think it would be for the best."

"But I so want to meet Shar. What poor timing . . . I mean . . . Derek's death and all while she's visiting you." Laney heard her begin to cry—intense and piercing sounds like the keening of the wind in March. Laney didn't know what to say so she waited. She finally heard Amanda blow her nose. "I'm a mess, Laney," she gulped. "But I'll see you tomorrow at one." Click.

If Amanda had remained on the line a bit longer, Laney was sure that she could have convinced her to postpone the luncheon until sometime after the funeral.

After shutting down the computer, Laney walked into the kitchen to find Shar wolfing a piece of gingerbread at the kitchen table. Just inside the pantry, Blackberry concentrated on removing every trace of meat from the table scraps. So much for a midnight snack, Laney mused, thinking of her uneaten steak.

"Caught me with my fingers in the whipped cream," Shar said, taking a finger swipe through the glob that topped her last bite of gingerbread. "M-m-m," she crooned, as she enveloped the sweet-topped finger with her mouth. The pink tip of her tongue made quick work of the residue on her upper lip.

"Where's Malcolm?" Laney asked.

"He kipped down."

"Excuse me?"

"That's what he said he was going to do when he went to his room. Think it means 'hit the sack,'" Shar said, slicing another square of cake. "Want some?" she asked, as she plopped it onto her plate.

"Guess not, since that's the last of it."

"Sorry. Who was that on the phone?"

"Amanda Taylor. She wants me to write the program for our high school reunion in July. Twenty years. I can't believe it."

"Went to mine two years ago in Pittsburgh along with all the other balding, stomach sucking, frosted hair graduates. I dragged Paulie with me. A big mistake. Caught him nuzzling the class wall-flower who had had her face lifted and breast implants inserted just in time for the reunion."

"Oh Shar."

While Shar put her empty plate in the dishwasher, Laney dashed back to the library and retrieved her class yearbook. She sat next to Shar and sipped at fresh coffee that Shar had made to go with her dessert.

Shar pointed to Laney's class picture. "There you are. Good Lord, woman, you've changed. Without your name underneath, I would never have known it was you."

"Look at that hair down to my butt."

"It's straight. How did you do that?"

"With straightener and an iron. It was the style back then. You remember. You're not that much older." She flipped through the graduates until she came to a montage of informal photographs that filled two pages.

"There's Gray. I'd know him anywhere." Shar pointed to a picture of four guys posing at a magnificent maple tree in front of the school.

"Wrong," Laney said. "That's Bart, Gray's twin brother that died in a car accident graduation night."

"How can you tell it's Bart?"

"Well, it was hard for most people but there was something about Gray, even back then. There was a softness in his eyes. I never had any trouble." Laney suddenly felt a chill. "Oh my God."

"Laney, what is it? Another hairball?"

It was a moment before Laney could speak. When she did, it was with a breathy voice that didn't sound like herself. This guy stand-ing in front of the tree . . ." Laney pointed to a bespectacled pale-faced teen with a short haircut."

"This geeky guy?"

"That's the guy that I told you hanged himself in November."

"Lordy, woman. Pete something, wasn't it?"

"Peter Sands. He left a wife, Tina, and two beautiful girls. They moved away from Hickory." It was a moment before she could look back at the photo. "See the guy hanging by his knees from that branch?"

"Hm-m."

"That's Derek Beale."

Shar turned the book upside down so she could see Derek's face better. "Drop dead gorgeous, even then. Sorry . . . wrong choice of words."

Laney shot bullets at Shar. "The point, 'Oh Compassionate One,' is that Bart, Peter and Derek are dead."

"Oo—ooh—ooh," Shar trilled, with wide spooky eyes. "'Something's Breaking Up That Old Gang of Mine,'" she sang, then sobered when she caught Laney's scowl. She looked back at the photo with renewed interest. "Who's the well fed guy with all the hair?"

"Chris Taylor," Laney said, clasping her cold arms.

"It's all a coincidence, Laney."

"I know," Laney said, and shivered.

6

After a restless night filled with disconnected bits and pieces of dreams, Laney awoke before dawn. In one dream, she was climbing the maple in front of St. Clair High School. She struggled through a maze of limbs, reaching ever deeper into a dark tunnel of swishing branches that took her higher and higher. Lost in the labyrinth, she finally thought she had found a winding way out only to discover Peter Sands hanging by his neck from a bough above her and Derek's body lying across a fork in the trunk below. When she awakened amid a tangle of damp bedclothes, she could hear a steady drizzle against her window. She showered and dressed in a pale pink T-shirt and denim jumper that hung almost to the tops of her sneakers. The crashing thunder and a suspicious trembling lump under her comforter predicted a stormy, gloomy day. Only when Laney began to strip the bed, did Blackberry venture from beneath the covers.

As Laney tiptoed through the kitchen, the gloom was briefly punctuated with quick flickers of lightning as though exploding flashbulbs lit her way, but the waning thunder assured her that the storm had played itself out. Blackberry ankle-nosed her as she padded down the hall to the library.

When she flipped the wall switch, the desk lamp with its creamy fringed shade cast its glow on the one room that never failed to comfort her. As always, her eyes were drawn to the leather bound books, most of which had belonged to her father. His love of reading, Laney realized only recently, had set the fire in her heart to write. Seeing the worn volumes in the rich mahogany bookcases kept Poppy alive in her mind. She still missed him, although he had died when she was only twelve, a victim of a massive heart attack which occurred in front of her mother, her sister and her.

Inspired by his presence, Laney booted up her computer, suddenly feeling bright-eyed and eager to begin writing. Only when she heard muted plumbing sounds overhead, did she check her watch and realize that she had been at it for three hours. She finished her paragraph, leaving her protagonist in an indefensible situation that she knew she would have to rewrite later.

Malcolm, as well as Shar, had opted for breakfast in the dining room. Laney suspected that their mutual attraction had been the reason they'd chosen breakfast in the dining room together instead of the alternative—single baskets at their bedroom doors.

She set two places at the mirror finish mahogany table. The crisp white linen place mats and matching napkins nestled intimately at one corner. When Laney heard Shar and Malcolm in the front hall, she poured steaming coffee into her large silver urn and placed it on the sideboard near a basket of warm marmalade muffins and a hot fruit compote made with dried fruits laced with white wine. She glanced into the heavy gold framed beveled mirror over the sideboard. The chandelier with crystal prisms sparkling like diamonds shined back at her. But below, her own image appeared sallow and strained—her brown eyes much too bright, her freckles blotches of shadow.

While the two love birds dallied over breakfast, Laney seared a rump roast in hot fat in her mother's vintage Dutch oven in the kitchen. She had stolen the cast iron pot when she left Hickory to attend the University of Pittsburgh almost twenty years before. Again she thought of her three high school classmates who had died. She made a mental note to devote one page of the reunion program to the alumni who were deceased. At that moment, she couldn't think of any others in her class who had died.

When the beef was a rich brown, she added a dozen small white onions and dropped on the lid. She was scraping the carrots when

Maddy walked into the kitchen with an armload of freezer containers. Her knit hat sparkled with raindrops.

"I let myself in with my key. Open the pantry freezer, will you?" she said.

"I was just thinking about all the delicious food you fix for me, and here you come with more. When do you find time to do it all and Hickory Dock too?" Laney asked, dashing into the pantry ahead of her mother and lifting the lid on the freezer.

Shaking off her dripping trench coat, Maddy hung it on a hook in the pantry and answered her daughter, "If it weren't for Guffy Haus, I'd really be pushed, but he works five mornings a week. That's when I do the cookin and bakin. Enough . . . what's this about Gray being questioned in Derek's murder?"

Laney pretended she hadn't heard and rushed back into the kitchen where she lifted the lid on her roast and dropped the whole baby carrots in. She added seasoned salt and pepper, some minced parsley, five peppercorns, three whole cloves, a bay leaf, a minced garlic clove and the last of the burgundy that Malcolm had brought the night before—about a cup. It all took about a minute or two. She planned to deliver the meal to Dory after lunch at the club. But after her mother's mention of Gray's questioning, her stomach churned when she thought of food.

Maddy snatched a mug hanging from a hook under a lead glass-fronted cabinet and poured the last of the coffee. She sat in one of the blond oak chairs at the round breakfast table facing Laney who stood at the stove across from her.

Maddy raised her brows. "Thought we decided to talk about things instead of buryin our heads in the sand." She tapped her foot. "I can outwait you."

"It's . . . it's just routine questioning," Laney said, unnecessarily lifting the heavy lid of the Dutch oven again. Steam dampened her cheeks. Her stomach churned.

"Police know Gray had that fight with Derek earlier."

"Yes."

"You worried?"

"No."

"Laney?"

"No!" Laney just wanted to be left alone—to be allowed to bury her head in the sand, if she wanted to. Her stomach churned.

Shar and Laney arrived at the country club before Amanda and deposited their umbrellas in the cloakroom of the women's powder room. Laney grimaced at her reflection in the vanity mirror. Above her flowing jade pants and matching knit silk tunic, her rambunctious hair blazed like a flare.

In contrast, Shar's strawberry blond pixie hugged her head neatly like a knit cap. She wore a royal blue jacketed jumpsuit, and another blue and red Hamilton plaid sash cinched her tiny waist. Around her neck a shiny silver thistle hung from a chain.

They waited for Amanda in the reception room while the rain continued to pelt the windows. They sat knee to knee on a wine colored damask sofa that matched the elegantly hung draperies at twin windows that overlooked the parking lot. Laney felt the squishy cushions shift as Shar squirmed uncomfortably in her seat. She couldn't imagine Shar ever feeling out of place and was about to ask her about it when the door suddenly opened and Amanda Taylor entered in a gust of blowing rain. Shoving the door closed, she removed her plastic rain hat, dripping water over the parquet foyer.

"There you are," Laney said, crossing the room and dragging Shar behind her. Laney gave Amanda a hug and introduced her to Shar.

"I saw you briefly at the farm yesterday," Amanda said, talking into Shar's left breast as she removed her raincoat. "I feel I already know you, thanks to Laney here."

Shar stooped a bit to catch the tiny woman's eyes. "You sure are close to the ground. Is it cooler down there?" she asked.

"Shar," Laney scolded.

"It's okay, Laney . . . really it is," Amanda said, forcing a smile. "I . . . I need someone to lighten me up."

It would take a tank of helium to lighten her up, Laney determined. Amanda's body sagged like a piece of wet cardboard that might fold into itself any second and her light brown hair hung in oily ringlets about her face. Amanda's veined hands smoothed at her ecru skirt and sweater that looked as though she had pulled them out of the go-to-the-cleaner's bag.

Amanda crammed her rain hat into her pocket and hooked the raincoat on a hall tree by the door. From the other pocket of her raincoat, she extracted a rolled up file. Shoving it into Laney's hand, she explained that it contained the completed alumni questionnaires for the reunion program.

The three of them moved into the dining room. The weather had kept the usual weekday lunch crowd down so they had their pick of the tables. The hostess led them to a round one that, on a clear day, would have had a view of the wooden patio deck and the golf course beyond. Today, rivulets of water formed an ever changing panorama of patterns on the windowpane.

Shar and Amanda ordered coffee and Laney, hot tea. While they sipped at their beverages, Shar twisted about in her seat, barraging Amanda with all kinds of questions like she was conducting an interview. By the time their salads came, Shar's interrogation had wrung enough information from Amanda for a short bio.

"You don't mean it. Tennis? You couldn't see over the net," Shar exclaimed, rubbing her body against the chair.

"In high school, Amanda went to the regionals twice, making it all the way to state our senior year," Laney added.

Leave it to Shar to perk things up, Laney mused, for Amanda seemed to have temporarily forgotten about whatever was tearing her up. Laney knew Derek's death had thrown Amanda, as it had everyone, but she thought her distress might also have something to do with the sale of her farm. She hoped that Shar wouldn't bring the Taylor Ridge listing up. She hoped for naught.

"I know you and your husband are selling Taylor Ridge and moving to town. Guess I can't blame you. The country is fun to visit, but I'd go loony toons if I had to live with the beasties and crawlies year round," Shar said.

"You love it, and you know it," Laney said, trying to divert Amanda's attention from the original subject, but she could see her face darkening and her small muscular body beginning to droop once more.

"That reminds me," Shar went on. "What in the hell are these itchy red bites all over my butt and other dark places that only my

three husbands had knowledge of?" She reached beneath the table
and scratched at her body.

"You must have chiggers," Laney laughed, knowing how tortur-
ous they could be. "You must have gotten them sitting in the grass
when we stopped to rest while bike riding. We'll get something for
them later," Laney said, distracted by Amanda who looked like she
was about to burst into tears. "Amanda, what is it?"

Before she could answer, the hostess approached the table and
leaned down and whispered into Amanda's ear. Amanda swallowed
back the tears, nodded at the woman and excused herself. She rose
to her feet, swayed unsteadily, but recovered enough to follow the
waitress to a door marked "office" near the entrance to the dining
room. The waitress opened the door and Amanda disappeared
inside.

"What in the hell is that all about?" Shar asked, still shifting
uncomfortably in her seat.

"I don't know, but I think she is about to lose it."

Laney focused on the door until she saw it open slowly. Amanda
inched out, her face appearing flushed, even from across the room.
She peered over at them, twisted and ran out into the reception
room.

"Let's go," Laney commanded. Without waiting for Shar, Laney
grabbed her bag and the reunion file and bolted through the dining
room after Amanda. When she reached the reception room, it was
empty. She was about to check the powder room but stopped when
she saw that the hall tree where Amanda had left her raincoat was
empty. She opened the door and caught Amanda's black Saab leaving twin fins of spray as it fishtailed out of the flooded parking lot.

Not stopping to knock, Laney swooped into the office. Shar, who
had caught up, followed her in. A woman, sipping coffee from a
mug, stood gazing through the window. She turned at the interrup-
tion—her expression a study in perplexity and concern.

"Oh Laney, it's you. What can I do for you?" she said, placing the
mug on a stack of papers on her desk. Her face brightened a bit and
she glanced curiously at Shar.

Laney didn't stop to introduce her friend. "Barbara . . . please, I
know this may be awkward for you, but Amanda's my friend. We
were having lunch. She just burst out of your office and took off like

a bat out of hell.'"

Barbara Hadden, a woman about middle age, shook her head, her fluttering right hand pulling her frosted pageboy behind one ear. The country club manager sat down in her desk chair and picked up a pen, pretending to study what looked like a billing statement. Laney could discern the account name at the top of the statement: Christopher Taylor.

"Laney, I can't discuss Amanda's personal business with you. You know that," Barbara said as Laney's eyes scanned down the page. Noticing Laney scrutinizing the bill, Barbara flipped the statement over.

"I thought maybe . . . she seemed so distraught," Laney added.

"I can't . . . really . . . I know you want to help," Barbara said, suddenly standing—obviously a signal the conversation was over.

Dismissed, Laney and Shar turned to leave. "Lunch was delicious, as always," Laney said over her shoulder.

"Thank you . . . and Laney . . . "

Laney swiveled. "Yes?"

"I realize that Amanda invited you for lunch, but would you mind signing for the tab? The Taylors are no longer members of the club."

7

"This whole thing is bugging me," Laney continued, as they climbed into the Whooptie. The rain had finally come to an end and the clouds were dispersing quickly in a light breeze.

"Don't mention bugs to me. I'm going out of my mind with these chiggers," Shar moaned. She scratched at her crotch indelicately.

"When we stop at Gray's, we'll get some chigger medicine from him."

"Praise the Lord. Now . . . about your friend, Amanda. If she's not a member of the club any longer, she must have just resigned while she was in the office talking to the manager. She certainly wouldn't have taken us to lunch at the country club if she had resigned earlier."

"If she resigned at all," Laney said.

"Did I miss something, woman?" Shar asked.

"I saw the Taylor's statement on Barbara's desk. I think she was kicked out of Hickory Country Club for non-payment of dues."

"Why you insidious snake in the grass. I can't believe you would sink so low as to read someone else's statement—what did it say?"

Laney grinned. "Past due 120 days."

Shar covered her ears with her hands. "I didn't hear that. So, the Taylor Ridge Taylors are flat broke."

"But how could that happen?" Laney said incredulously.

"Bad investments? A relative sucking them dry? Gambling? Deep pockets? Blackmail?"

"Can't imagine any of the above. They are the most prudent and restrained couple I know."

"Just like my first husband, Jake, except I had another name for him—'Cheap.'"

Laney pulled into the clinic parking lot and parked next to Gray's 1958 restored pink Buick. The sun flashed brightly off the car's exaggerated chrome fins and draping. When Shar saw it, she let out a cry of awe.

"Look at that, will you? So there it is in all its splendor. When you told me about it last year, you didn't do it justice, woman." She elbowed the stubborn door twice and uncoiled from the Whooptie's front seat. Laney knew she'd be a while checking out Gray's car so she went inside the clinic.

Her eyes needed a minute to adjust from the glare outside to the dimness of the waiting room.

"Laney, good to see you," Natine Sullivan, Gray's secretary, called from her desk inside a partitioned alcove across the room. Her dimpled bronze face slowly came into focus.

"Hi. Where's Gray?" Laney asked. She still couldn't believe the woman was forty. She looked like a teenager.

"You don't want to see him today," Natine said with a scowl that scrunched her brow and made her dimples disappear. "He's been torn up ever since he got back from the court house."

"Well, I have to face him sooner or later." Her heart began to dance an unstable tango.

"He's in the post-op. Go on back, but be on guard."

"Send Shar back if she ever tears herself away from Gray's Buick," Laney said.

Laney strode down the hall, past the pharmacy supply room, examining rooms and surgery. The sound of barking canines filtered through a metal door from the runs outside. She opened the post-op door slowly and peered in. Gray was petting Puccini who was lying on his side on a stainless steel table in the center of the room. Gray looked up as she entered. The swelling in his eye had subsided, but every shade of green was now evident—pea, olive, spinach and chartreuse—all splotched with mustard gold. His face looked pinched, his recent Florida tan, washed out and pasty. His normally soft pliant mouth forced a tight smile.

"Hi," he said.

"Hi," she said. "I forgot about Puccini's surgery this morning. He looks like he did all right. You look worse than he does."

"Thanks."

"The questioning . . . pretty rough?"

"Pretty rough."

"That's all you're going to say?"

"That's all I'm going to say . . . right now."

Shar knocked and peeked in the door. "Can I come in?"

"Sure," Gray said, petting his cat. Puccini didn't seem to be in any pain and his copper eyes blinked sleepily at Shar. Losing interest, he bent over and began to lick the stitches.

"Will the operation change his personality?" Shar inquired. "After Paulie had his vasectomy, that's when he started screwing around."

Gray's face reddened and he cleared his throat. "Vasectomies aren't castrations, Shar. Men can still perform normally after a vas," he explained patiently. "However, Puccini's catting around days are over and the neutering definitely should calm him down some."

"Calm him down? If he gets any calmer, he'll quit breathing. All he does is catnap on your dashboard. Shar stroked between Puccini's ears. "Poor wretched pussy," she crooned. She glanced at her watch. "May I use your phone? Malcolm said he would be back at the farm this afternoon. He wants to take me out for dinner."

"Use the phone in my office just off the waiting room," Gray said.

After Shar left, Gray picked up Puccini and unlatched the door of a large unit in a middle tier of cages against the wall and placed him inside. The cat shut his eyes. Gray latched the door, strode deliberately to Laney and pulled her to him roughly. His arms pinned hers to her side and he buried his face between her jaw and her shoulder while his breath whispered chills on her neck.

"Laney, be patient with me through this," he murmured. "I need your trust . . . your loyalty. I love you so much."

Laney thought she felt a wetness on her neck.

Jessica Mills met them at the door.

"Jesse, I completely forgot you were coming today," Laney said. Jesse cleaned every week for her as she had done for her sister, Cara.

"I'm on my way out. I'll be back Thursday to finish up my six hours before I go to the Finish Line. That Malcolm guy is on the screened porch. See ya." She waved and ran out to her gray station wagon before Shar could say "hi."

Shar leaped by Laney and made for her bedroom, chigger medicine bottle in hand, her long legs eating up the staircase like she was pursued by the monster mite itself. Laney headed for the kitchen where she removed a large casserole dish from the refrigerator. Lifting the lid, she smelled the fragrant roast, carrots, pearl onions, and browned potatoes. Grabbing a basket in the pantry, she lined it with a new terry cloth towel covered with sunny daffodils. She placed the labeled dish inside, along with a quart mason jar filled with the glistening rich dark brown gravy. She tucked in a bag of her mother's yeast rolls from the pantry freezer and added a pint jar of Cara's piccalilli. As she closed the pantry cabinet door, she noted sadly that Cara's canned goods were fast being depleted.

Before she left for Dory's, she peeked out on the porch where Shar had joined Malcolm and saw that they were in intense conversation, their elbows resting on the round metal table with noses practically touching. Blackberry lay at Shar's feet. Shar had kicked off her flats and one long slender foot swept back and forth along the collie's back. Apparently, she had stopped itching after applying the chigger medicine that Gray had given her. Seeing Laney, Malcolm straightened.

"I've made an offer on Taylor Ridge, Laney," he said. "I should know something by this time tomorrow." His brown eyes were bright with expectation.

"I'm happy for you, Malcolm," Laney said, but she was not really happy at all. Malcolm's high spirits were the result of Chris and Amanda's misfortune, whatever that could be. A heaviness enveloped her as she said goodbye and hefted the basket for Dory.

Laney swung a right through the entrance of Hickory Pike Farm. When she came to the Y in the lane, she was tempted to take the right fork and visit with Woody, Terry and Melinda to see how they were tolerating the rabies shots. Mary hadn't handled the foal so didn't have to go through the series of five shots spread over twenty-eight days. When she had seen Gray earlier, he had told her that he had already taken his boosters.

Thinking of Gray, Laney brooded about his comment to her and the tears she was sure she had felt. What had happened at the sheriff's department that made him feel so threatened and vulnerable? Why did he feel it necessary to ask for her support? If only he would confide in her. She buried the thoughts inside as she braced herself for what she knew would be a painful visit with Dory.

The drive to the house was breathtaking. Along the curving lane, groups of dogwood and redbud trees that were just beginning to bud mingled with ancient shagbark hickories. Usually overgrown, the sides of the drive had been freshly mowed and any old branches or tree limbs that had fallen during the winter had been hauled away. Groups of daffodils scattered their gold here and there beneath the trees. As Laney wove her way forward, she caught glimpses of the two-story house with Flemish bond brick patterns. Slipping from the forested drive, she saw the house in its entirety appear in front of her. It lay back of a circle drive like her own Victorian, but the house was considerably larger. She was surprised to see that the weary antebellum house that for years had cried out for care had finally been tuck pointed and the trim and shutters had been repaired and freshly painted.

Several vehicles lined the curved drive. Laney parked behind a shiny new navy Lexus with temporary St. Clair County plates. Derek's old red Porsche was parked out of the way in a short carport to the side of the house but she didn't see Dory's white station wagon or Derek's vet truck.

While crossing the pillared portico, the pungent smell of the shaped dark green boxwoods met her nostrils. She shifted the heavy food basket and rang the front bell. From somewhere behind the house came the sound of heavy machinery.

Dory answered the door. Behind her, a teenage boy, galloping down the stairs, pulled up short. His expression turned sour when he saw Laney at the door, obviously hoping she had been someone else. Laney immediately recognized Dory's son by an earlier marriage, even though she hadn't seen him in several years because he had usually been away at school whenever she had visited Cara.

"Laney, how thoughtful," Dory said, as she accepted the basket. Without searching the contents, she transferred the basket to the teen, who looked remarkably like his mother. "Walker, dear, would you take this out to Mary in the kitchen?"

Woody's wife must be helping out during the funeral, Laney concluded. Walker pouted and slouched down the hallway beside the staircase before Laney could say hello. Dory turned back to Laney. "Please do come in and chat awhile," she said in a silvery, genial voice.

Chat awhile? Her husband was just murdered, for God's sake, Laney thought in astonishment.

As Laney shadowed her out of the entrance hall and through a front parlor, she realized that the interior of the house had also been newly decorated. When they entered the back parlor, Dory indicated with a wave of her hand for Laney to be seated on a gold damask covered settee sitting perpendicular to the fireplace that was faced with a gleaming white mantel. Shazam, Laney said to herself. The old ruin has been done over. However, she was happy to see that the original French hand-blocked scenic wallpaper above the mantle and covering all the walls in the room hadn't been disturbed. Dory sat opposite Laney in a ruby colored Queen Ann wing chair whose twin rested beside the mahogany and maple sewing table separating them. Laney recognized the chairs as those that used to be covered in faded blue silk. Several other pieces in the room were familiar to her but clearly had been reupholstered. What a great improvement it was from the deteriorated state the home had been in when Derek inherited it from his mother.

Dory smiled at Laney. "Laney, everyone has been so kind. Thank you again for your neighborliness." Laney scrutinized Dory's face, but for the life of her, she couldn't detect any evidence of sadness.

But then her flawless face was carefully made up and everyone expresses their sorrow differently, she admonished herself.

"I'm so very sorry, Dory. Is there anything I can do to help you? Perhaps make some calls for you or offer my home for any out-of-town relatives or guests that may be coming for the funeral. I know I should have offered before now."

Dory waved the offer away as she answered. "No. The only relatives are my son, of course, and my mother and brother who arrived shortly before you. They are upstairs getting dressed for the visitation. As you know, Derek's parents are deceased." The engine noises began again but were louder now. Laney turned toward the sound that seemed to be originating through French doors that opened onto a patio.

Evidently picking up on Laney's distraction, Dory began, "Please forgive the disturbance, Laney, but Derek had already begun the swimming pool before he died and you know how hard it is to keep workmen these days. It's not too insensitive of me to continue with it, do you think?"

Why no, let's have a pool party, Laney thought to herself. "I . . . suppose—"

"Laney," Dory interrupted, looking at her gold watch. "I must be going. Visitation is from six until nine this evening. The funeral is graveside at eleven in the morning." She stood and tugged at her black dress. The pearls around her neck looked real.

Laney followed her perfect figure back into the foyer where Dory paused in front of a beveled mirror that hung above a drop-leaf Hepplewhite table and patted her glistening, dark brown pageboy. Her green eyes shone. She was the most stunning widow Laney had ever seen. Dory thanked her again and urged her toward the door. As the door closed behind her, she heard voices inside.

As Laney started the car, Dory, Walker, and a man and an older woman whom she assumed were Dory's brother and mother, hurried out the immense paneled door. What she saw next left her open-mouthed. While the rest of the family chatted and dallied on the portico, Dory slipped behind the wheel of the luxurious Lexus that was parked in front of Laney. Laney's foot slipped off the clutch, and with a lurch, the Whooptie stalled.

"Double shazam," Laney exclaimed, pretending to adjust her

mirror through the open window while she watched the rest of Dory's family pile into the expensive car and glide away from the rock curb. Only when the Lexus passed from view into the shadowy trees, did Laney recover enough to restart the Whooptie.

8

"What do you think?" Freddie asked.

"I think Gray was telling the truth when he said he didn't have the tape," Gordon said.

"Maybe that empty case was already there on the ledge before Derek fell to his death," Freddie said, sweeping another tortilla chip through the hot salsa. He looked up when he felt Gordon's eyes on him. The sheriff's lips were parted in amazement. "Want some?" Freddie asked, offering the almost empty bag of chips.

"Are you kidding? That's why I gave Maddy's salsa to you. Every batch comes with warning and a fire extinguisher. One of these days your gut's going to incinerate," Gordon said, as he settled back in his chair. "Back to the empty cassette case. It was clean . . . no weather on it. The lab said the partial thumbprint looks like Derek's."

Gordon stood and walked around his battleship gray desk and sat on a corner facing Freddie who crunched the last chip and sipped at his Ale-8. After the last gurgling swallow, the deputy added another sticky ring to the desk top when he slammed the green bottle down.

The work day for them was over and they were catching breathers before going home. They had already questioned Gray, golf pro Charlie Breathitt, Woody Wakefield, and Chris Taylor.

"You know what I think?" Freddie said, crunching the bag and missing a free throw into the gray waste can by the door. "I think maybe Derek's fall dislodged the cassette tape from his pocket, flipped the case open when it hit the ledge, and popped the tape into the creek. That's what I think." He tipped back in his gray chair and lifted first one heavy foot then the other onto the desk with a satisfied grunt.

"Not a bad scenario," Gordon said. "Could have flipped way out."

"Has the water patrol come up with anything yet."

"No, but they'll find it if it's out there," Gordon said.

"Do you think if there's a tape, it's significant?"

"Who knows. Maybe it could supply a motive for Beale's murder."

"Forgetting the tape. What about an act of passion? Everyone knows Beale was no angel. Hardly a gal in the county he hasn't handled."

"You thinking maybe Dory Beale got wind of one of his infidelities? Come on. She has her own spicy track record," Gordon said.

"Are these the legs of a murderer, Your Honor?" Freddie crossed his legs demurely and feminized his voice coyishly.

Gordon laughed, "She's a knockout all right, but the coroner said Derek probably died between eleven and twelve-thirty. Dory had taken Mary Wakefield and her children to church with her in Hickory and it didn't even let out until past noon."

"Only takes a second to cut a rope."

"I still think the tape holds the answer," Gordon said.

"Hate to play devil's advocate with you, but Gray did have opportunity and motive. He drove out to the farm to tell Woody that the foal had rabies."

"Then, just as soon as Gray told him, Woody had a motive just like Gray," Gordon said. "And he lives right on the farm."

"Woody said he mowed until three o'clock on the other side of the farm after Gray left at eleven," Freddie said. "And what about Gray's alibi? He has none . . . said he just rode around until one-thirty. And Laney didn't see him until three o'clock."

"I admit it does look bad for Gray. But Gray couldn't kill anyone," Gordon said as he stood and stretched.

"That brings me back to Dory Beale," Freddie said. "There's something about that widow woman. She's always struck me as being like one of those statues I saw once in a museum that had a red velvet rope protecting it. She's up there sitting pretty but she's as cold and bloodless as a block of marble. Hardly shed a tear when we told her about her husband. I say she did him in."

"Yeah, but like you said, her legs are not the legs of a murderer." Gordon quipped.

When Laney arrived home, she changed into her jeans, a red cotton sweater, and sneakers. She was about to begin working on her novel when Blackberry's high-spirited antics persuaded her to give in to a little diversion by taking a short walk—maybe even a canoe ride. The Border collie led her down the path behind the carriage house toward the springhouse. Fingers of shadow were venturing from beneath the trees, climbing the hill and chasing the sun behind the house. The familiar path to the springhouse seemed to lure the dog. She ran forward, then backtracked, urging Laney on with wags, whines, and wiggles until they finally stood on the small floating dock. The canoe lay nearby in the grass, turned upside down, the two paddles resting against the side where she and Gray had left them after the ruined picnic the day before. One look at Stoney Creek changed her mind about canoeing. Although it wasn't swift, the water was the color of mocha cream and bits of debris bobbed near the banks.

She was about to return to the house, when she heard the familiar sound of Cutty Bell's trolling motor approaching from upstream. Smiling to herself, she decided to wait. She was quite fond of the fellow. One of several local characters and an avid fisherman, hardly a day went by that you couldn't find the Vietnam veteran somewhere on the creek that wound through the county and swiped at Hickory on its way north. But Laney knew that the two and a half miles that snaked through Stoney Creek Farm were Cutty's favorite haunt.

"Say Laney," he called to her as he came into view from behind some weeds along the bank. He raised a denim covered arm and waved and chugged toward the dock. Laney could picture his spider web tattoo under his jacket. He killed the motor and drifted toward the dock. Laney caught the towline and wrapped it around a cleat a couple of turns.

"I haven't seen you for awhile. What have you been up to?" Laney asked as the battered johnboat nudged the carpet shielded edge of the dock.

"Ain't been up to much. Just fishin," he said, standing up in the rocking boat and turning his back to Laney. He tugged at his jeans that exposed the crack in his butt and gave him his nickname, "Droopy Drawers." From out of the corner of her eye, Laney saw a yellow stream and heard the spout hit the water. She reeled, her face flaming. When she heard the zip, she cautiously turned back, stooped and began to pet Blackberry as though she hadn't heard or seen a thing.

"If you're wantin to take the canoe out, head downstream. Water patrol's workin upstream where Doc Beale got kilt." He reached into his grimy cooler, retrieved a beer and snapped the lid.

Laney suddenly straightened and peered anxiously at Cutty. "What are they doing?"

"Dredgin the creek for a tape."

"They told you that?"

"Not zackly. My nephew works for em and he told me."

"What kind of tape?"

"One of those audio ones. They found a empty cassette case on the ledge near Doc Beale's body. Cops think it might help find who kilt him." Cutty bent over, unwound the towline and tossed it into the bottom of the boat. "Better be goin if I'm gonna to get outta here before dark. I put in at Jeff Irwin's. I hope they let me back through."

Cutty's belly peeked out in blubbery folds below a skimpy T-shirt. He switched on the motor, backed the boat away from the dock and turned the throttle to the right. With a wave of his camouflage cap, Cutty headed back upstream.

Laney and Blackberry took a long walk after seeing Cutty. Darkness was closing in as they traveled back toward the house. While she walked, she wondered why the police were taking the empty cassette case so seriously—so seriously, in fact, they were dredging the creek for the chance there had been a cassette inside. For heaven's sake, she thought, the case could have already been there when Derek fell. The phone was ringing as Laney let herself in the house and the grandfather clock in the front hall chimed nine o'clock in an incongruous harmony. She grabbed up the phone in the library. It was her farm manager

"Miss Laney, this is Aaron. Unreasonable is getting ready to foal. I know you wanted to see it," he said.

"Be right there," Laney said breathlessly. Damn, she thought. I wanted Shar to see this. She scribbled a quick note, taped it to the front door and locked up. She sped down the lane in the Whooptie, knowing how quickly foaling can happen. Aaron was on the phone when she rushed into the office. Through the observation glass, Laney could see the gray mare pacing the stall. A vehicle braked in front of the office. Laney ran to the window next to the door and saw Shar and Malcolm alight from his rented green Oldsmobile.

"Are we too late?" Shar asked as they entered the room.

Aaron, who had just hung up the phone, rushed by the three of them, his green eyes briefly darting to Laney's. "I've called Dr. Prescott on his mobile. I think we have a problem," he called back at them.

"What does he mean?" Malcolm asked Laney. She felt her heart skitter in her chest like she had had too much caffeine.

"All I know is that Aaron wouldn't call Gray if it weren't an emergency." She looked anxiously through the window at the gray mare. Aaron was hooking the shank to her halter, and her rump was facing the window. Laney got a chill. Blood oozing from the mare's vulva and trickling down her hind legs, splashed onto the bright straw in scarlet drops. She had witnessed several foalings this spring but she had never seen that much blood before. She wished Gray would hurry.

As though Gray had read her thoughts, she heard the sound of another vehicle and she jumped to the office window. "Thank God."

The three of them watched from the viewing window as Gray entered the stall. His face was a study in concern as he checked the mare. Unreasonable strained—her right hind leg lifting in pain.

"Oh Laney!" Shar cried. "What's that?"

From the dilated vulva emerged a bloody red protuberance.

Through the barred glass, Laney saw Gray's mouth form the dreaded words, "Placenta previa."

He flew out of the stall and was back in a few seconds, but even in that short interval of time, the mass had grown to the size of a football. As Unreasonable strained, the bag seemed to grow even larger. Shar let out a cry and covered her eyes with her hands. Laney dashed out of the office and stood in the stall door opening, in case Gray needed her.

With a strong downward sweep of the scalpel, Gray slashed open the monstrous crimson bulge. As the pouch collapsed, a white membrane-covered projection came into view. He cut through the sack, revealing two front hooves and a nose. Gray tugged at the legs, frantically clearing the nose and mouth at intervals as the foal inched out. Aaron held the shank tightly while talking softly to the mare, who remained standing. With Gray's final protracted pull, the foal slipped into his arms and he lowered it to the straw. It lay lifeless.

"Laney, take the shank from Aaron! Aaron, my ambu bag and Dopram!"

Aaron knew instantly what to do and flung the shank into Laney's outstretched hand.

Gray dropped to his knees and began to rub the foal's chest and throat vigorously—his other hand squeezing mucus from its nose and running sweeping fingers deep into its mouth and throat.

Still the foal did not breathe.

Aaron returned with the ambu bag, stethoscope and syringe. Grabbing the stethoscope, Gray listened at the foal's chest. "A heartbeat . . . but it's fast." He opened a long-lashed eyelid of the foal and touched the eyeball lightly. "No eye reflex," he said, and placed the mask of the ambu over the foal's mouth and nose. Gray's large muscled hand began to squeeze the bag—in and out, in and out. There was no response from the tiny body.

"Aaron, the Dopram!" Gray said with outstretched hand. He

slowly released the respiration stimulant into the jugular of the foal, then continued squeezing the bag.

Laney's eyes riveted on the foal's chest. But from the tiny mouth it came—first, a clouding of the clear plastic mask, then a gasp, then another. The narrow chest rose and fell, then rose and fell, again and again. The foal began to struggle and Gray pulled the mask away. Lifting its head, the colt whinnied. Unreasonable turned her head and nickered.

Laney walked to the polyphon in the corner of the parlor and selected a disc from the cabinet below. She lifted the burl lid, dropped the fifteen and one half inch tin record into place and carefully wound the handle. The "Wine, Woman and Song" waltz by Strauss tinkled through the room like music from a carousel. Exhausted from the emotional ordeal, everyone lulled sluggishly about the cocoa colored room. Shar was the first to speak.

"Woman, you sure didn't tell me a foaling would be so hairy," Shar said, sitting on the floor in front of the red damask sofa and leaning against Malcolm's legs.

"It's been an eventful day for all of us," Laney said, settling on Gray's lap in the green leather Morris chair and sipping her Bloody Mary. Gray was on his second bourbon and water, and Malcolm and Shar savored snifters of brandy. The fringed lamps on the highly polished mahogany end tables cast a dusky glow on the wooden floors and brightly colored oriental rug.

"At least the mare and her wee foal made it all right," Malcolm said. "Thanks to Gray, here." He lifted his glass and toasted the vet.

"Did Chris and Amanda accept your offer, Malcolm?" Laney asked.

"Sally was to call me if they signed. I haven't heard as yet," he said.

"Well I heard something interesting today," Laney said, then told them about the cassette case that was found near Derek's body and that according to Cutty, the water patrol was searching the creek for the missing tape. She felt Gray's body stiffen, then he gently pushed her off his lap, stood, and strode over to the credenza to freshen his drink. "I didn't notice a cassette case on the cliff, did you, Gray?" Laney asked.

"Funny you should ask," he answered. "Police asked me the same question today. Since I was the one who discovered the body, they wanted to know if I had taken the tape. Wouldn't be surprised if they got a search warrant and went through my apartment."

"Gray, they wouldn't," Laney said vehemently. "Well . . . evidently, now they think it may have flipped into the creek because they were out there today looking. I wonder if the tape could be significant evidence in the murder."

"Probably just a tape of Tiny Tim singing, 'Tiptoe Through the Tulips,' " Shar quipped. Everyone laughed, except Gray.

"Listen, you guys, I'm beat," he said. "I'll talk at you later." Gray gulped the rest of his drink and excused himself. Laney walked him to the door.

"This really has you upset," she said when they stepped onto the front porch. It sounded more like a question.

"Damn straight!" he roared. "Who wouldn't be? Barron grilled me like I was a goddamned suspect."

"Who's Barron?"

"Detective Fuller Barron," he said hatefully. "They've called in a homicide investigating officer from Frankfort. You should have heard him, Laney. I know he already has me pegged as the killer."

Laney reached out her arms to hold Gray, but he pushed her away. "Got to go." He snatched up the bloody coveralls he had peeled off after the foaling, charged off the porch, and stomped to his Grand Cherokee. She heard the sporadic scream of the Jeep's tires all the way to the front gate.

Laney sensed Shar's presence behind her and a long slender arm stretched around her waist. Laney let her head tilt and rest on Shar's shoulder.

"God, Shar, what's happening to him? He's losing control. I want to help him but he won't let me. He's shutting me out."

"Do you think it's just about Derek's murder?"

"No, I think his best friend's financial situation is eating at him."

"Chris Taylor?" Shar straightened and peered down into Laney's eyes.

"Yes. Ever since our canoe ride when I told him about Chris listing Taylor Ridge, he's been different. I think he feels hurt that Chris didn't confide in him about it."

"Why do you think Chris didn't?"

"Got me . . . unless it's his pride—"

"Or some deep secret Chris doesn't want anyone to know about." Shar nudged Laney with her elbow.

"Oh, I get you. We're back to 'relative sucking them dry . . . gambling . . . bad investments.'"

"You forgot one," Shar said, her eyes narrowing, her pixie face suddenly appearing wicked in the yellow porch light.

"What?"

"Blackmail, woman."

"Someone blackmailing Chris? . . . who? . . . get out of here!" Laney gave her a playful shove and started into the house. She was on the threshold when she braked hard. Shar slammed into her backside with an "oof." Laney wheeled, seized Shar's willowy arm and dragged her reeling into the parlor.

Laney furiously tossed ice into a tumbler at the credenza and splashed a hefty measure of vodka over it. She added a tad of V8 and squeezed a wedge of lime. Taking a goblet from the cabinet below, she filled it halfway with brandy. Her hands shook as though she had a chill.

"Lordy, woman, you'll get me sozzled. What are the reinforcements for?" Shar asked, snatching up her goblet.

Laney moved to the red sofa and snuggled into a corner. She slapped a pillow in her lap and patted the cushion next to her. Shar kicked off her open-toed flats, took the opposite corner and flung her right leg over the back of the sofa. She rested her left foot on the pillow in Laney's lap. Her toes wiggled restlessly and her toenails flashed amethyst—the color of her matching slacks and blouse.

Shar swigged her brandy and choked, making her gray eyes spurt. "Enlighten me, woman," she said in squeaky falsetto.

"What you said on the porch . . . I first discounted it—"

"Blackmail?" Shar interrupted, her voice back to normal.

"I haven't had time to tell you about my visit with Dory. You won't believe this, Shar."

Laney related how the Beale's house had been remodeled including a new pool. She described the well kept grounds. "Derek had always moaned about how keeping up the old house was like dropping money into a black hole . . . that as long as the roof didn't leak, he had better things to do with his money."

"Sounds like he changed his mind, big time."

"But where would he get the money, Shar? Big time change takes big bucks—bucks I don't think he had," Laney said.

"Didn't he make a good living at that vet clinic where he worked?"

"A good living, yes. But enough money to pay for all the help it takes to keep a farm like that manicured, the house tuck pointed and painted inside and out, new upholstered furniture, a swimming pool? . . . and all in the last few months." Laney was counting off the improvements that she remembered on Shar's toes. "Oh Shar, I forgot! She drove away this afternoon in a brand new Lexus!"

"A Lexus? Woman, they cost fifty-thou. Are you sure it was hers?" Shar's pupils were getting larger. Laney wasn't sure if it was because of mentioning the Lexus or too much brandy.

"It had St. Clair County plates."

"Hmm . . . remember at the races, I saw him betting at the five hundred dollar window several times? Wait a minute. Are you saying that maybe Derek got all this money by blackmailing Chris?" Shar asked, popping both her feet onto the floor. Her brandy, a miniature tsunami, swished high in the goblet.

Laney's mouth opened as realization hit her. "I . . . I guess I am."

"Then this deep dark secret would have to be pretty bad if Chris would pay blackmail to Derek to keep it quiet," Shar said, plopping down on the sofa again.

"And giving up his farm, the house, the country club and who knows what else to pay it," Laney said. She was silent for a minute. Abruptly, she jumped to her feet, throwing the pillow into the sofa. "This just doesn't make sense. I can't imagine Chris doing anything so immoral or illegal that he would pay blackmail to Derek to keep it quiet. He's just too straight and narrow."

"I guess . . . and they're friends, anyway," Shar conceded. "They played golf only two days ago and went to the Blue Grass Stakes together on Saturday. Why would Chris have anything to do with Derek if he were blackmailing him?"

"You're right." Laney was winding down—the Bloody taking the wind out of her sails. "Unless . . . he didn't know who was blackmailing him."

"Guess it could happen that way." Shar yawned and leaned her head back on the sofa.

"Right . . . but not likely, huh?" Laney said, shutting her eyes.

"Whole thing's silly."

"Right. . . ."

Laney awakened when she heard the grandfather clock chime three times. She was at one end of the sofa hugging the pillow and a long foot with purple toenails. Her friend was at the other end spread eagle, her right foot still flung over the back of the sofa. Her mouth sagged open and she emitted a soft "ca . . . ca . . . ca" with every exhalation.

Laney groaned and slid off the sofa onto the floor, trying not to waken Shar. She muddled to the front door and let in Blackberry, who was asleep on the front door mat. She locked up, turned out all the lights and was slaking her thirst with a second tumbler of ice water when her drinking partner staggered into the kitchen.

"Want some?" Laney said, thumbing at the water jug.

Shar unscrewed the lid and guzzled right out of the jar.

"Say, what ever happened to Malcolm?" Laney asked.

"Kipped down earlier . . . alone again. I don't understand the guy. He hasn't given me as much as a smooch. You don't think he's . . . well . . . ?"

"Malcolm? . . . not on your life. I just think he likes you too much."

"That's a new one on me."

"Think about it," Laney yawned. "I think I'm going to call it a night. I don't remember doing that little scene since college."

Shar wiped her mouth with the front of her hand and dumped the rest of the water into the sink.

"Sure was an interesting theory we came up with," Shar said.

"Sure was."

"Just a theory, wasn't it?"

"Sure," Laney said with her fingers crossed.

9

Laney was sitting at her vanity table trying her best to control the fiery beast on her head when Shar knocked and peeked in her bedroom door. Shar was already dressed in a scarlet skort and matching long jacket—her favorite plaid fashioned into a long woven scarf that she wore draped under the jacket's notched collar. Two gold thistle pins sprouted on her left lapel.

"Hi. May I come in?" Shar asked, bouncing through the door and looking around the smoky blue bedroom. "Say, this is all right."

"I love this room. It was Cara's," Laney said.

"That bisque doll you said Gray got repaired for you looks just like your sister," Shar said, picking up a silver oval framed picture of Cara and comparing it to the old fashioned doll in a child's wicker rocking chair by the fireplace. "He loves you a lot you know."

"I know." Laney slipped off her robe and dropped it on the bed. Walking to the closet, she yanked a black knit A-line dress off the hanger and slipped it over her head. Shar zipped it up the back.

"Funeral this morning, huh?" Shar said.

"Yes, and I'd rather take a beating than go. Only going because of Chris and Amanda. I just don't think Dory needs any support."

"Maybe she did the dirty deed," Shar said.

"Sharlene Hamilton."

"Like it never crossed your mind."

"Of course n . . . well . . . maybe yesterday when I heard the workmen laboring on her swimming pool. Enough . . . what's on the agenda for you and Malcolm while I'm at the funeral?"

"He's taking me to an early breakfast at the Finish Line. Then he wants to hang around here until he hears from Sally about his offer on Taylor Ridge. But sometime today we're going down to the foaling stall to see Thistle."

"Who's Thistle?"

"That's what we named the new colt."

"I hate to burst your Scottish bubble, but thoroughbreds don't get named until they are ready to race."

"Well . . . since we had such an emotional involvement in his prickly birth, we will make an exception, won't we?"

Laney laughed. "Thistle it is."

"Malcolm told me he is planning to return to Florida if the Taylors accept his offer," Laney said, noticing the lights dimming in Shar's eyes as she spoke.

"Woman, I can't bear the thought."

Somewhere deep in Shar's somber gray eyes, flickered some underlying devilment. Shar's mouth twitched at the corners. She's up to something, Laney thought.

They both heard Malcolm rattling coffee cups in the kitchen at the same time. Shar gave Laney a hug and bounced to the door. "I'll connect with you later," she said, and was gone. Laney listened to her long strides down the hall.

Back at her vanity, Laney studied her image. Puffy crescent bags beneath her eyes broadcasted too many Bloodies the night before and instantly her jaws clinched as she thought about what Shar and she had discussed. Could Derek have been blackmailing Chris? The theory seemed absurd last night. Blackmail just didn't make sense. But now, with her mind clearer, she could see that perhaps it could be true. A paradox to solve or bury away? She knew what she wanted to do. She really didn't want to deal with it.

The telephone on her bed table rang, startling her. She lifted the receiver and heard Gray say her name.

"Could I go with you to the funeral?" he asked.

"I was going to call you and suggest that," she said, noting the weariness in his voice. "What if I come now and bring breakfast."

"That would be nice. I've canceled all my calls this morning and given Natine the morning off."

"See you in about a half hour," Laney said.

Laney walked through the kitchen garden toward the carriage house. The sky was melted sapphires and a light wind kept redesigning the billowy clouds. When Laney reached the red door, Blackberry pulled up and sat, her brown eyes cheerless, as all hope for her expected walk was dashed. Laney reached into her straw carry-all, felt for the pan of hot scones and removed a triangle. She laid it on the path in front of the Border collie. Blackberry almost smiled as she cased the area for any threat to her "people food."

Laney made the drive to Hickory in about ten minutes. The clinic parking lot was empty except for Gray's Jeep and pink Buick. Laney collected her carry-all and as she approached the clinic, she noticed a cardboard carton the size of a deep manuscript box in front of the door. She rang the bell and heard Gray's footsteps on the stairway, then a fumbling with the lock.

"Hi," he said, as the door opened. He tucked his hands under his armpits and smiled shyly. "What's going on?"

He seems so much more relaxed, Laney thought, remembering his outburst the night before and his screeching exit down the lane.

"You have a package out here," she said, and stepped over the box into the waiting room. Gray shoved the door open with his hip and stooped and retrieved the carton. Puccini, who had just curled into a ball on one of the waiting room chairs, abruptly came to life and circled Gray's legs.

"Mew."

"That wasn't Puccini," Laney said, placing her sack on a nearby chair and rushing back to unfold the cardboard lid. "Gray, look. It's a kitten."

"Damn it," Gray said, holding the box high so that Puccini couldn't get to it. Gray's cat was circling him, emitting strange noises from deep in his throat. "People do this to me all the time. They drop off all kinds of animals here, thinking I can find homes for them."

"There's a note." Laney snatched up a piece of note paper folded against the inside of the box and read the typewritten message out loud:

YOUR CAT KNOCKED UP MY CAT.
I HATE DEADBEAT DADS.

Laney and Gray's eyes locked for a long moment, then they burst into laughter. Tears ran down Laney's cheeks.

Laney reached into the box and lifted the kitten. The fluffy animal with faint gray tabby markings meowed and his copper eyes blinked. "Oh Gray, he looks a lot like Puccini. Look at the eyes." Gray placed the box on a chair and took the cat out of her hands. Holding him up, he stared into the kitten's face.

"I'm afraid it's true, Puccini. No denying this one." He handed the kitten back to Laney.

"I wonder who wrote the note," Laney pondered.

"Now that could be a puzzle forever unsolved. Puccini has been wandering away from the Jeep ever since the first of the year. I could think of at least a dozen farms where he's gone off catting around. And most of my farm clients have cats."

"At least he won't sire anymore kittens," Laney laughed.

"Let's eat. I'm starved," he said, and they climbed the stairs to his apartment—Laney still holding the kitten and Puccini racing ahead of them to claim his territory.

"I want to run something by you," Laney said, as she poured them more hot coffee from her large carafe. They had been scarfing down Maddy's warm cream scones and the rest of the fruit compote left over from the day before.

"Sure," Gray said, stirring cream into his coffee. He was dressed in his funeral clothes—a navy suit with a white button down shirt and red and navy striped tie. The tie had a small stain about mid chest and the shirt was slightly frayed about the collar.

The kitten was on the floor lapping at a saucer Laney had filled with cream. He must have been weaned as he knew exactly what to do with his little pink tongue. Puccini—his nose out of joint—was nowhere in sight.

"Shar and I were talking last night about Derek." Gray's face darkened as though the lights had dimmed, but Laney continued. She went on to tell him about her visit to Dory's and of the recent acquisitions and improvements.

"Maybe she got a life insurance advance."

"Gray, Derek died just three days ago. The work on the house must have started months ago. Do you want to know what Shar and I came up with last night?"

He shrugged. "Why not?" His caustic tone had returned.

"What if Derek had blackmailed Chris? That would explain why Chris would have to sell Taylor Ridge."

Gray paled. His mouth opened, then closed. He swallowed—the usually silent function loud in the quiet room.

"Laney," he said, his turquoise eyes immense. The shiner blanched with the intensity of their color. "What . . . how?"

"I know this sounds crazy, but couldn't it be? It would explain the Beales' heavy spending and the Taylors' financial problems. Amanda and Chris have even been dropped from the club for non-payment of dues."

Gray blinked. "Wait a minute. The four of them were close friends, for God's sake!"

"What if Chris didn't know who the blackmailer was?"

"Laney—"

"Maybe there's some deep secret Chris doesn't want revealed."

Gray jumped to his feet and held up his hand, palm outward. "Laney! Stop it!" he said, the veins in his neck ballooning. Downstairs, the front doorbell chimed. "I have to answer that. I ordered some drugs that must be refrigerated." He galloped down the stairs.

Laney waited and she waited. Becoming concerned, she scooped up the kitten, who had fallen asleep at her feet, and ran down the stairs. The waiting room was empty. She unlocked the door and peered outside. Gray's Jeep was gone from the lot. Closing the door, she walked back to Gray's office off the waiting room. The clinic was silent except for some canine sounds down the hall where the kennel cages were.

Returning to the waiting room, Laney checked Natine's alcove. A hastily scribbled note lay on the partition that doubled as a counter:

> *Laney,*
> *Gordon was here. More questioning. If drugs come, please put in fridge. Lock up. I'll call you. I love you.*
> *Gray*

The Rolodex lay next to the note. She didn't know why she looked at it except that the address and telephone file was usually on Natine's desk. Her eyes scanned the opened entry: Marshall U. Knight, Attorney.

10

The funeral was held in the St. Clair County Cemetery, the same beautiful setting on the outskirts of Hickory that held the graves of Poppy, Cara, and Joe. Laney had remained at the clinic to wait for Gray's drug order so the service was already in progress when she arrived. The crowd was large and cars lined the winding lane through the cemetery. She searched for Gray's Jeep, with no avail. She had to park quite a distance away from the green tent set up for the service. She felt heads turn as she crept as close to the awning as she could. Dory and her son, Walker, and Dory's mother sat facing the casket in the front row. Laney recognized five of the pall bearers standing just outside the tent and behind the casket. Three of them were partners in the vet clinic in Lexington where Derek had worked, one was Dory's brother who she had seen on the portico at Dory's the day before, and the other man was Chris Taylor.

She was shocked at Chris's appearance. Always a stocky guy— even in high school—he looked as though he had lost twenty pounds. When Laney had last seen him at the races on Saturday, he had been seated with his back toward her. My God, she thought, staring at his wan face, something is certainly doing a number on him. Chris's eyes suddenly locked with hers and instead of his usually warm smile, she felt his cold look of aversion. His gaze quickly veered to the casket. What's all that about, Laney thought, dumbfounded and hurt.

Amanda sat in the second row of metal chairs, the ringlets of her light brown hair vibrating as she sobbed silently. These two friends are going through an excruciating time, Laney thought. I wonder if Gray has talked to Chris about it. Damn it, I bet he hasn't and that's exactly what I'm going to do when this service is over. Enough of this pussyfooting around.

Pussyfooting reminded her of the orphan kitten she had left in the car. She'd parked under a shady hackberry tree and had cracked the windows, so she believed he would be all right, but she wanted to get back to him as quickly as possible.

The service ended and many in the crowd converged on the widow. Dory, still dry-eyed, was receiving everyone gracefully. Laney watched as Chris gave her a hug and whispered in her ear before walking rapidly toward his white Honda. Amanda got into her black Saab, unaware that Laney had been trying to reach her in the crush of people.

Dory and her family finally climbed into the funeral home limousine. Laney rushed toward Chris's Honda, but he moved forward behind the motorcade that was inching its way out of the cemetery. She hurried back to the Whooptie and followed the column of cars. When Chris reached the entrance to the cemetery, she saw him turn left toward Lexington. "Bet he's going to work," she thought, and turned left herself when she arrived at the stop sign.

Traffic was heavy on Addison Pike and she eventually lost sight of the Honda. However, she knew the way to the University since she had been in Chris's office and lab on several occasions.

The box on the passenger's seat moved and she heard the kitten scratch the cardboard.

"Poor baby," she said reaching into the box with her right hand and lifting the kitten. For the rest of the trip, Laney struggled with confining the animal to her lap.

When she reached the chemistry-physics building, she spotted Chris's car in an A sticker parking spot. Classes were in session so there were no available parking spaces. She was about to resort to the parking structure across the street when a red Camry backed out of a metered spot on Funkhouser Drive and she quickly slipped in. She placed the kitten back into the box and popped the ring on the last can of Kitty Komforts that she had snitched from Puccini's larder at Gray's. Dropping the can in the box, she hoped that the kitten wasn't too young to eat it.

As soon as her two quarters clanked in the meter, Laney climbed the concrete steps to the first floor of the building. She raced through the second set of double doors when she spotted Chris coming out of the chemistry department office with a handful of mail. He turned left and while walking away from her, he sifted anxiously through the pile. Laney was just about to call out his name when he suddenly fumbled at a letter and stopped dead as though he had just slammed into a wall.

"Jesus Christ!" he said, his face blanching.

Chris's head jerked upwards searching for observers to his outburst, and Laney ducked into a chemistry lab and flattened herself against the wall. The lab instructor paused in mid-sentence. A second later, she peeked out and watched as Chris continued down the empty hall, tearing open the envelope as he went.

She took a deep breath, relieved that he hadn't seen her. What could have triggered his strong reaction to a piece of mail, she wondered.

Laney suspected he was going to his office. When he turned right at the hall intersection, she was sure of it.

"Young lady, do you belong in this class?" the instructor asked.

"Sorry," Laney muttered and stepped out into the hall. She hurried to the corner and watched as Chris unlocked his door and stepped inside. The slam of the door echoed in the empty hallway. She rushed to the door and through its glass insert, she saw Chris throw the mail on his desk, sit in his chair and scan the letter. The hand holding the paper dropped to the desk then slowly devoured the note, as though Chris's fist were eating it alive. Venomously, he threw the crushed note into the waste basket by his desk and dropped his head into his arms, his body heaving great sobs.

"May I help you?" a voice behind her asked. Laney straightened and spun around so quickly that her elbow caught the corner of a young woman's notebook and sent it flying to the floor. Papers scattered. So engrossed in Chris's behavior, Laney had completely overlooked the possibility that someone might see her staring through the glass window. The girl, evidently an undergraduate by the gigantic backpack she was lugging, gave Laney an inquisitive look.

"Oh . . . I'm so sorry . . . let me help . . .I'm such a klutz," Laney said, feeling her face flush. "I saw Dr. Taylor on the phone and was waiting for him to finish his call." The lie flowed from her lips much too easily.

They stooped together and gathered up the papers, trying to straighten the edges. Laney handed the sheets to the girl.

"It's all right . . . honestly," the girl said, sensing her embarrassment. "You're lucky to find Dr. Taylor in. He was my advisor last year."

She thinks I'm a student here, Laney thought. The twelve-fifty bell rang and the girl smiled and traveled on down the hallway, shoving the papers into her notebook as she went. One o'clock classes were about to begin and the halls suddenly filled with students. Laney turned back to the door and before she could take another glance inside, it opened and Chris stood in the opening, glaring at her.

"What are you doing here?" he growled. His face showed the ravages of the emotional episode and too little sleep. Never one who cared much about his appearance, today Chris struck Laney as totally indifferent to the way he looked. Because of the considerable weight he had lost, heavy creases crossed his black trousers at the hips and his belt gathered in the extra fullness in untidy pleats. He had removed his jacket, exposing a sweaty white shirt that clung to his sagging frame. His hand combed through the light brown hair that hung over his collar, and a shadow of a beard told of a hurried shave before the funeral. Laney ached to hold him and make everything all right.

"Chris . . . please talk to me," she attempted, shouldering her way into the room. He grasped her arm spinning her around, anger flooding his tortured face.

"Laney . . . I don't have time . . . please go . . . now!" he said, pointing to the door with his free hand. Laney thought his face would explode any moment. She pulled her arm free and grabbed an arm chair in front of the desk and bounced into it.

"I'm not leaving until you talk to me," she said, folding her arms across her chest and feeling a lot less unshakable than she sounded.

Chris looked at his watch, then walked around his desk to his chair. She could hear his heavy snorting breaths like he had just run the fifty yard dash. His color changed by the second. She feared he would have a heart attack.

Chris sat on the edge of his chair and placed the tips of his fingers on the edge of the desk like he was about to play the piano. "I have five minutes before my lab, Laney. Say what you want to say and get out." His words were precise and stinted.

"You are in some kind of trouble. I can tell. How can I help?" Laney asked.

"What are you talking about?" He wouldn't look at her. His fingers tapped an octave and back.

"The farm . . . Taylor Ridge . . . you said you would never sell it."

Again his cheeks reddened and his teeth clinched. "I've changed my mind." He checked his watch again and stood.

"You're snubbing me . . . why?" Laney asked.

"Not you."

"Who—"

"That's all the time I have," he interrupted. He strode to the door and held it open for her. She had no choice but to leave. He followed her out and banged the door shut behind her. He turned abruptly to the right and purposefully walked in the direction they had come. When he turned left at the corner, Laney pivoted and ran back to Chris's office. She turned the knob, fully expecting the lock to have automatically engaged. To her surprise, it clicked open and she slipped inside.

She dashed to the waste basket and sorted crazily through the waste. Evidently, Chris made tiny basketballs of all his paper. The one o'clock bell stopped her heart. So afraid that someone would find her there sifting through Chris's trash, she scooped up all the wadded paper she could find and stuffed it into her purse. With her shoulder bag bulging and unable to snap it closed, she hugged it to her body and darted to the door. She opened it slowly and glanced up and down the hall. The halls were still clear. She wove the maze of hallways until she found her way to a Rose Street exit and ran back to her car.

Throwing her bag into the back seat of the Whooptie, she hopped in. The kitten hadn't eaten his food and he was panting on the passenger side floorboard. Dismayed because she had never seen a kitten pant before, she swung through McDonald's on Limestone and ordered a #1 and a vanilla milkshake. Pulling into a parking place, she poured part of the shake into the lid, and the kitten went to town on it. She started up the Whooptie and decided to beat it back to Hickory as the odor of something other than her Big Mac struck her nostrils.

With so much whirling about in her head, the trip to Hickory seemed to take but a few minutes. She wondered if Chris was snubbing her because he thought Gray was somehow responsible for his friend's death. Remembering Gray's note that morning had said that he had gone in for another round of questioning, Laney's intuition told her something new had come up in the investigation.

She dropped by the clinic but Natine told her she hadn't seen Gray all day. When Natine had returned from Chris's funeral, Gray had already left on calls. She pointed to the full schedule in her appointment book.

Laney swung through town and stopped at Hickory Dock. Maddy was readying the pavilion for the season by scrubbing down the white plastic tables and chairs under the scarlet awning. When all threat of a late spring frost had passed, baskets overflowing with cascading geraniums would be hung from brackets at each support. Laney saw two paddle boats thrashing side by side along the bank. The two teenage boys whomped water at each other, prompting squeals and giggles from their girlfriends.

Maddy had just sat down on one of the chairs she had cleaned when she saw Laney approach with the kitten.

"Look at that, would you?" she said, reaching for the animal. "Where did you get that little one?"

"Someone left it at Gray's. According to the note, I'm afraid Puccini is the daddy," Laney said as she handed the kitten to her mother.

Laney stroked the kitten as Maddy buried her face in its softness. "Mother," Laney said, "speaking of Gray, has Gordon said anything to you about any new evidence in Derek's murder?"

"Gordon doesn't tell me anything unless it's public knowledge."

Having a sudden inspiration, Laney quickly snatched the kitten from her mother and started for the car.

"Laney, honey, you just got here," Maddy pouted.

"Mother, please call Shar for me and tell her I'll be home in about an hour. Okay?"

Not waiting for her answer, Laney spun gravel on her way out of the parking lot, knowing that she would have to answer for that later.

11

When Laney saw the teenagers in the paddle boats, it occurred to her that if the police had uncovered any new evidence in the creek search, Cutty Bell just might have the lowdown. She knew that Cutty lived on the water so she turned left at the entrance to Hickory Dock and drove slowly along Chester Avenue that followed Stoney Creek through town. Chester Avenue was a spotty street where you could find an expensive home with a wraparound deck and pontoon boat on the water, next door to a moldy shack on stilts. It didn't matter whether you were rich or poor when the love of living on the water was concerned. She passed two upscale homes and as she drove on, the neighborhood turned considerably shabbier.

The name on the battered rural mailbox was printed freehand with a wide brush: C. BELL—the final L trailing around to the lid of the box.

Laney moved cautiously into a dirt driveway of sorts, doing her best to fake out potholes that could have ingested a school bus. In fact, the orange hulk of one rested in a mammoth clump of Johnson grass behind a dilapidated building that looked like a machine shop. Scores of used tires were crammed tight against every window inside the bus like treadless rubber children on their way to Goodyear school. Rusted farm machinery, the front half of a Ford Falcon and the carcass of a Volkswagen beetle lay almost hidden in the high grass. An odd apparatus that looked like a child's swing set dangled a motor on a chain hoist connected to an I beam. Almost hidden behind a rippled plastic greenhouse with a rotting wooden frame was a travel trailer perched dangerously near the creek bank. At least if high water threatens, Cutty's home can be moved to higher ground in a hurry, Laney thought.

She stopped the car and scrambled to find the kitten that had disappeared somewhere under the passenger seat. She grabbed the furry body but not before her hand swept over something soft and gooey. The sugar in that shake must not have agreed with him, she thought, as she wiped the side of her hand on some weeds near a flight of rickety steps that led to the open door of the shop. As she climbed, she stepped around a water pump and what looked like a gas tank for a weed eater. When she reached the landing, she called Cutty's name.

"C'mon in," a voice yelled from the dim interior.

She crossed the threshold onto a oily wood plank floor. The odor of cut lumber and motor oil was strong. A single light bulb hung from a ceiling latticed in cobwebs that had caught the sawdust created from a table saw to the right of the door. Cutty stood at a bench working on a generator in the center of the plywood walled room.

"Say, Laney," Cutty said, smiling broadly and lifting the screwdriver in a wave.

"Thought you might be out on the creek," Laney said, petting the kitten.

"Just got back a little while ago. Have to finish fixin this here generator before five. Whatcha got there?"

"Kitten."

"Blackberry ain't gonna to like that. That's one smart dog." He hiked at his filthy jeans.

"I hope to pawn him off on my friend Shar, who's visiting me this week."

"Ain't met that one." He reached inside one of the open grimy cardboard boxes lying on the floor and pulled out a handful of assorted nuts and bolts. "Know this ain't no social call. Whatcha want?"

Laney went for it, thinking that Cutty rather liked her. "Have you heard if the police found anything in the creek yet?" she ventured.

Cutty looked up at her for a second, then went back to the generator. His camouflaged cap shaded his eyes. "Maybe."

"The tape they were looking for?"

"How'd ya know 'bout that?"

"You told me yesterday. Remember?"

"I forgot. They found it all right."

Laney felt goosebumps.

"Ain't gonna help none."

Laney placed the kitten on the bench and he sniffed at a bolt. "Why not?" she asked.

"Ain't no tape."

"You just said—"

"The cassette ain't no count. Cartridge was tore up and the tape inside was missin. They couldn't find it no how. Some turtle or fish musta got caught up in it . . . run off with it."

"Could that happen?"

"Sure . . . happens with trot lines and jug fishin all the time." He hiked his jeans again. "Somethin was written on the cassette. Just four letters: 'TONG.' Rest of the ink was washed off." Cutty stopped tinkering for a moment as though he was debating about something. "I'll tell you 'bout another thing if you swear you won't tell nobody. Don't wanna give my nephew on water patrol no grief."

"I swear."

"They found somethin else. Coulda been the murder weapon."

"Huh?" Laney interrupted her idle nut-turning on a bolt.

"A pair of dehorners stuck in the muddy bottom below the cliff. Coulda been what cut the rope and kilt Doc Beale."

"No way," Laney exclaimed.

"Had Doc's name on em."

"Derek worked cattle," Laney explained.

"Not that Doc . . . Doc Prescott's."

Cutty's grubby T-shirt faded in and out and something pinged in Laney's ears. Her hands snatched up the kitten and she backed towards the door.

"Th-thanks . . . Cutty . . . got to go," she stammered.

"Remember . . . you swore," Cutty called after her.

Still in a fog, Laney drove by rote through town but as she started out Hickory Pike, the kitten on her lap began to purr against her
stomach, reminding her that she was low on milk. Backtracking, she
stopped at the mini-mall. When she grabbed at her bag, the wadded
waste paper from Chris's office spilled out over the seat and floor.
She let it lie where it fell and ran into the grocery and stopped next
door at Walmart to pick up a litter box.

The clock on the Whooptie's dash said three-fifteen when she
turned into the Stoney Creek Farm entrance. As she broke out of
the alley of trees, Unreasonable's paddock was empty on her left.
Aaron always kept a mare and her new foal in the foaling stall for
the first few days. A couple of days in the adjoining paddock,
weather permitting, then he would turn her out with the other
mares and foals.

Gray's Jeep met her nose to nose between the front pilasters to the
house. They both skidded to a stop and she saw Gray's hand lunge
for Puccini to prevent him from slipping off the dash. Gray backed
up to let Laney in.

Laney couldn't stop herself from leaping from the car and rushing into his arms.

"What's all this about? Only saw you this morning," he said.

"Gray . . . your note. It scared me to death." Laney nuzzled his
neck, then quickly straightened and kissed his soft lips. He drew her
snugly against him but the moment lasted but a few seconds before
he wrenched his mouth from hers.

"Laney, we need to talk." He grasped her hand and began to lead
her toward the porch when she remembered the kitten in the front
seat of the car. She broke his clasp and ran to the Whooptie, gathered up the kitten and caught up to Gray. Blackberry was nowhere
in sight.

They sat on the porch swing, as close as they could sit, the striped
kitty exploring the porch.

"Gordon questioned me again this morning. Water patrol found my dehorners in the creek below the cliff. They think they cut Derek's rope," Gray said.

The statement coming from Gray's lips seemed almost like an admission, Laney thought. Admission? Dear God, of what? Murder?

As though perceiving her inner fear, he said, "Laney, I didn't kill him. Derek borrowed my dehorners early this spring when one of the wooden handles on his broke just before he had to do a large herd in Fayette County. He picked mine up at the clinic early one morning on his way to Lexington. They were an old pair that I didn't use anymore. I told him to keep them since I had bought a newer style."

"Do you think Gordon believes you?"

Gray didn't answer for a period of time. In the interlude, the porch swing creaked back and forth—an irritating, haunting sound. "Doesn't matter what he believes, Laney. I'm their prime suspect."

A tiny gray paw slapped at a lengthy frond of a Boston fern on a low wicker stand against the wall. Laney tried to focus on the sweet kitten, but Gray's alarming words hammered away at her. She wanted so to minimize the importance of Gray's statement—to preserve things as they had been. But he went on, building on her fear.

"Detective Barron believes I had the motive and opportunity and now there's this added evidence—my dehorners found near the scene of the murder."

"Motive?" Laney cried. "What possible motive?"

Gray was calm, almost resigned. "Laney . . . remember the incident at the Bluegrass Stakes when Derek tried to humiliate me by agreeing to do the mare inducement when I refused? Several people witnessed it. And then I took a punch at Derek at the country club the day of his murder after I discovered the foal was rabid. Everyone knows how angry I was." He shook his head, slowly. "I was a damn fool."

Laney clasped his hand tighter. "But angry enough to kill . . . ? You couldn't . . . you wouldn't."

"The police can only see my out of control rage at the country club just an hour before Derek was murdered."

"But what about opportunity, Gray?" She was searching for something—anything.

"I told the investigators that I went out to Woody's to tell him about the rabid foal and that he and the children would have to be immunized. That was around eleven o'clock. Woody was out mowing in a pasture. I heard the tractor and followed the sound to the paddock, climbed the fence and met him in the middle of the field. He told the investigators he saw me about eleven-ten. I left the farm then but he didn't see me go. My whereabouts are a mystery to everyone but me from about eleven-fifteen to three-fifteen when you came to the clinic. Four hours, Laney! No one saw me for four hours!" He sprang to his feet in frustration.

"Gray . . . you've never told me . . . where? . . . where were you?" She remembered that when she had seen him at the clinic that day, he said he had returned about one-thirty and had taken a nap until she rang the bell.

Gray stooped and lifted the kitten that was immediately swallowed up in his broad hands. Holding the kitten in his palm, he stroked his belly gently with a forefinger. "I just drove around the county, Laney."

"But someone must have seen you—"

"He does look like Puccini, doesn't he?" Gray said, clearly finished with his explanation. "What shall we do with him? Puccini won't stand for any feline rivalry—his son or not."

"I can't see Puccini sharing his dashboard with a kitten, anyway," Laney said, glancing out at Puccini back under the windshield of the Cherokee. "And I don't think Blackberry will give him the red-carpet treatment either. I'm hoping that maybe Shar will bond with him and take him back to Pittsburgh with her."

"Speak of the devil," Gray said, trying hard to be glib, while the shadow of fear still inhabited his eyes.

Malcolm's rented Olds swept up the lane from the lower barn and Laney took the moment before they pulled into the circle to give Gray another kiss. She felt his lips tremble beneath hers. Why can't this be over, she thought. At that moment, Laney wished that Shar weren't there so that she could devote all her attention to Gray.

"Laney, I have a call," Gray stepped back, his hand squeezing hers to reassure her, but it didn't put her mind to rest. He handed her the kitten and strode swiftly to his Jeep as though he didn't want to stop to talk with Shar and Malcolm.

Blackberry beat Malcolm's car to the house by cutting across the lawn. She arrived seconds before the Oldsmobile came to a stop behind the Whooptie. Gray waved to them and drove around the circle and out the entrance.

"Something I did?" Shar remarked, bouncing out of the car and glancing at Gray's quick departure.

"He hasn't had the best of days. I'll explain later," Laney said.

"What do you have there?" Malcolm said, being the first to arrive on the porch. Blackberry was doing a frenzied dance of death around Laney's feet.

"Shar, put Blackberry in the house . . . quickly!" The cat was digging her claws into her chest as she tried to shield him from the dog.

After Blackberry was banished to the dark interior of the front hall, Shar swept the kitten away from Laney and that was that. When Laney explained how he had arrived at Gray's clinic in a box with a note, she let out a whoop.

"Can I have him?" she asked, the kitten climbing inside her jacket front and burying under her arm. "The little bastard couldn't be any harder to take care of than the three I married."

Malcolm laughed heartily. He's not so stuffy after all, Laney thought, giggling along with him.

"It's toddy time," Malcolm announced, looking at his watch and producing a pint of Cutty Sark Scotch whisky from the side pocket of his tweed jacket.

"Mal has something to celebrate," Shar said, leading everyone into the parlor. Laney disappeared into the kitchen to get ice, Blackberry following her in for an afternoon treat. After slipping the dog a milk bone in the pantry and closing the door, Laney joined Shar and Malcolm in the parlor. Malcolm did the honors with the drinks and after everyone had theirs, he held his Scotch and water high.

"Here's to my new farm, Taylor Ridge," he said, his teeth blazing white against his brown goatee and trim mustache.

Laney's heart sank in her chest but she did her best to smile. So, Chris and Amanda had accepted Malcolm's offer, she thought. Her earlier encounter with Chris flashed through her mind. Poor Chris and Amanda. Although she had only lived at Stoney Creek Farm for a year, she knew she would be devastated if she had to move.

"When will you close, Malcolm?" she asked.

"In thirty days. Mr. Taylor added 'time is of the essence' on the contract."

Chris must really need the money, Laney thought.

"I'm leaving tomorrow to go back to Florida," Malcolm said. "I hope I may stay at your establishment when I return for the closing."

"Your room will be longing for you. Be sure to give me the date before you leave so I can reserve it. Beginning next Friday, we are full through Derby Day. When you return the middle of May, the schools let out for the summer and tourist season begins. That reminds me, please excuse me while I check for any messages. Shar, I bought a litter box for the kitten. It's in the car."

Laney retrieved her messages in the library and returned two calls for reservations, one for three days starting the Monday after the race and the other for the weekend after. She looked longingly at her computer. "I'll get back to you as soon as I can," she promised, patting the monitor as she left the room.

When Laney returned to the parlor to freshen her drink, she found the room empty. Shar called to her from the kitchen. She found her sitting on the quarry tile floor, the kitten in her lap. The litter box was filled and against the wall near the pantry.

"Where's Malcolm?" Laney asked.

"He drove to town to pick up pizza at Tony Belini's. He didn't want you to cook tonight. Anyway, I'm having pizza withdrawals. In Pittsburgh, I eat it three times a week."

"How do you do that and stay so thin?"

"Good genes. Mother's side. She's seventy years old and wears the same size six she wore when she got married. I got my height from good old Dad. He was six-six and weighed two fifty when he died four years ago. My Scottish grandfather topped him by an inch."

"I remember when your father died. You had just started to work at *Three Rivers Magazine.*"

Shar looked pensive. "I still miss the old man." Then she immediately brightened like she had never thought of him. Laney wished that she could do that. Shar didn't let anything get her down for long.

Shar unkinked her legs, stood and started down the hall to the back stairs, the kitten inside her jacket. "By the way, woman," Laney heard her yell back at her as she climbed the stairs, "you really need to do something about the Whooptie. A malodorous stench greeted my nostrils when I opened the door and the interior hankers for a litter bag."

Remembering the kitty messes, Laney armed herself with paper towels, disinfectant, and a couple of grocery sacks, and after releasing Blackberry from the pantry, she spent the next fifteen minutes cleaning out the car. She dropped Chris's paper wads into a plastic sack, planning to look for the letter after dinner.

The evening was perfect with a faint breeze rippling the creek and rustling the trees so they ate on the screen porch at the round iron table. They ate Belini's thick crust pizza with everything, including anchovies that Laney and Malcolm picked off their slices and piled on Shar's. Laney tossed a crisp salad laced with her mother's tangy Roquefort dressing. Completely satiated, the three of them gaped torpidly at the greasy paper plates in front of them.

Laney yawned. "What are you going to name your kitten? Thistle is already taken," she said thickly.

As though he knew he was the topic of conversation, the kitten poked his two copper eyes out of the top of Shar's zippered sweatshirt that she had changed into before dinner.

"I think I have an appropriate name for the wee one," Malcolm announced. "He reminds me of a serious weed called kudzu that grows in the South. It has long runners that grow a foot a day and clings faithfully to whatever gets in its way—just the way the puss is clinging to Shar."

"I've seen that weed," Laney said. "It's creeping into southern Kentucky."

"Kudzu. I like that, Mal," Shar said. She unzipped her sweatshirt, lifted the kitten and stared at him nose to nose. "Kudzu, just don't grow a foot a day."

"Now if you will excuse me," Malcolm said. "I have some calls to make. Is it all right if I use your phone and charge them to my calling card?" Malcolm asked Laney.

"Sure, Malcolm. Use the phone in the library."

As soon as Malcolm left, Shar didn't lose any time getting the scoop on the funeral that morning. And when Laney told her about following Chris to the university, Shar got fired up.

"Woman, what in the world made you do that?"

"It was the hostile look he gave me at the funeral . . . and that he looked like death warmed over. And poor Amanda. You saw how frazzled she was on Tuesday at the country club. I wanted to see if I could help, but she drove away before I could talk with her." Laney retrieved a trash bag from the kitchen.

"Laney, spit it out! Did you talk to him?"

"I'll get to that," Laney said as she stacked the paper plates. "I saw Chris completely come apart when he read a letter in his office."

"In front of you?"

"Not exactly . . . through the glass in his door."

"You spied on him?" Shar's eyes got large.

"Well . . ."

"Come clean, woman." Shar licked her lips in anticipation.

"That's really it, Shar. When I finally forced my way into his office, he gave me five minutes . . . really not even that long. He didn't tell me a thing except that I was mistaken believing that he was in trouble."

"Yeah, sure. . . ."

"But I have proof now." Laney dropped the paper plates into the trash bag and twisted a tie. She plopped the bag outside the screen door and ran through the kitchen into her bedroom. When she returned to the porch, she turned a white plastic grocery sack upside down, spilling the wads of paper onto the seat of the wicker rocker next to the table.

"Resorting to trash collection?" Shar asked.

"Just Chris's trash." Laney explained that after she saw Chris throw the letter into the waste can, she sneaked back into the office and collected the contents.

"You shameless gumshoe," Shar said, taking a swipe at Laney. "Let's get at it."

Most of the items were computer paper, departmental memos, notices of committee meetings, and inquiries for research materials.

"Look at this," Shar said excitedly. It's his statement from the University Credit Union. Uh oh . . . a couple transactions here."

Shar showed it to Laney. The statement showed that on March twelfth, ten thousand dollars was taken from Chris's account, leaving a zero balance. The following week, on the nineteenth, Chris took out a loan for ten thousand dollars.

"Do you think this is what upset Chris so badly?" Shar asked.

"It couldn't be. This statement is dated April first. Today is the sixteenth. It's a couple weeks old. He must have just cleaned off his desk. Anyway, he knew about these transactions. He made them himself. If you had seen his face when he opened that letter. . . ."

Laney grabbed the last wad of paper and smoothed it out. "Damn . . . just a university policy memo. Shar, I didn't get it." She wanted to cry.

"Don't cry, Miss Marple, let's go back out to the Whooptie. Maybe you forgot one."

"I'm sure I didn't," Laney whined, but followed Shar's long strides out to the car.

Shar handed Kudzu to Laney and wrenched open the door on the passenger side. She bent double, her head almost touching the floor, her body a boomerang with her denim covered butt saluting the dash. One elastic arm swiped under the seat, her left hand grasping the seat cushion in a death grip.

"Another one!" Shar screamed, holding it high when she finally unraveled. Laney thrust Kudzu into Shar's middle, leaped and snatched the paper clump out of her hand and ran into the house, Shar on her tail. "Don't you dare read it without me," Shar threatened.

Laney had it smoothed out by the time they both reached the screened porch, both of them breathless. Their eyes scanned the sheet. At first, Laney thought the paper was blank, then her eyes caught an inch of small type centered on the page:

20-10-10-M

"What the hell is this?" Laney said, her hopes dashed all over again. She sank into a wrought iron chair.

"Maybe a code? . . . although it looks a lot like a fertilizer mix."

"What do you mean?"

Shar jerked it out of Laney's fingers. "When I was a kid, the old man had a garden and he used to buy fertilizer in sacks that gave the percentage of nitrogen, phosphorus, and potassium in three numbers like this."

"Get real, Shar. Chris wouldn't get upset over a fertilizer mix, unless—like you say—it's actually a code for blackmail." Laney plucked the note from Shar's hand. "The letter M. It could stand for Monday. But what could the numbers mean?"

Shar grabbed it back. "If M stands for Monday, I say the number before the M would be the time. That's the most logical sequence— ten o'clock, Monday."

Laney yanked the paper away from Shar. "Say, we're getting good. Let's see . . . if this is a blackmail note, you would have to know where and how much?" If we have the time down, which number would be the amount, twenty or ten?"

"I say, go for the ten . . . remember the loan at the credit union? And the withdrawal was for the same amount the week before," Shar said.

"That leaves the twenty . . . the where. A locker number? But it doesn't say where the locker is."

"If this is a blackmail note, we know it couldn't have been the first one Chris received. Ten or twenty thou wouldn't be enough to force him to put his farm on the market. He probably received initial instructions in another note—where the locker is located. In the mysteries I read, a blackmailer has the victim leave the money in a locker at a bus station or airport."

"Too obvious. How about somewhere on campus where Chris works?"

"Or in a mall."

"The possibilities are endless. There's only one way we could discover where—follow him." Laney became pensive. "But remember our theory last night? If Chris received another blackmail note today, if that's what this is, it blows it all to hell. Derek can't be the blackmailer if he's dead."

"Did I hear the word blackmail?" Malcolm asked, as he came out on the porch.

Shar's face lit up like a flare when she saw him. "Mal, we think Chris is being blackmailed—hence the reason he sold Taylor Ridge."

The little man's fingers combed through his beard and a frown above his glasses drew his eyes together.

"That's pretty heavy stuff," he said. "Who would do that? The person would have to have some knowledge of some wrongdoing of Mr. Taylor's. Maybe even some tangible proof. And it would have to be bad enough that Mr. Taylor would submit to extortion to prevent its exposure."

"Assuming it's true that Chris is being blackmailed, we first thought that it might be Derek Beale bleeding him dry. Recently he seemed to have come into an unaccountable source of funds. But now we believe the blackmail continues, even after Derek's death," Shar explained.

Malcolm slipped his hands into the front pockets of his oatmeal-colored Shetland wool cardigan. "I'm not much into intrigue, but allowing myself to reflect for a moment, perhaps this tape that you spoke about last night . . . the one that the police think may be a clue in Dr. Beale's death, could also be the link in the blackmail."

"But . . . the tape—" Laney was about to reveal that the tape had been destroyed when she remembered her promise to Cutty.

"Yes?" Shar began.

"Nothing," Laney said. Shar snatched up the last cold square of pizza just before Laney gathered up the pizza carton and carried it into the kitchen. Laney's recollection of her promise to Cutty had suddenly brought back her conversation with Gray about his dehorners being found in the creek. Gray was a suspect in Derek's murder. She felt her nose burn, her eyes begin to fill. And she was beginning to believe that the police weren't the only ones that thought he was suspect. After Chris's cold shoulder today, she was sure that he also thought Gray had killed Derek. She felt her head began its journey into the sand—familiar territory. To hell with worrying about a damn tape.

12

It seemed to Laney that she had awakened every hour during the night. Strangely, she didn't remember her dreams, only that whenever her eyes snapped open, her heart was racing as though she had been fighting the current in the swiftest part of a stream. When she finally struggled out of bed about three-thirty, her arms ached with a heavy tiredness and she had an overwhelming longing to hear Gray's voice, to touch him, to hold him. She lifted the receiver of the telephone, dialed and lay back upon the bed.

When his soft voice answered, "Yes," it was as though he knew it would be her.

"Gray?" She spoke his name quietly.

His tone changed. "Laney, is something wrong?" She sensed his anxiety.

"No . . . I . . . I just had to hear you . . . feel you near me. Do you think me mad—calling you at this hour?"

"I was awake . . . thinking of you . . . loving you in my mind."

"I'm afraid, Gray . . . for you . . . I have this sense of foreboding. I can't make it stop." She began to cry. "Gray, make it stop."

"Laney, I'm there holding you . . . touching your hair, your mouth, kissing your eyes . . . making the tears go away."

Suddenly, he was. She felt his arms about her, his broad hands cupping her face, stroking her hair, his soft mouth covering hers.

"I treasure you, Laney. I'll always be here for you, I promise. God, but I love you," he whispered.

His words washed gently over her as though she were drifting in a soothing sea of his love. "Gray, it's gone . . . the dread . . . it's gone."

Laney rubbed her eyes. The computer screen blurred in front of her. The grandfather clock in the front hall chimed seven times. She checked her watch. Three hours. When she had hung up the phone after talking to Gray, it had been almost four and she had dressed and been at the computer ever since.

Her fingers pressed the six magical keys that formed the bewitching words that terminated five months of work: The End. Her first draft was finished and she felt—what did she feel? Satisfaction? Relief? Or was it sadness? She couldn't put her finger on it. Perhaps she felt all of those emotions.

She was pondering whether or not to begin immediately on a second draft, when she heard the sound. Actually, Blackberry heard it first. Curled on the oriental carpet, she suddenly lifted her head, her ears perked and she cocked her head to the right, then to the left. Barely perceptible and distant, the intonation struck Laney as musical. Thinking that perhaps Malcolm or Shar had the kitchen radio on, she opened the library door and listened. It didn't appear to be coming from within the house. She ran to the library window and peered out into the yard. A heavy gray fog lay low over the lawn obscuring all but the dim shapes of the closest dogwoods.

"Laney, do you hear it?"

Laney spun around to see Malcolm standing in the open doorway, his hands thrust into the pockets of his blue, green, and black Lamont tartan robe. On his tiny feet, he wore green suede slippers.

"Malcolm, what is it?"

His face was alight with excitement. "We must go outside," he announced, then turned quickly and disappeared down the hall toward the sound that was becoming more audible—yet, to Laney—still not identifiable.

She scampered after him and Blackberry followed, the dog's toe-nails clicking on the hardwood floors where the Persian rug ended near the stairs. When Laney reached the kitchen, Malcolm opened the French doors wide, and instantly the undeniable drone of bag-pipes met Laney's ears, although it was still distant. Blackberry began a mournful whining noise deep in her throat and Laney held her collar as Malcolm opened the screen door to the yard and stepped outside. Laney slipped out behind him, leaving the Border collie whimpering on the porch. As though hypnotized by the mod-ulation of the chanter, Malcolm hurried toward the music, covering the flagstone path faster than Laney could believe possible for some-one so short. Below his robe, his muscular calves rippled with every stride. The fog began to disperse with the morning sun and swirled like fingers of smoke down the steep path to Stoney Creek. When they reached the limestone springhouse, the reverberating harmony seemed to be originating from the creek itself and Malcolm drew up short, breathing hard with his efforts and pointing toward the wooded valley in front of them.

"Ach lass, 'tis like we're mid th' misty birks of Aberfeldy," he gasped, his words tumbling into a form of Gaelic dialect.

Then out of the thicket of sycamore, ash, and oak the piper came, whorls of vaporous fog about her tall figure. Shar cracked no smile of recognition, nor did she communicate, even subtly, that she was even aware of her observers gawking on the path.

The Hamilton tartan kilt swished the tops of her knees as Shar paced. Below the kilt, matching hose rose from black laced gillies, wet with dew. Behind the bagpipes, the silver, diamond-shaped but-tons on her black velvet vest flashed in the breaking mist and a long-sleeved white blouse rippled lace at the cuffs and jabot at her throat. The snug headband of Shar's blue tam-o'-shanter circled her upper brow at an angle and a red pom-pom peeked over the flat circular crown.

Shar cut through the ground clouds like an apparition, her mouth closed tight over the blowpipe—the three drones, connect-ed by gold cording, rested high on her left shoulder. Below, her left arm pumped the bag against her side and the pads of her fingers danced over the double reed chanter keys playing some ancient melody.

An acute feeling of excitement swept over Laney and she began to tremble with emotion. Clearly, Malcolm was also enchanted.

When had Shar learned to play the pipes, Laney wondered? Then it came to her—the hazy recollection that when she worked at *Three Rivers Magazine*, Shar would never go anywhere with her on Wednesday nights because of taking some kind of music instruction from a Hamilton relative. "Bagpipes!"

Laney and Malcolm followed the piper back up the flagstone steps where the two of them sank to a concrete bench in the kitchen garden, while Shar completed the chant in front of them. With the final note, the silence was total. Then gradually, like trickling applause at the end of a great performance grows in intensity, the songs of finches and warblers picked up the void. Shar removed the blowpipe from her mouth and smiled at Malcolm.

"My dear," he said with emotion. "My dear."

Silently, Laney retreated to the screened porch.

Laney prepared a breakfast of Maddy's baked apples with dates and coffee crumb cake—both out of the freezer and heated through in the oven until piping hot. Reluctantly, she called the lovebirds to the screened porch. Shar laid her pipes on the wicker love seat and ran up to her room. She returned toting Kudzu and the curious brown leather case that Laney had stowed in the trunk of the Whooptie upon Shar's arrival at Bluegrass Airport. Laying the case open on the porch floor, Shar folded back the drones and wrapped them and the chanter carefully in felt and lay them inside the case. Carefully expelling any remaining air from the blue velvet covered elk-hide bag, she folded and tucked it almost reverently on top before snapping the case closed.

Laney poured the hot coffee and collapsed into one of the wrought iron chairs at the round table. The day promised to be another sunny one and the temperature was quite pleasant for the third week in April.

"Shar Hamilton, you have to be the most enigmatic person I've ever met. That you play the bagpipes so well and I wasn't even aware of it . . . ." Laney could only shake her head in wonder.

Shar smiled almost modestly, "I've been taking lessons for five years. I must admit, I didn't advertise the fact. Afraid, I guess, that someone would ask me to play before I was proficient enough."

"You are proficient enough," Malcolm said, finally jumping into the conversation. His brown eyes intensified through his thick lenses. "For a moment, I was transported to the glen of Aberfeldy, not far north of Edinburg where I was born." He cleared his throat and Laney thought she detected tears in his eyes. "Sharlene, thank you," he choked. He cleared his throat. "You . . . you must excuse me while I dress. My flight leaves in a couple of hours." He patted his lips with the white linen napkin and stood.

Seeing the tragic expression on Shar's face, Laney asked, quickly, "Malcolm, are you sure I can't persuade you to stay a few more days?"

"Laney, I surely wish I could," he said, glancing at Shar. "But my farm affairs need attending. And of course I must make the many arrangements for my move to Kentucky."

Back to the problems at hand, Laney thought, Malcolm's comment immediately reminding her of Chris and Amanda's misfortune, Derek's death, and that Gray was a suspect.

"I'd better change also," Shar said. "Kudzu is doing his best to see what I wear under the kilt." The kitten had just about disappeared into the opening in her kilt beneath a giant thistle pin.

When the two of them were gone, Laney quickly stowed the breakfast plates in the dishwasher and made a pot of tea. She was on her way down the front hall to the library when the doorbell rang.

"Hi." Jesse stood on the porch. In her right hand, she held her dust witch—a feathered long handled, extendible cleaning tool. She carried the gadget with her to all her cleaning clients' homes just like a pool shark totes his own personal cue stick. She took a swipe at a spider web above the door. She shivered. "The only thing I don't like about the country. Where do you want me to start, Laney?"

"Malcolm is leaving in a few minutes and I'll need the bed stripped and the room and bath cleaned," Laney said. "By the way, Jesse, can you spare me any extra time next week? Beginning Friday, all six rooms will be filled almost every night for awhile."

"I'll see what I can work out. Maybe Carolyn can help."

Jesse's older sister, Carolyn Hendricks, sometimes filled in for Jesse at the bed and breakfast when a conflict arose with Jesse's regular job at the Finish Line.

"Wonderful. I don't know how you manage two jobs, Jesse."

"The same way you do, I guess. You learn to juggle your time."

Laney held the door open and caught a whiff of Hombre Rose as Jesse strode down the hall. Her jeans clutched her shapely legs in a seductive grip.

After fixing a tea tray for herself, Laney settled at her desk in the library, resisting the temptation to bring her manuscript up on the computer. Instead, she reached for her high school yearbook. "Better get started on the reunion program," she grumbled.

As she flipped through the 1977 yearbook, the book opened naturally to the two pages with the composite photos that she and Shar had looked at a couple of nights before. The same photo of the four young men stared out at her with youthful, expectant faces. Even Derek, hanging upside down from the branch of the maple tree, looked confident and eager. He did accomplish much in his short life, she thought. Eight years of college to become a veterinarian was nothing to sneeze at. Even though she didn't believe he had worked at his potential, he'd had a goal and had accomplished it. But Bart, Gray's brother, hadn't even had a chance—his life snuffed out while driving drunk on graduation night. She poured herself a cup of tea, squeezed a wedge of lemon and shook in a packet of artificial sweetener.

As she stirred her tea, she studied the figure of Peter Sands. He stood in front of the tree, his hands stiffly at his side. Pete, the idealist—so principled and controlled. She remembered his high-minded causes in school and his rigid work ethic after college when he worked at an engineering company in Lexington. Even in high school, he was way ahead of anyone in his class in electronic know-how.

Laney turned to the back of the year book where the senior class pictures were in alphabetical order by last name. Beneath Pete's photo was the short verse:

Pete Sands' future is assured,
Nothing for him to fear,

Every company will keep an open door
For St. Clair's electrical engineer.

"God, did I write that?" she moaned. Guess I have to claim it, she thought, recalling that she had volunteered to write the poems for all ninety-seven graduates.

"Write what?" Shar's pixie face peeped in the door. She had changed into a long Hamilton plaid jumper that almost reached her ankles and a white long sleeved cotton blouse. A pair of blue leather loafers covered her long feet and two copper eyes gazed out from one of the ample patch pockets.

"Oh Shar, I was moaning over this poem I wrote twenty years ago when I was editor-in-chief of the *St. Clair High School Journal.* Shar looked over her shoulder.

"You're right, it is sorry—but you were only a hack writer of poems back then. Once, when I was assigned a two line rhyme for homework at Taylor Allderdice, I forgot all about it until I got into class. Miss Burster called on me first and I made it up on the spot:

'He went down the street
To get a piece of meat.' "

"Shar, you didn't." Laney laughed out loud.

"I did, and a couple of the guys broke up and before it was over the class was out of control. 'Bugsy,' the name we gave the English teacher because she scratched at herself incessantly, banished me from the room because she thought I had made up the vulgar rhyme purposely."

"Oh Shar, you were outrageous even back then," Laney hooted. "Did you?"

"What? Make it up on purpose? Certainly not . . . at least not that time. Say . . . that poem. Why did you write that about Pete?"

"Because he was a genius when it came to high-fidelity systems. From ninth grade on, he always brought in his own stuff for any musical programs or plays at the school—amplifiers, speaker systems, recorders and the like. I know the school missed him big time when he left for college."

"Did he ever become an engineer?" Shar probed.

"He sure did. He was an electrical engineer for Martin Electronic Engineering until just before he killed himself." Laney caught the expression on Shar's face. The look was the same one that she had seen the day before when she sensed that Shar was secretly planning something for Malcolm.

"What's up kiddo?"

"I was just trying to make some kind of connection between the tape that the police were dredging the creek for and Peter Sands' electronic background."

"I thought that's what you were doing."

There was a light tap at the door, and this time it was Malcolm who peered in.

"I have to be leaving. My plane leaves at one." His eyes locked with Shar's and he sighed.

They walked him to his rental car and Laney gave him a buss on the cheek and said goodbye. While he loaded his luggage in the trunk, Laney retreated to the library. Blackberry padded behind her. Poor Shar, she couldn't remember Shar ever looking so distressed. She really must care for Malcolm.

Now, back to this program. She opened a new word processing document on her computer and typed the title at the top of the page: *IN MEMORIAM*

She was listing the names of the three deceased graduates when Shar and Kudzu joined her in the library. Shar scooted a chair next to Laney.

"Is he gone?" Laney asked, pausing to gaze at her friend.

Shar nodded, feverishly petting the kitten in her lap as though if she stopped the diversion, she would burst into tears.

"How would you like to take a trip to Washington?" Laney asked.

"The state or DC?" Shar asked, stiffening as Blackberry stood and approached, her nose in sniffing gear. Kudzu's eyes, the color of shiny pennies, locked with Blackberry's amber brown ones.

"Neither. Washington, Kentucky," Laney said, nudging Shar with her elbow.

"Didn't know there was such a place."

"Most people don't."

Blackberry's and Kudzu's noses connected in a double snuffle. Blackberry's tongue washed the kitten's ear and Kudzu returned the favor and rolled over onto his back in Shar's lap. Blackberry checked out the rest of the kitten with impudent strategic licks and swipes, then sat on her haunches wagging her tail as though she were waiting for Kudzu to come out and play.

Shar complied cautiously by placing the kitten on the floor. Blackberry instantly dropped to a deep bow—her nose on the floor, rump-in-the-air stance. Her helicopter tail threatened to lift her skyward.

Kudzu bounced about the dog in a kind of basketball ballet, springing straight legged from her tiny white mittens. Blackberry played "one on one" with Kudzu, dodging the kitten's leaps and bounds until the kitten plopped onto the oriental and curled into a ball. The Border collie, clearly not finished with her game, nudged Kudzu and repeatedly did her rump-in-the-air stance to no avail. She finally dropped to the floor next to the sleeping kitten and lay on her side, a paw resting against the kitten's back.

"As I was saying . . . " Laney continued, laughing along with Shar. Tears ran down her friend's face and Laney knew that they weren't all over Malcolm's departure. "Washington is a tiny pioneer village of restored log buildings. Lots of antiques, history, and a couple good restaurants. It's near Maysville on the Ohio. A good friend of mine lives there. Maybe she can meet us for lunch." Laney looked up the number in her address book on the desk and dialed.

"Tina?" Laney saw Shar's brows go up. "This is Laney. I'm fine. Listen, a friend of mine is here from Pittsburgh and we thought we would take a day trip to Washington. How about meeting us for lunch at Marshall Key's Tavern on Saturday? Good. One o'clock it is. It's been too long, Tina. I can't wait to see you." She replaced the receiver.

"This Tina you just called," Shar began. "She wouldn't be the widow of Peter Sands who committed suicide, would she?"

"Well, maybe." Laney hedged.

"Are you kicking around the idea there may be a connection between the tape and Pete's electronic background?"

Laney agonized over her promise to Cutty and whether she should confide in Shar. She would be leaving for Pittsburgh on Sunday, she rationalized. What would it hurt?

"What the hell. Will you promise not to tell a soul about what I am about to tell you?" Laney asked, already feeling guilty.

Shar raised her right hand. "I swear on my last prenuptial agreement," she said, excitement in her eyes.

Laney related her visit to Cutty Bell's and that he had told her that the tape cassette cartridge had been recovered but the tape had been lost. While she was at it, she told her about Gray's dehorners being found below the cliff.

"What are dehorners?"

"They look like hedge clippers . . . long wooden handles for leverage, but with curved blades to cut the horns off cattle."

"Sounds like a rather grisly operation."

"It is," Laney said. "But in this case, the police believe they were used to cut Derek's rappelling rope—another rather grisly procedure."

Shar's mouth dropped. "You must be worried sick about this," Shar said, covering Laney's hand with her own.

"I feel compelled to help Gray any way I can." Laney was pensive. "Maybe there *is* a connection between Peter and the tape."

"But now we know there isn't any tape. Does Gray know?"

"He didn't mention anything to me about the tape after he was questioned yesterday by the police and I was afraid to tell him because of my promise to Cutty."

"Laney, he's your guy. What harm would it do?"

"It might mess up the police investigation."

"How?"

"I think the police may be keeping the tape's condition under wraps."

"Why would they do that?"

"When I was researching my novel, I read somewhere that interrogators don't always disclose everything they know to suspects. They sometimes hold back knowledge that could perhaps link the suspect and the crime. And I'm sure Gray wasn't the only person they questioned."

"Oh, I get you. You're saying if the murderer believes that the police may have potential damaging evidence, the killer could get nervous and do something stupid."

"Right. Police may have a plan to catch the killer. I sure as hell don't want to screw that up by telling Gray. He might let it slip to the wrong person—"

"Like Cutty did by telling you," Shar interrupted, with a knowing smirk on her face.

"Thanks a lot."

Shar gave Laney a playful shove. "Listen, I don't know if snooping around up in Washington will help Gray, but even if we don't come up with anything, it will still be a fun trip."

Secretly, Laney wondered just how much fun she could really have, under the circumstances.

13

A duet from Bizet's *The Pearl Fishers*, soared to the rafters of Gray's tiny apartment above the clinic. He shook the final crumbs of Rice Krispies into his last clean cereal bowl and dropped two stale slices of bread into the toaster. While the coffee perked, he rinsed a used mug out with hot water—the last drops of dish washing liquid gone after a thinning of water for a week. Have to get myself to the market or we'll starve, he thought, eyeing Puccini bolting down his last can of tuna.

"God, my life's a mess," he said, while he buttered the toast and sat down at the small kitchen table. He took one slurpy bite of snap, crackle, and pop downgraded to squish, squash, and sog and ran to the sink where he spat the cereal and sour milk over the week's fermenting dishes.

Had Gray tuned the volume on Jusse Bjoerling's and Robert Merrill's duet any higher, he would have missed hearing his telephone ring. He turned it down and picked up the receiver.

"Gray!" Natine cried. "Better get down here, pronto!" Click.

"Cr-ap! Now what?" he said, flinging the phone down on its cradle. He jammed his feet into his penny loafers, grabbed his cat and galloped down the apartment steps, two at a time.

"Easy now, calm down," Natine said. "Someone has broken into the clinic. I think we need to call the police."

"What? Goddamn it!" He shoved by her and strode through the waiting room to Natine's alcove. His eyes scanned the nook. "Where? . . . nothing amiss here, Natine. What—"

"Gray . . . your office . . . don't touch anything."

He stormed by her again. The door to his office was ajar. He pulled up short when he reached the threshold and clutched Puccini to his chest as though to shield him. "My God . . . call Gordon, Natine."

She pivoted and rushed back to her alcove, while he stood studying the room, paralyzed. Every veterinarian book he owned had been thrown from the bookshelves onto the floor. The desk drawers had been emptied, even his framed licenses, diplomas, and certifications had been ripped from the wall. A wooden box that a classmate at Auburn had carved was turned upside-down on his desk. The computer was untouched but software boxes that he kept on the desk had been opened and dumped. His stereo player was on the floor along with scattered opera tapes and CDs.

He was still standing there when Natine returned.

"Nothing seems to be missing," Gray said. What about the pharmacy?"

"I hadn't gotten that far. Police are on their way."

"Natine, check on the animals . . . the run out back."

She raced on down the hall while Gray rushed to the pharmacy storage room. Puccini jumped out of his arms and scooted after Natine. The door was ajar but everything looked as he had left it— the incubator still cooking a couple of cultures, a plastic bag of dirty syringes in the trash can from a herd he had worked yesterday, the cattle brands lined up on the top shelf. The ear tags, boxes of sized syringes and tubes of wormer were as he had left them—rather, as Natine had left them, he rethought. Every evening before leaving for home, she straightened the storage room, knowing how his numerous quick trips to restock his truck during the day left it in chaos.

He reached to open the refrigerator.

"Don't touch that."

Gray snapped his hand back and spun around. Gordon stood in the doorway.

"After last year, I thought you knew crime scene procedure,

Inspector Clouseau," Gordon quipped.

"Sorry."

Freddie appeared at the door. "Source of entry was the back door," he said. "It was open. The locks around here aren't too challenging. A credit card would do it."

Natine popped her head in. "Animals are okay."

"Can you tell if anything's missing?" Gordon asked Gray.

"So far, nothing. I was just about to check the fridge."

Gordon donned a pair of rubber gloves that he pulled from a wad in his pocket. A single glove fell to the floor, its fingers turned under like a fist. Gray stooped and put it on his right hand.

Gordon snapped the refrigerator door open. Gray scrutinized the shelves. All looked in order at first: Bottles of tetanus antitoxin, equine flu vaccine, oxytocin, pasteurella bacterin.

"Uh-oh," he said.

"Something missing?" Gordon asked.

"Not that I can see. But . . . it's . . . it's like it's been sorted through. The bottles and boxes are shoved around like someone was looking for something." He straightened a large jar of boluses with his gloved hand.

"Maybe someone looking for a particular drug to get high on?"

"Can't imagine shooting up with equine rhinopneumonitis influenza vaccine," Gray laughed hollowly. He scanned the bottom shelf. "No . . . nothing missing . . . just moved around."

"Gray?" Natine popped her head in again.

"Yeah."

"Do you have your truck keys?"

"Aren't they on the counter where I always leave them?" Gray said, jamming his hands into his pockets and searching anyway.

"No."

"Run upstairs and see if I took them up with me when I changed last night. Wouldn't be the first time," Gray said.

"Where were you last night when all this was going on?" Gordon asked, while they walked back down the hallway to the waiting room. Deputy Rudd was busy taking notes in Gray's office. Another deputy was dusting for prints.

"Went to the movies." Gray sat down next to Gordon.

"With . . . ?"

"Me, myself, and I. Needed some time alone with my shadow. Been a grueling week, as you know."

"Detective Barron tough on you, huh?"

"Yep. Still can't believe you all think—"

"I can't discuss it, Doc."

"Sorry."

"What time did you leave here?"

"Don't know exactly. Was a few minutes late for the eight-ten feature showing of *The Devil's Own* at Movie Ten. You figure it."

Gordon took a few notes. "I assume everything was all right when you left."

"I assume. Showered and dressed but didn't check the clinic."

"What about when you got home?"

"Guess it was about ten-thirty or so. Got a sundae at the Finish Line just before they closed. Let myself in this door and went right upstairs to bed."

"Hear anything?"

"Nope. But then canines could have a dogcatcher protest down here and I wouldn't hear it." Gordon wrote a bit more in his notebook.

Natine bounced down the stairs into the waiting room. Her mahogany colored face glowed with sweat and she huffed from all the exertion. A grimace had replaced her double dimples.

"They're not there. I only found the keys to the Buick," she said, handing them to Gray.

Puccini jumped into Gray's lap and turned on his back, wanting to be scratched. Gray dropped him to the floor and stood.

"What did you drive last night, Doc?" Gordon asked.

Gray dangled the Buick keys at him.

"Maybe we'd better check the Buick and the Jeep, if they were parked here all night."

Natine, inside her alcove, dug in her purse. "Here's a second set of keys you gave me for emergencies," she said. "Guess you would call this one of those times." She flipped a ring with two keys over the counter.

Gordon and Gray hurried out to the clinic parking lot, where the Grand Cherokee sat parked next to the pink Buick. Two patrol cars were parked behind the two vehicles. It didn't take but a moment to see that the Buick was spotless inside.

"Just as I left it," Gray said.

They approached the rear of the Jeep and Gray unlatched the swing-out mounted spare, unlocked and raised the liftgate.

A longer search of his vet truck led Gray to believe nothing was out of place there either. A pungent odor emanated from a plastic bag containing manure covered plastic sleeves and Betadine stained wads of cotton where Gray had left it after his last call of the day at Merimont Farm.

"Guess I just mislaid my keys somewhere. They'll turn up."

Gordon check his watch. "Well, I've got to be going. If you miss anything at all, tell Freddie or give me a ring. He'll be around here for a while." He climbed into his patrol car and with a wave, drove out of the lot.

Gray sat down on the bumper edge of the flat cargo floor, his khaki covered legs stretched out in front of him, his back against the vet bed. Puccini, finding the clinic door open, wandered out into the lot and jumped into the cargo bay next to Gray. He stroked the cat, wondering who and why someone had broken into his clinic if nothing was missing. His energy was gone—as though he had been at it all day instead of just starting out. He sighed and contemplated canceling his calls but remembered the two palpations and cultures scheduled at Overland Farm.

"What do you think, copper eyes? Want to get on the road?" As though understanding the request, the tabby leaped onto the top of the vet bed and poised to leap across the back seat to his spot on the dash. As he jumped, something clanged beside Gray. He turned and looked down. His keys! His original set of four keys—the ignition and door keys for the Jeep, the clinic key, and a small key that fitted a drawer lock in the vet bed.

How? I know I didn't leave these here, he mulled. If I had, I couldn't have gotten into the clinic after the movie last night. He scratched his head. As he focused on the ring of keys, he was suddenly gripped with a raw uneasiness. "Surely not," he thought out loud, a chill ripping down his spine. Separating the smallest key, he inserted it into the only drawer that was equipped with a lock. A quick twist and the drawer snapped open.

"God, no!" It was empty.

14

"I'm getting used to this cycling," Shar said, gasping for breath. "Either that or I'm becoming desensitized to pain and suffering." She hopped off her bike and dropped it into the grass next to Laney's. Blackberry continued on down the lane, her tail flowing behind her like a white tipped black banner. Laney knew she was on her way to the crossing to cool off with a quick dip.

Out in the nearest paddock, Aaron was leading Unreasonable and her foal toward the gate nearest the foaling barn. Three youngsters were perched on the plank fencing next to the gate. Laney recognized Aaron's son, Eric, by his apricot colored hair and long skinny limbs. On Eric's left, on the same top rail, sat Woody Wakefield's son, Terry. Terry's sister, Melinda, stood on the lowest rail, her tiny hands clutching the top plank with all her might. She was staring up at Eric with adoring eyes.

Laney and Shar approached the children. When Melinda saw them, she hopped down from the rail and ran over.

"Miss Vey, do you see Fissle?" Shar's and Laney's eyes linked for a second and they smiled at the child's enunciation.

"Thistle is really something, isn't he?" Laney said. Laney unhooked the gate and held it open while Aaron brought the mare and foal through. As soon as they were in the clean stall, all of them piled into the office to observe the colt through the observation window and have cold drinks from the small refrigerator. Shar did the honors, passing out frosty cans of soda pop.

The gray mare ate oats from a corner bucket while the foal had his dinner from one of two swollen teats below.

"How many shots have you had, Terry?" Laney asked, careful not to say the dreaded word, rabies.

"Two," he said, not looking at her. He stared through the observation window.

"Just two? I thought you got seven of them in the stomach," Laney said, surprised.

Aaron looked over at Laney, his face coloring. She never understood why he blushed whenever he spoke to her.

"They give five of them in the arm, now," Aaron said. "Day zero, the third, seventh, fourteenth, and the twenty-eighth day. They also give a human rabies immune globulin on the first day."

"My arm hurts," Melinda said as she nodded, her golden curls bobbing as she showed her arm to Laney and Shar. She lifted the sleeve of her T-shirt. The site looked swollen and red.

"Won't be long before it's over with," Shar said. "Your daddy has been getting them too, hasn't he?"

Melinda nodded her head again. "Daddy is mad . . . mad at Mommy too," she said. Terry gave her a punch on her sore arm and she began to cry. "Terwy, you hurt me."

"Shut up," Terry said to his sister.

Aaron gave Laney a severe look and shook his head as though warning Laney to lay off the subject.

"Do ya wanna see our peacock?" Eric asked Melinda, trying to get her to stop crying.

A smile struggled its way out of Melinda's down-turned mouth. "A real one with pretty feathers?" she asked, wiping her blue eyes and taking Eric's hand.

"Yeah. If we can get him to come down out of the rafters, he might spread them," he said.

"Can I go too?" Shar asked, already bolting for the door.

The boys didn't look too thrilled with the idea of Shar tagging along but she was already out the door.

After they left, Aaron sat down at the desk and opened the large check ledger and began to make out bills from a pile of statements, while Laney sat down on the Naugahyde sofa and dangled a leg over the arm.

"Aaron, what was that look all about when Melinda said that her father was mad at her mother?" Laney asked. Aaron looked over at her and blushed to the roots of his short blond hair. His eyes were a startling shade of green.

"I believe the kids' parents are having problems," he said. "Eric told me last week that Terry told him that they might divorce."

"Aw, no."

"I have a feeling that Terry may know more than he lets on. Things must be kind of unpleasant at home. Since this is spring break, I've been picking up the children to play with Eric quite often. They seem happy enough to be away from home right now."

"I'm shocked. I thought the two of them were devoted to each other."

"I thought so too . . . but ever since Mary started working at the Beales, I think . . ."

"Aaron? What?"

"I better not say." He went back to his check writing.

"Aaron, you were about to tell me something." Laney stood and leaned over the desk, forcing Aaron to look up at her. The flush on his face erupted into beads of sweat.

"I . . . I saw them once when I delivered a load of last year's hay to one of the barns at Hickory Pike Farm," Aaron stuttered.

"Who? Woody and Mary?"

"No. Mary and Derek. I . . . I think . . . you know." Aaron made a mistake, wrote VOID on the check and slammed the ledger shut. "I'd better check on the kids." Then he was gone.

"Well, what do you know," Laney said. "Mary and Derek."

"Thought you ought to hear it from me instead of on the news," Gray said, standing in the hallway inside the front door—his hands, as usual, tucked under his arms.

"Gray, did they take anything?" she asked, grabbing his arm and drawing him into the parlor. She fixed him a bourbon and water, stirring it with her finger because she had forgotten a spoon when she had filled the ice bucket for toddies. He took it eagerly and drank deeply.

"No . . . I don't think so," he said, his eyes darting here and there as though he expected something or someone to surprise him.

He sat on the red sofa and crossed his legs. His top leg pumped away and he chewed on the inside of his cheek.

All this is taking a toll on him, Laney stewed to herself, noting his paleness. She wanted to fix a Bloody for herself but didn't want to leave his side for as long as it would take.

"What could they have wanted?" Laney asked, clasping his free hand.

"Who knows. Some of the drugs were disturbed but they didn't take anything in the fridge. Natine took an inventory. My office was a wreck. It was though they were looking for something specific." He snatched his hand away from hers and ran it through his brown hair. Wiry ends curled around his ears. She detected the gray for the first time.

"Could I have another?" he asked, reaching out with his glass. She took it from his trembling hand.

"What did Gordon think?" she asked, as she fixed another drink for him and a Bloody for herself.

"Doesn't have a clue." Gray walked to the window and looked down to the creek. "Laney, what would you think of moving away from here?"

The drinks sloshed over the rims as she walked toward him. Her hand trembled as she handed him his tumbler.

"Gray, why? . . . where?"

"Anywhere." He downed half of the glass in one gulp. "This hasn't been a good year for either of us, has it?"

"Now you sound like me last year about this time? It was you that helped me go through all the pain of losing my sister. What can I do?" She placed her glass on the window sill and placed her hands on his shoulders, massaging his tightness.

"No one can help."

She laid her head upon his chest. She heard his heart thudding through his surgery scrubs. One muscular arm encircled her shoulders and she heard the clink of ice as he drank from his glass above her head. Her heart silently cried out to him. He's being destroyed by this, she thought. I've got to help him.

"Yoo-hoo . . . you in there?" Shar said, lifting one of Laney's closed eyelids.

Laney, stretched out on the sofa ever since Gray had left, hadn't heard Shar come into the parlor. She rolled to her side, snuggled a needlepoint pillow, and closed her eyes again. "No, I don't think I am," she mumbled.

"How about another Bloody?" Shar asked, grabbing Laney's glass off the window sill on her way to the credenza.

"No thanks. One's enough for me. I'm borderline depressed as it is."

"Was that Gray I saw pulling out the drive?"

"Hm . . . what you saw wasn't really him." Laney sat up still embracing the pillow. "Shar, he's worried to death about this investigation."

"If he didn't do anything wrong, why is he so worried?" Shar said, as she dropped ice into her tumbler.

"I think what bothers him the most about it is that he's afraid people might think he did it. It goes back to his father, G.W., who's an alcoholic. Somehow he feels that he has to live down his dad's irresponsible past behavior."

"He's still living?" Shar lay on the carpet on her side, her head propped on an arm. She sipped her drink.

"Yes, he pops into town occasionally and bugs Gray until he gives him enough money to leave town again."

"That Chris won't speak to him must be hitting Gray hard."

"They were good friends, at least I thought so. By the way, the reason Gray came over was to tell me about a break-in at the clinic last night."

"Woman, no wonder he's so distracted. Was anything taken?"

"Gray says not but he believes someone was looking for something. Stuff was moved around. Do you know what I'm thinking?"

"I think so, but you go at it."

Laney jumped from the sofa, the pillow falling to the floor. She fixed a second Bloody, stirred with her finger, and then stuck the finger into her mouth. "What if the killer was looking for the tape at Gray's? Remember, the cops still haven't let it out that it was destroyed."

"I thought that's what you were thinking," Shar said, her eyes shooting sparks.

"Shar, maybe Derek was blackmailing Chris and someone else knew about the blackmail and continued it after he was murdered.

"Like Derek's wife, Dory."

Laney nodded. "Then maybe she thought Gray found the tape when he found the body, so she broke into the clinic to retrieve it."

"That would explain the break-in, but who murdered Derek?"

"After our bike ride to see Thistle, I can think of several suspects," Laney said, placing her nearly full glass on the marble topped center table. She told Shar about Aaron catching Derek and Mary in the barn and Terry telling Eric that his parents may get a divorce.

"So that's what Melinda's remark about her daddy being mad at her mommy was all about."

"If Woody knew about their affair, that sure could give him a motive for murder," Laney said.

"That and Derek's indifference about the foal that ended up having rabies would give him a doozie of a motive," Shar said. Kudzu meandered into the parlor and began to play with the fringe on the oriental carpet.

"If Dory knew about the affair, that would give her one, also," Laney said. "Not to say that if Mary thought Derek was just using her for a diversion, she might have done him in, herself."

"Do you think that's all it was—a diversion?"

"You've never met Mary but she's a country girl—a very pretty country girl, mind you—but not very sophisticated. Not Derek's type at all. And my sister had told me of other Derek liaisons through the years."

"Damn it, woman, quit! This gets more bedlamizing by the minute. Sounds like a lot of people could have had motives to kill Derek."

"But I still say the tape was the key to the blackmail and the murder," Laney said.

"And it's no more," Shar had to add.

Nancy West stood in the doorway to Gordon's courthouse office. "Gray Prescott just phoned to say that he found his keys at the clinic. He had just misplaced them," she said.

"Thanks, Nancy. Would you close the door, please?" Gordon asked.

"Yeah, sure." The sheriff's department deputy gave the door a kick and it slammed behind her.

Gordon winced. "Does she do that on purpose?" he asked Freddie absently.

His deputy shrugged. The sheriff asked him the question every time Nancy slammed it. Freddie peeled down the wrapper of a Milky Way and took a bite. A bridge of caramel sagged between the candy and his mouth until it severed and swung down over his double chin.

"I still think there's a connection between the break-in and the murder. Barron thinks so too. What do you think, Freddie?" Gordon asked, creaking back in his chair, hands behind his head.

"Since the public doesn't know about the ruined tape, there's a chance the murderer thinks it's still out there somewhere," he answered, wiping the candy off his chin and licking it off his finger. "Maybe that tape was what the burglar was after, although I don't understand why he searched the fridge, unless he could have been looking for drugs too."

Gordon leaned forward in his chair and leaned his elbows on the desk.

"Freddie, you saw Doc's office. Every possible hiding spot was searched. I say he wasn't looking for drugs. He was looking for the tape. There was something on it that was important enough to kill for. I'm sure of it." He hit the desk with his fist. "Damn, if only we had found that tape intact."

"Well, we didn't. So, what else do we have?"

"Not much. No prints. No nothin.'"

"So the burglar wore gloves, and no one saw him enter or leave,"

Freddie said as he finished the last of the chocolate bar. "Something doesn't add up here. If the murderer was after the tape when he broke into the Doc's clinic, then Doc's in the clear."

"You would think so, wouldn't you?"

"You mean you guys still think Doc did it?" Freddie's eyes grew wide.

"Not me. I think the murderer broke in to find the tape. Barron has his own theory about what happened. He believes Doc may have staged the whole thing to take the suspicion off of him."

"No shit."

"He said it would be simple for Doc to go off to the movies, come home, mess things up a little, force the back door with a credit card, then go to bed and wait until Natine discovered the clinic in shambles in the morning."

Freddie was speechless. That didn't happen too often and Gordon was enjoying it.

15

Every time Laney awakened during the night, she heard the rain beating against the window next to her bed. Fortunately, the severe storms that were predicted missed the county and hit northeast of St. Clair County. But enough distant rumbling triggered Blackberry to jump onto the bed and burrow as close to Laney's body as she could.

To some extent, Laney's grumpy mood was the result of her lack of sleep and gray skies overhead. As she dressed, she was tempted to call Tina and cancel their luncheon but the thought that Shar was leaving the next day—the main reason for her grouchiness—made her push herself to make the best of the dreary day.

She dressed in lime green and white checked seersucker pants and matching jacket that she slipped over a white short sleeved chemise. She harnessed her heavy hair, galloping recklessly into frizzy ringlets, into a long single braid.

Shar had already made coffee and was in her red peignoir playing with Kudzu when Laney dragged into the kitchen. Laney poured coffee and slumped into a chair at the round oak table. Blackberry gave the kitten in Shar's lap a swipe with her tongue, then wagged her body at the French doors to be let out. Shar obliged. They heard her barking at a squirrel in the front yard, a moment later.

"The sky to the west looks like it may clear before long, so cheer up, woman," Shar said.

"It's not just the weather, Shar. I don't want you to leave tomorrow."

"Leave? Who's leaving tomorrow?"

Laney's chin snapped up.

Shar wrapped her bony arms around Laney's neck from behind
and gave her shoulders a squeeze. "You're not going to get rid of me
that easily. If you think I'm going to leave you to sort out this
cliffhanger by yourself, you're of unsound mind."

Laney leapt from her chair, bopping Shar on the chin on her way
up. "Your job? Will John give you extra vacation time?"

"He wouldn't dare nix the request," Shar said rubbing her chin.
"Especially when you do the asking." Her mouth twitched into a
smirk.

"Me?"

"Bernard thinks you hung the moon."

"Yeah, sure, and all nine planets, but I'll do anything to get you
to stay a little longer." She seized Kudzu from Shar and danced
around the kitchen.

"Call him while I get dressed," Shar said, snatching the kitten
back and running down the back hallway. Laney heard her galloping legs take the stairs two at a time.

It wasn't as hard as she thought it would be. Two Pitt students
were interning at *Three Rivers Magazine* for the spring semester and
they would help fill in the gap until Shar returned.

"I knew it," Shar said, when Laney told her that Bernard agreed
to give Shar another week of her vacation time. "The petulant pub-
lisher still pants for you."

Laney flashed her a cynical glance and resumed slicing a
muskmelon. She sprinkled fresh blueberries over the juicy slices.
The two of them were just sitting down to the fruit and toasted cinnamon bread when Laney heard her mother's whistle as she let herself in with her key, arms laden with more of her freezer goodies.

"Shar, I haven't been avoidin you, but the dock has been extra
busy because of the nice weather. I hate I haven't seen you and now
you are gettin ready to leave." Maddy hurried into the pantry and
took a minute to organize the freezer.

"Good news, Mother," Laney called. "Shar's staying on for an extra week."

"Well, you may have to put her to work when all your guests start pourin in next week," Maddy said, carrying a cardboard box as she exited the pantry. "What do you want me to do with this box. It was on the freezer."

"Oh that's the box Kudzu and the note were left in," Laney said.

"Who in the world would give you kudzu?"

"Kudzu's what Mal named the kitten," Shar said, pulling the kitten from her lap under the table.

Maddy laughed. "I never did read that note."

"Me either. Where is it?" Shar asked Laney.

"It's probably at Gray's . . . or maybe it's still in the box," Laney said.

Maddy peered inside the box. She pulled out a ragged, terry cloth towel and her fingers scratched against the bottom of the box as she retrieved a wrinkled sheet of paper folded in half. "Is this it?"

"Looks like it," Laney replied.

Shar stood, crossed over and read over Maddy's shoulder.

"If that doesn't beat all," Maddy said, laying the carton on one of the kitchen chairs. Her freckled face stretched into smiles and her brown eyes danced. "I wonder who wrote this."

"Whoever owns Puccini's little trollop of a mother, I'd say," Shar laughed.

"Well, that could be a hard nut to crack. Puccini goes with Gray on every call and almost every farm has a cat or two," Laney said, pouring the coffee. "Mother, want a cup?"

"No, honey, will be goin. I'm glad you're stayin on awhile, Shar." She waved and went on down the front hall.

Shar sat back down at the table and laid the note down on the table. She stirred sugar into her coffee as Laney, sitting next to her, re-read the note.

"Hmm . . . be right back," Laney said. She scooted her chair away from the table and skipped down the hall and disappeared into the library. She was back in a flash, clutching the wrinkled note that Chris had thrown into his trash can. She smoothed it farther and placed it next to the kitten note.

"Eat your breakfast, woman. We have to be on the road soon," Shar said. She washed a bite of toast down with her coffee.

"Both look like regular eight and a half by eleven typing paper," Laney said.

"Mmm. This toast is scrumptious."

Laney lifted the two sheets and carried them over to the range, then held one, then the other up to the hood light. "Look at this, Shar. They're both Mead erasable bond."

Curiosity getting the best of her, Shar took a final gulp of her coffee and followed Laney over to the range and peered at the two sheets of paper that Laney held.

"See the watermark coming through in the light?" Laney said.

"I read Mead erasable all right. But isn't that garden-variety paper?"

"I guess it is but look at the top of the sheets . . . that red edge. They both came from a tablet, Shar. There's even a piece of the sticky red tape left on the corner of the kitten sheet." Laney felt butterflies in her stomach.

"Let's compare the type," Shar said. Her eyes glowed. They scrambled to the breakfast table and Laney removed the plates and laid the notes side by side on the table under the brass and cut-glass hanging lamp.

The two of them scanned the two notes for a few seconds:

YOUR CAT KNOCKED UP MY CAT.   *20-10-10-M*
I HATE DEADBEAT DADS.

"The type is the same size in both notes," said Shar excitedly.

"I see that . . . and the kitten note is all in capitals," Laney said.

"So is the M in the blackmail note," Shar said.

"Shar, look at the M in MY in the kitten note and the M in the blackmail note," Laney said, her face hot with emotion.

"The tops of the M's aren't clear. In fact, all the tops of the letters and numbers are faded . . . like the ribbon on the typewriter was worn." Shar grinned at Laney. "What do you think, Agatha?"

"I do believe we've made a breakthrough, my dear Watson," Laney said, with a shameful British accent. Her heart thumped in her throat.

Laney dumped their cold coffee in the sink and poured fresh. A puddle of sunshine flooded the counter like a sign. She shivered with the knowledge that it was possible that whoever had sent Kudzu and the note to Gray's clinic had also sent the blackmail note to Chris.

By the time Laney and Shar got on the road, they were already behind schedule. After breakfast, Laney had tried to call Amanda for the third time since the fiasco lunch at the country club on Tuesday to see how she was getting along. She was concerned how her friend was coping with the sale of the farm and the ordeal of Derek's funeral. The first two times she had called, she hadn't gotten an answer, but this morning, she was relieved when she heard Chris answer the phone. As soon as she asked for Amanda, he curtly told her she couldn't come to the phone and abruptly hung up. She was hurt and empathized with Gray over his loss of Chris's friendship.

They also took time to run down to the barn to let Aaron know they would be gone for most of the day and to ask him to feed Blackberry and Kudzu if they hadn't returned by six. She gave Aaron a key and told him that he would find the kitten in the pantry. During the day, Blackberry remained outdoors.

As they climbed back into the Whooptie parked in front of the horse barn, the smell in the air was a mixture of wet grass and horse manure. The sky flashed a brilliant blue under fast moving flocculent clouds as the car circled around the yard and down the lane. With each passing day, the canopy of maple leaves over the blacktop grew denser and was gradually turning from light to dark green. On opposite sides of the road, two young men swung weed eaters to keep up with the rapid spring growth.

"How far is Washington from Hickory?" Shar asked. She had already kicked off her flats and was wiggling her stockinged00 feet in time to a ditty from a K.T. Oslin tape that she had brought from Pittsburgh entitled *Songs From An Aging Sex Bomb*.

"It's just down the road a piece," Laney replied with a mischievous smirk.

An hour and a half later, they were parked in front of a orange cone barricade just outside of Washington while a utilities crew finished creating Lincoln logs out of a huge tree that had fallen across the roadway during the storm the night before.

"Just down the road a piece, huh?" Shar groaned. "I'm fast catching on to the local lingo. And I'm really beginning to worry because that guy with the chain saw just said the road would be 'cleared directly.' "

"Look, he's waving us on, Shar," Laney said, and started up the Whooptie. Shar blew a kiss to the workman holding a cone under each arm.

Laney pulled into a parking slot in front of Washington Hall at ten after one. A finger sign pointed to the left of the building and they followed the steep wooden steps down to the whitewashed basement level of the Marshall Key's Tavern.

Tina Sands was seated at an antique tavern table covered with a red and white checked tablecloth. This was the first time Laney had dined at the restaurant. The original tavern had been built in seventeen ninety-five but had burned early in the nineteenth century. The second structure had been built as a fine hotel on the original foundation in eighteen forty-five. The first floor now held an antique store.

Tina jumped to her feet when she spotted Laney. Their shoes clicked as they crossed the uneven polished brick floors. Laney embraced Tina enthusiastically and introduced Shar. They settled into the Hitchcock chairs and all began talking at once.

"Shar, Tina moved here from Hickory after her husband died in November of last year. I'm ashamed to say I haven't seen her since then but we do talk on the phone often," Laney explained.

"We're going to have to change that," Tina said. "I want you to see my little house that I've turned into a gift and antique shop. Mom lives right next door and she works for me part-time. She seems to have a new lease on life now that she has something to do."

Laney noticed that Tina seemed to have one too. She smiled much more readily than she used to and her eyes were shining when she spoke about the shop. Also, a light touch of blush and mascara had defined her pale features and she had highlighted her brown hair with shiny golden streaks. Her blue silk blazer matched her eyes.

"Would you have anything in your shop with thistles on it?" Shar asked, always looking to add to her collection.

"Thistles . . . let me see. Yes, I do know of a piece of depression glass with a thistle pattern on it. You must come over after we eat."

They ordered their lunches and the light conversation abruptly turned when Laney asked, "I didn't see you at Derek's funeral on Wednesday, Tina. Were you there?"

Tina lurched backward in her chair as though she had been struck and she grabbed at her napkin, covering her mouth with both hands. Laney knew immediately that she wasn't aware of his murder.

"Dear God, I didn't know you weren't informed. I assumed that Dory . . . perhaps I should have called you myself. You didn't read about his murder in the obituary? . . . see it on the news? Forgive me."

Tina reached over and grabbed Laney's arm. Her eyes were huge. "Murdered? He was murdered?" She was completely stunned. Laney allowed her time to recover. The waiter brought their lunches to a silent table. After a few moments when the only sounds were the chattering of other diners at the nearest table, Tina finally spoke, though her voice cracked with emotion.

"It's all right, Laney. I'm all right . . . it's just . . . a shock." She swallowed some ice water and sighed to the bottom of her toes. "I've been so busy with the shop opening, I didn't see or read a newspaper all week. And Mom, who's usually on top of things like that, obviously didn't either. I've kept her so busy. I'm sure my new friends here didn't make the connection if they even heard about it." She stared at Laney and shook her head—that she had been so out of touch. "Please tell me all about it," she said in a quiet voice.

Laney started from the beginning—the Blue Grass Stakes. She told her everything, including Gray's being a suspect in Derek's murder.

The pupils of Tina's blue eyes shrunk to hard points of steel. "Gray could not do this," she said vehemently. She turned and looked at Shar. "I've known Graham since we were children." Her expression softened. "All this since last Saturday? Laney will never get you back to Kentucky."

"Like hell she won't. Most exciting vacation I've ever had. I haven't had such drama since I played Martha in *Who's Afraid of Virginia Woolf?* at college. But forget that. I met the most wonderful guest at Laney's bed and breakfast . . . ." She rattled on about Malcolm for several minutes, her eyes dancing with the thoughts of him. Finally realizing that she was monopolizing the conversation, she braked. "Woman, I'm sure I've convinced you that Malcolm is the next best thing to heather."

Tina was smiling for the first time since Laney had told her about Derek's murder. "Will you see him again soon?" she asked politely.

"Right now we're communicating by Ma Bell but Laney may have a permanent house guest after he moves to his new farm in about a month or so," Shar chuckled.

"He's bought a farm?"

"He bought Taylor Ridge from Chris and Amanda," Laney said.

Tina sat back in her chair as though slapped. "You don't mean it."

"I'm afraid so." Laney hadn't meant to get into her blackmail theory, but it was the perfect opportunity to bring up some questions she had about Tina's late husband. To be honest with herself, she knew that was the real reason she had called Tina and arranged to meet. She plopped the last decadent bite of her Marshall Key pie into her mouth while she finished telling Tina her theory.

"It's just a hunch, mind you, that if the tape were found, it might hold a clue to the blackmail and the murder," Laney said, pushing her plate aside and wiping her mouth with her napkin. She was screaming inside to tell Tina that the police had found the destroyed tape but she already felt enough guilt that she had betrayed Cutty's confidence by telling Shar.

"This is all fascinating stuff, but I really don't know how I can help you, Laney," Tina said as the waiter brought their checks. "Let's have coffee at my house and we'll talk some more there."

Shar insisted on running into several of the antique shops on Old Main Street and gave a whoop when she found a folding, leather picture frame embossed with thistles in the last shop. She was still crowing over her purchase when they hopped into the Whooptie and followed Tina's van to her house on Green Street, that ran perpendicular to South Court.

"Just look at that," Shar said, when she saw the two story log and stone structure, her enthusiasm as unending as a treadmill. But in this case, Laney shared in her delight when she saw Tina's house. Below every casement, purple pansies and white phlox over-whelmed each dark green window box. Behind the house, slate gray clouds were descending like a velvet curtain over a backdrop of blue sky.

"The log section and part of the stone section is original—early eighteenth century," Tina said, as she led them through the build-ing. "Its restoration and the limestone additions were done in the nineteen sixties. It's had five owners since then."

Tina introduced Shar to her mother, whom they interrupted from her dusting of the many antiques and collectibles that filled every nook and cranny in the log rooms. Laney hugged Lucille, whom she hadn't seen since Peter's funeral in November. Lucille Fowler had lived in Maysville all her life, but when Peter died and Tina moved to Washington, Lucille also moved there to be closer to her only grandchildren, Aggie and Cilla. It was spring break and Laney learned that the children were off visiting their Aunt Margaret in Ripley, Ohio.

After a tour of the three log rooms that were devoted to the busi-ness—one up and two down, Tina led them into the section that she and the girls used as their living quarters.

"This is fabulous, Tina," Laney said, as the three of them settled around the table in the snug little kitchen. "The log section reminds me of the log cabin on your farm in Hickory." As soon as she made the comparison, she was sorry. Tina's face dropped and she quickly busied herself filling the coffee pot at the sink.

"I'm sorry . . . I really have been putting my foot in my mouth today, haven't I?" Laney grimaced and Shar crossed her eyes at her behind Tina's back.

"I've dealt with Pete's suicide, Laney," Tina said. "It's the mention of the farm that has me troubled. If it weren't for the capital gains, I would sell it. My estate planner insists that I keep it as an invest-ment for the girls. Taxes would take a huge bite. Personally, I have no sentimental attachment to the place anymore, mostly because Peter died in the cabin there."

Shar threatened to lurch right out of her chair. "You mean your husband killed himself right there on your farm?" she asked, her right land flying through her short blond hair.

Tina poured the coffee into blue speckled Bybee pottery mugs and placed them on blue checked place mats. Two early red tulips nodded from a pitcher—another Bybee piece—on the center of the table.

The wooden chair grated against the red brick floor as Tina sat down. She passed the cream and sugar. "Yes he did, Shar . . . in a remote cabin on the place." She spooned one sugar into her cup and stirred in widening circles. "I haven't really spoken to anyone about it much. For several months, I blamed myself . . . something that I've discovered is normal behavior according to my therapist. In hindsight, I remember numerous signs that something was very wrong. When his company downsized and he was pink slipped, I guess I should have been on my guard. But you had to know Peter. He was always very emotionally controlled and secretive about himself, so when he began to go to the cabin more often during the weeks before he died, I first thought it was just his way of coping with disappointment. And he also told me he was using the time out there to prepare résumés and letters of introduction for new employment."

"Did you ever go out to the cabin to see him any of the times he was there?" Laney probed.

"Oh yes, several times. But he always acted as though I were an intruder."

"Did the girls ever go with you?" Shar asked.

"Cilla used to ride her bike to the cabin and she would always come home hurt because her father would have the door locked. He would yell to her that he was busy with his résumés."

"What did he do out there all that time?" Laney asked. "Was he actually preparing for interviews?"

"After he died, I never found a single résumé. Cilla thought he watched movies or listened to audio tapes out there. She said she listened at the door a couple times and thought she heard a video or audio tape she had heard a couple times before. He had all the latest electronic equipment out there." Shar kicked Laney under the table a little too hard and she winced.

"This is awfully personal, Tina, but did . . . did he leave—"

"Leave a note? Oh, yes," Tina said.

"Did it explain why he did it?" Laney asked gently.

"Well . . . not really . . . I mean . . . I think he thought it did, but in his depressed frame of mind it really wasn't very clear to me." Tina's eyes pooled for a moment. "I've read it over and over, trying hard to read between the lines so I could understand what was so oppressive about his life that he couldn't bare to live in this world any more."

"So you still have the note?" Laney asked.

"Oh yes. Would you like to see it?" She rose and walked down the hall to the stairway and climbed.

"Lordy, woman," Shar exclaimed. "There's no way I can read the last words of someone who was about to give himself a necktie party." She stood and spotted what looked like the door to the bathroom under the staircase and made her fast retreat as Laney heard Tina's returning steps.

Tina didn't seem to realize that Shar had left the room. She held a worn sheet of stationery that she placed in front of Laney. She sat back down in the chair and observed Laney while she read the handwritten note:

> *Forgive me. I can't take it anymore.*
> *After this, you will understand.*
> *Peter*

Laney looked into Tina's gray eyes. She expected sadness, but instead she found resignation. Acceptance.

"This is it?" Laney asked. "You were supposed to understand with *this?*"

For an instant, Tina's eyes wavered, then hardened back into resolution. But Laney had caught her hesitation.

"You think there is something more, don't you?" Laney asked. "Tell me, Tina."

"Laney, I think Pete believed his death would be all the explanation needed. With this ultimate act of despair, I would understand the pain he was in . . . his lost job after fifteen years at Martin Electronic Engineering."

"Bull crap!"

"Laney!"

"He says, 'After this, you will understand.' 'After this' . . . after what, Tina? There has to be more."

Tina began to cry. Huge pent-up sobs.

"When you found him, where was the note?"

"I didn't find him."

Laney staggered to her feet. "Surely not the girls . . . my God, no!"

"No, not the girls."

"Who then?"

"Derek Beale."

Laney felt all the blood in her body turn to ice then melt in an instant and run molten to her brain like a hot flash. She began to shake, collapsing into her chair.

"How . . . how did Derek come to be there?"

"Derek told the police that Pete had called him that morning from the house and asked him to meet him at the cabin that evening . . . that he wanted to talk to him. Later, police thought that it was part of Pete's plan so that I wouldn't be the one to find his body."

"Then what happened?"

"When Derek got to the cabin it was almost dark. Pete's car was parked in the driveway and he could see that the lights were on in the cabin. Derek knocked and when Pete didn't come to the door, he turned the knob. The door was unlocked. He found Peter hanging from a rafter. A chair lay on its side. Derek immediately called the police from his cell phone." Lifting the note, Tina read it again, though Laney was positive Pete's final words were etched permanently upon her brain. She folded it and slipped it into the pocket of her jacket.

"I don't remember reading anything in the paper about Derek being the one to find him, so most people assumed you had been the one."

Tina wiped her eyes with a paper napkin and blew her nose. "Gordon was very kind to suppress as much as possible, out of respect for me and the children."

Gordon would do that, Laney reasoned, recalling how much he loved children. "Did Gordon tell you what he found when he reached the cabin?"

"He tried to spare me as much as possible. He gave me the note that he said he found on the desk . . . and Pete's eyeglasses. He found them on the floor next to the desk. Rather unlike Pete. He was always so . . . so orderly."

Shar, who had been standing in the doorway for some time, inched her way back into the kitchen. Her pixie face was ashen.

"Tina, the note . . . the part that says, 'after this, you will understand.' Could Pete have been referring to a tape—a video or audio tape?" Laney asked.

"He left no tape for me," Tina said bitterly, wishing in her eyes that he had. So much anger still there, Laney thought.

"But what if he had?" Shar added.

"Then where is it?" Tina implored in a childlike whine as though Shar could produce it at will.

"Tina, honey, we don't know if there was ever any tape, but if there was, only one person could have taken it," Laney said.

"The person who found Peter!" Tina said, as realization struck her.

"Yes," Laney said.

"But why would he take something so personal, a man's dying words, so to speak, and not tell me?" asked Tina.

"Perhaps he played it on Pete's electronic equipment and discovered what was on the tape. Peter's high fidelity equipment was right there in the room, wasn't it?" Shar asked.

"Brilliant, Shar!" Laney said. Shar grew another half inch.

"It's no use speculating if you don't have the tape," Tina said, "unless . . ."

"Unless what?" Laney probed unenthusiastically, suddenly tired—wanting to be through with it all. She waved the whole thought away with her hand.

"Unless Pete had made a copy."

"A copy? . . . what copy? . . . a copy!" Laney grabbed Tina's arm. "Tina, could you have any of Pete's old tapes?"

"I have loads of his tapes, in the basement."

"Could we look through them?"

"If you'd like," she said, crossing to a door, "but I warn you. There are at least three cartons full of them." She flipped a wall switch and led them down a steep flight of stairs into a large concrete basement. Through the tiny rectangular windows, Laney saw the wind gusting the grass and they heard distant thunder.

Antiques filled most of the cellar—waiting their turn to replenish the shop upstairs, Laney determined. Tina dragged three cartons from under a trestle table against the right wall. "Help yourself," she said. "Just be glad that they're here in this newer basement built in the sixties instead of the dungeon under the log section. If you'll excuse me, I must relieve Mom in the shop. Take your time." She climbed the stairs and Laney followed the sound of her footsteps overhead until they disappeared.

"Okay, woman, let's get at it," Shar said.

They used the trestle table for a work station. They sat on a couple of wobbly slat-back chairs and began sorting through the cassettes. Peter's taste in music ran strictly to the classical, featuring mainly pianists performing Schumann, Rachmaninov, Liszt, and Chopin.

"If I find one more Vladimir Horowitz tape, I'm going to barf. What's wrong with Yanni? At least he's easy on the eyes," complained Shar. She curled her lip at the cassette cover depicting an aging Horowitz in concert in Moscow.

"This is a lost cause, Shar. All the tapes in this box are of well-known artists. I haven't found a single one that doesn't have a commercial label on it."

"Me either. There are loads of CDs too," she said as she stretched her long arm into the bottom of the final carton. "Say, look at this," Shar said, holding up a Reba McIntire tape. "The girls must have slipped one in on Pete."

Laney smiled, wondering how the girls were handling the suicide. "Well, that's it," Laney said, as she began tossing the tapes and CDs back into the boxes. "Look what time it is," she said as she checked her watch. We won't get home until late."

They scooted the boxes back under the table, climbed the steps and turned out the light. They found Tina turning the closed sign around in the front window. Her mother had gone back to her little house next door.

"No luck?"

"No, and we're tired and I know you are too. So we're going. I hope I didn't stir up too many painful memories for you, today." Laney embraced Tina and heard her sigh deeply.

"I've got a handle on my life, Laney, even if I never find out all the reasons Peter ended his life. I've got my girls and my shop and I've met a man who lives in Maysville. We go to dinner sometimes."

Laney felt her nose begin to sting and she choked back the tears. "Tina, that's wonderful. Give my love to Aggie and Cilla, will you?"

"Is this the depression glass piece you were speaking of?" Shar asked, lifting a pale peach covered butter dish from Tina's desk.

"Oh dear, I almost forgot. I found that while you were in the basement. I do believe that's a thistle design on the lid."

"Tina . . . it is!" Shar inspected every inch of the piece. "I love it." She paid for the treasure and Tina wrapped it carefully.

Laney had started the Whooptie and had shifted into reverse to back out of the driveway when Shar said, "Hold it." The Whooptie stalled.

Tina was waving to them as she ran out the door. Laney rolled down the window.

"Here are the keys to the farm gate and the cabin. Check out the cabin. Maybe I didn't find all the tapes." She dropped the keys into Laney's hand and blew them a kiss.

16

Gray was on his second drink when Marshall Knight walked timidly through the door of the Sports Page Bar & Grill in Hickory. Marshall squinted through the smoke and rubbernecked until he spotted Gray, the only one seated at the bar. Everyone else seemed to be either out on the dance floor or in the back alcove watching the finals of a dart tournament that was culminating after three consecutive Saturday night play-offs. A local country band calling itself Hickory Smoke was playing a fast number. The place was hopping.

Gray watched the scrawny little attorney making his way around the tables and chairs. His unfastened galoshes flapped at his pant legs and he wrapped his black raincoat close to his body as though something in the sleazy place might contaminate it.

"Thanks for coming out," Gray said. He scooted the bar stool out next to him so that Marshall could sit, but he remained standing.

"Can't we sit at a place more private?" Marshall's eyes darted uncomfortably about the room.

"Can't be any more private than this. We're the only ones at the bar."

Marshall's fingers combed through the thin strands of his yellow gray hair, and he reluctantly stepped on the bar rail, and with a little hop up, sat down. His legs dangled. "I was just leaving my office to go home when you called. It sounded urgent, otherwise I never would have consented to meet you in such a place." Marshall pulled a pack of Camels out of his raincoat pocket and lit up.

"Realize that and I'm sorry, Marshall, but I wanted to get this off my chest before I lose my nerve. Your wife said you were at the office. Guess I'm not the only one who has to work Saturday nights sometimes. Gray looked down at his blood spattered overalls. "Emergency C-section."

The bartender walked from the other end of the bar where he was watching the tournament between filling waitresses' drink orders. Marshall had successfully defended Lester in a marijuana possession case recently.

"What can I get you, Mr. Knight?" Lester asked.

"Nothing for me, thank you." He waited until the bartender returned to the tournament. "What do you need to tell me that takes courage? Pray it's not a confession. No attorney wants to hear that." Marshall crushed out his cigarette in an overflowing ashtray.

Gray searched to each side of him before he spoke, "The break-in the other night . . ."

"Yes?"

"Discovered something missing after Gordon left."

"Heavens, it's not what I'm thinking." Marshall lit another Camel and dragged long.

"Not the tape, Marshall."

"Thank goodness." Marshall relaxed a hair and stared at the lit end of his cigarette.

"However, may be more serious than that."

"Please, tell me."

"A restricted drug—"

"So someone *was* looking for drugs. But what could they take? Some worming boluses?" Marshall slapped his thigh after his funny remark.

"Marshall, you don't understand the significance here. My two hundred fifty milliliter bottle of Thanatol is gone."

"Thanatol? Does it get you high?"

"It gets you low, Marshall. Dead low. It's my euthanasia drug. There's no antidote."

Gray watched Marshall's face turn pasty in the darkened bar. "Why for heaven's sake didn't you tell the police as soon as you discovered it missing?" the lawyer gasped.

"I'm already under suspicion for one death. How do you think it would have looked if I'd reported the drug that I use exclusively for death was missing?"

"And now the delay in reporting the theft of a restricted drug—" Marshall began. He waved to the bartender. "I've changed my mind. Would you be so kind as to pour a beer for me?" he asked politely. After his request, his frown returned.

One look at Marshall's face told him what he already knew. Gray shrugged. "So, I should have . . . and I didn't." Gray stuck up a finger for another drink and swallowed the last of his last one. "So, where do I go from here?"

Lester delivered Marshall's beer.

"You go to the police." Marshall sucked deeply on his cigarette and exhaled little smoke.

"Detective Barron doesn't believe a thing I say, the cynical bastard. He believes I killed Derek. Thinks I fabricated the story about giving Derek the dehorners. Thinks I either have some damn tape or got rid of it." Gray took a giant swallow from his fresh bourbon and water.

Marshall wrapped his bony fingers around the handle of the frosted mug and took a swill. He licked at the foam on his upper lip. "Something else has occurred to me, Gray. I wouldn't be surprised if he thought you rearranged your own clinic to throw the police off."

"Sounds just like something Barron would think. Throw in a little obstruction of justice. So . . . I go to the cops."

"We go to the cops."

"You'll go with me?"

"I don't want you to talk to the authorities without me present."

"Getting that serious?"

"It's getting that serious."

17

Blackberry sulked on the front porch while her new furry friend traveled toward the Nissan via Shar's tunic pocket. Laney just couldn't stand leaving the dog behind.

"Want to go for a ride, girl?" Laney called, opening the back door. The dog needed no prodding. She was a black and white blur from the porch steps until she settled upright in the back seat next to the open window. They took off.

After the rain the day before, the air sparkled with freshness and many of the long-awaited creamy white blooms of the dogwoods had finally opened. But unhappily, Laney only discerned the day as painfully vivid—like a raw nerve. She squinted against the piercing blue sky and intense green grass. She knew the experiences of the past week were the reasons she felt galled and set on edge. And she missed Gray's warmth and cheer. Damn it, she thought, if there was only a copy of the tape somewhere, maybe it would explain why Pete killed himself, why Chris was being blackmailed, and finally— the most important thing—somehow clear Gray of any suspicion of murder.

As they sped toward Hickory, Laney observed Blackberry through the rearview mirror. A third of the dog's body protruded from the window—the wind streamlining her face into a G-force grin and flattening her ears against her skull Snoopy style.

Laney felt Shar's eyes on her as they drove toward the town.

"You're really counting on finding something, aren't you, woman?" Shar asked, petting Kudzu who had ventured from the confining pocket.

"I know it's a long shot, Shar, but that's all I have to go on right now. If this doesn't pan out, I may resort to tailing Chris until he makes a money drop somewhere."

"You seem absolutely positive that he is being blackmailed."

"Shar, I saw his face when he opened that letter. He was devastated. And I saw him bawling like a baby in his office. I'm convinced someone has something on the man that is so threatening to him that he's paying them big bucks. The extortion has become a detriment to his health."

"I wonder if Amanda knows about it."

"The blackmail? . . . I bet not."

"Why not? . . . the selling of her home . . . the loss of the country club membership. Chris had to have explained all that to her."

"I'm sure he told her something, but not that he was being blackmailed. Amanda is one of those submissive wives that doesn't know squat about her husband's finances. She told me once that she didn't even know how much money Chris made at the university. Can you believe that?"

"Did the women's movement pass her by or what?"

"She's one gal that never burned her bra. Chris always protected her and she seems to like it that way. She always does whatever Chris tells her to do."

"Humph . . . I bet Chris likes her that way, too."

Laney turned onto the bypass and at the first caution light, swung a right onto Squire Road. After about a mile, she switched on her signal, turned left onto a gravel driveway, and stopped in front of an iron cattle gate with a lock and chain. She dangled Tina's two keys in front of Shar's nose.

"I'm driving, so you have to open the gate," Laney announced. "Lock it after I go through."

Shar dumped Kudzu in Laney's lap and scrambled out of the car. While Laney waited for Shar to comply, she recalled that the lane didn't use to have a gate. *I guess when Tina moved to Washington, she had one installed for security reasons,* Laney thought.

"Okay woman, let's get at it," Shar said, crunching the door shut after gathering her limbs inside. Kudzu made a leap into her lap.

Even with the recent rains, the Whooptie left a light trail of dust behind as they followed the packed dirt road with a high grassy center for a quarter of a mile through a pasture where a herd of Charolais cattle were grazing. The lane abruptly came to an end in front of a gate—another one that Laney didn't remember—but this one wasn't locked. Shar obliged again, giving Laney a dirty look. The surface of the road on the other side of the gate was blacktop and it branched in two directions. To the right, it followed a ridge and disappeared over a hill where Laney knew the main house was located. There, Laney recalled, a second driveway wound its way to Squire Road. As soon as Shar was back in the car, Laney took the left fork that swiftly descended into a dark wood of evergreens. The Whooptie pitched, rolled, curved and looped it's way down through the trees as though the car were a metal ball in a pinball game. The car continued its descent and after one final hairpin curve, Laney turned the wheel sharply to the right onto a concrete bridge that crossed the north fork of Stoney Creek.

"Whew!" Shar gasped. "That's better than the Jackrabbit coaster at Kennywood Park."

Midway across the bridge, Laney abruptly stopped the car. Elevated from the rain, the water slapped at the sides of the concrete, and rivulets of water dribbled over the edge.

"Woman, don't stop here! There are no sides!" Shar screamed. Her eyes were giant gray balls of fear, her hands, like claws, grasped at the dash.

Laney, observing her near panic terror, shifted the Whooptie into first and pulled off the causeway.

"I'm sorry, Shar," Laney said, stopping again at the far end of the bridge, then dropped her head to the steering wheel.

Shar stretched out a trembling hand to her friend. "I've always been terrified of bridges, but you . . . you're coming apart at the seams. Laney, what is it?"

Laney couldn't answer for a minute; the recollection was so vivid in her mind. When she eventually lifted her head from the steering wheel, she could only zero in on the reflection of the bridge behind her in the rearview mirror. She wondered how she had forgotten what happened that night.

"Bart . . . that's where he died," she choked.

Following Laney's gaze in the mirror, Shar spun her head back to the bridge. "The car accident? . . . he was killed here?" Shar gasped. She clenched Kudzu in a smothering hold.

Laney nodded. "I haven't been here since before it happened. I read that the car careened out of control down this road, left the bridge, and plunged into the creek."

"My God, Laney."

The whole chilling story came back to Laney, just as though she were reading the details in the newspaper two days after graduation night.

"You said he had been at a party," Shar said softly.

Laney nodded. "Bart had been drinking heavily all night. We all had. A couple of us tried to get Bart's keys away from him. But Bart had bought the Chevy Vega that very day after saving up from various jobs for two years. No one was going to take his keys away."

Laney knew she hadn't been an angel that night either. After drinking a great deal herself, she had fallen asleep on the sofa and when she had awakened, the sun was filtering through the antique satin drapes. The soused bodies of several of her classmates were scattered about on the gold shag carpeting in the Blair's living room. Mrs. Blair had been sensitive enough to call all the parents when she'd discovered them passed out on her floor about two o'clock in the morning.

"But why did Bart come *here* that night?"

"Who knows?" Laney shrugged. "He was drunk. He wasn't missed until morning."

"Didn't Gray's parents miss him?"

"It was graduation night. Parties everywhere. No one expects you home until dawn or later." She shuddered with the memory. "The water was high like today and the car sunk to the bottom. The newspaper said he was still in the car when they found him."

Laney started up the car again. Her hands gripped the wheel like clamps to keep them from shaking. Shar, unsteady herself, was quiet, her hands stroking the kitten with quick nervous movements.

The Whooptie cut to the right and struggled up the opposite grade—a duplication of the sine curves they had driven on the other side of the bridge.

Shar ended her silence. "Who planted all these pines and white spruce?"

"Peter's father did when he bought the place right after he married. Peter told me he had planned to sell Christmas trees for extra income but liked them so much, couldn't bear to cut any of them down. Beautiful, aren't they?"

"Breathtaking. It's so shadowy and still—almost spooky."

Near the crest of the hill, the road leveled and Laney made a final swing through a grove of dense hemlocks, halting in front of a small square-log cabin. A tiny frame addition jutted out on the right and a wide stone chimney was visible behind the weathered gray shake roof. When Laney cut the engine, a jam session exploded around them. Spring warblers, the rat-tat-tat of woodpeckers, and chattering squirrels all blended into a concert of living instruments. Blackberry, well-behaved up to this point, abruptly shot out of the window and began to explore. Shar tucked the kitten back into her pocket and unwound stiffly from the car. The yard around the cabin was unkempt with wild onion and dandelions beginning to sprout from lack of mowing.

Laney retrieved the keys from Shar and inserted the larger into the keyhole. After several tries, the key turned to the right. Laney had to knock her hip against the door before it gave and grated open, leaving a fresh scrape on the dusty pine floor. Stepping inside, she was met with the musty smell of old air and dampness. Behind her, Shar had a death hold on Laney's belt.

"Shar!" Laney yelped, unexpectedly spotting their reflections in the horse hame mirror on the right wall. Shar practically ripped her belt out of the belt loops before she, too, saw their images. She began to giggle.

"We look like Nancy Drew and Bess Marvin," Shar sputtered. Laney broke up at Shar's comparison and laughed until weak in the knees. Shar released her hold on Laney and dropped Kudzu to the floor.

"It shouldn't be too difficult to search the place," Laney said. "There are only two rooms and a bathroom. Her eyes shot to the bookcase that filled the wall to her left. "It's gone, Shar. Pete's stereo equipment took up practically half of this space," she said, pointing to the empty shelves.

"Surely you didn't expect it to still be here, did you? Someone would have ripped it off."

"Yeah, I guess so. Tina must have sold it. Come to think of it, a lot of the furniture is gone. I remember a couple of mission chairs on either side of the bookcase and a matching sofa here with crackled leather cushions." Laney spun right and stared at the fireplace, the stone surrounding the gaping opening black from hundreds of fires. "My favorite piece was a red painted settle next to the fireplace." She turned toward an oak table used as a desk to the right of the front door. I wonder if Peter wrote his note here, she thought. The back of a ladder back chair unnaturally faced the desk. Her eyes instinctively traveled upwards to the crossbeam rafters in the open ceiling. There was no indication that a rope once coiled tight around one of them. Cobwebs were beginning to form around the spokes of the wagon wheel chandelier hanging from the center beam.

"Let's start with the bedroom and bathroom," Laney announced. She disappeared into the dark hallway. "You better run out and get the flashlight for the bathroom, Shar. There are no windows in there." Laney moved into the bedroom and opened the louvers of the shutters covering the twin windows at the front of the house. She peeked through but couldn't see Blackberry anywhere. Shar was stretching her frame inside the Whooptie.

Laney searched the room in just a few minutes. The only furniture remaining, was a marred maple dresser and a dusty bed frame. Laney checked the drawers that were swollen tight with dampness. She had to get on the floor and prop her feet against the dresser to get the leverage she needed to get the bottom drawer open. Instead, the front of the drawer came off in her hands. Empty like the others. She hammered the drawer front back on with her fist and walked to the tiny closet. Other than a few wooden hangers, it was bare. Kudzu wandered inside as she ran her hand along the high shelf. When she withdrew her hand, mouse droppings clung to her palm. "Yuck. No wonder the kitten was drawn to the closet."

Shar burst into the room. "That bathroom's so tiny, if you turn around too fast, you get hair in your mouth."

Laney grinned. "Nothing here either. Let's hit the main room."

Shar searched the small kitchenette in the corner of the log room next to the opening to the hallway, while Laney combed through the drawer in the desk and recessed coat cubicle adjacent to the front door. Nothing.

"This is it, Laney," Shar said, as she opened a knotty pine cabinet door below the bookcases. The base cabinets stretched across the width of the bookcase units. Laney started at the right wall and worked toward Shar. The cabinets were mostly filled with stacks of magazines, yellowed newspapers, and odds and ends of pots and bowls that the tiny kitchen couldn't hold. Kudzu climbed inside and sniffed around as they searched.

"A box!" Laney cried, but after dragging it out, found only *National Geographic Magazines* inside.

Shar had almost vanished except for her wiggling rear end as she struggled with something deep inside. When the rest of her body emerged, her face was red and she was panting. She dragged a cardboard carton in front of her and she squeezed it through the opening and dropped it a couple of inches to the floor.

Laney pounced on the carton and slapped the cardboard flaps open.

"Shazam! . . . I think," she said as an afterthought. The box was filled to the brim with audio tape cassettes. They dragged it to the open front door where they had lots of light.

"Laney, I think these are more of the same . . . actual artist tape recordings . . . more Horowitz," she said wryly while holding up one of the pianist's cassettes.

Laney had to agree that they had come to the end of the search—until she found two large plastic cases at the bottom of the carton.

"Look at this, will you?" Laney waved a case with a photo of Rod Stewart on the cover.

"It's an eight track tape," Shar said. "I had a zillion of them when I was a teen."

"So did I." Laney tossed it back into the box. "Look at this one, Shar!" She held up a black case with a white label.

"Lordy woman, it's a blank eight track that you can record on, just like you can now with blank cassettes," she squealed, snatching it out of Laney's hands and jumping up and down like a banshee. Kudzu took off out the door and into the trees. Shar dropped the tape into Laney's lap and scrambled after her cat.

Laney looked at the tape. She had no idea that blank eight tracks ever existed. But, if anyone would have had that knowledge and access to such a tape, it would have been Peter.

Shar broke through two hemlocks with Kudzu in tow and Blackberry close behind. Shar sat down on the stone step in front of Laney. The dog and cat shared a patch of sunlight.

"Shar, did you ever hear of an eight track recorder that you could record blank tapes on?"

"I'd heard of recorders, but never knew anyone who had one. But if this Peter guy was the electronic wizard you say he was, acquiring one and hooking it up to his equipment shouldn't have been a problem."

Laney turned the tape over. The label was imprinted with eight lines. On the line next to track one, two words were written in ink: *Tongue Twisters.*

18

"Shar, do you see what I see?" Laney said, nudging her napping friend. Shar didn't move, so soundly was she sleeping. Her head lay back on the headrest and she was snoring big time. Kudzu and Blackberry were in the back seat—the dog quivering for the car to come to a stop so she could cut loose through the window, the kitten, asleep on his back with white paws curled under. Laney punched Shar a second time.

"Hmm . . . quit . . . for pity's sake." Shar stretched her long legs against the sack of fresh vegetables that they had purchased on their way through Hickory. She slowly opened her eyes as Laney braked behind a familiar green Oldsmobile parked in the circle drive in front of her house. Toenails clicked and scraped against the window frame as Blackberry made her escape.

"Mal!" Shar whooped, shoving the stubborn door ajar. Like an distending party favor, she unfurled in one graceful motion and hurtled down the brick path toward the porch. The little guy stood at the railing with a beam on his face that imperiled the sun, his arms outstretched in spite of himself. Shar rushed into his arms, nearly bowling the two of them into the bed of English ivy. He's been gone all of three days—absence does . . . , Laney thought. There's definitely something going on here.

Embarrassed by his unaccustomed show of emotion, Malcolm

busied himself by straightening his gray sweater vest while Laney approached the porch.

"Where did you come from, you sight for sore eyes?" Shar blurted, while clinging to Malcolm's hand.

"Why, Ocala, of course," he said. "When my farm manager made arrangements to see the Taylor Ridge farm and manager's house, and you informed me by phone yesterday morning that you were extending your stay here, I thought it the perfect opportunity to accompany him and see the two of you again." His eyes swept over Shar quickly and Shar actually blushed, her pale lashes fluttering.

"Where's your manager?" Laney inquired.

"I dropped Smitty and his wife off at Hickory House in town, where I shall also lodge for this visit," Malcolm said.

"You will not!" Laney retorted. "You will stay right here—in your old room."

A subtle look of relief passed over Malcolm's features. Still, he protested, "But your guests—"

"My guests don't arrive until Friday, so enough said," Laney replied. "In fact, your farm manager and his wife may also stay here if they like."

"They are quite comfortable at the hotel. But thank you, I certainly would love spending a few more days here in your lovely home."

"Now that it's settled, lug in your things, Malcolm, and we'll have toddies," Laney said. "You have a lot of catching up to do."

Malcolm carried his single suitcase to his room while Laney freshened up from their cabin search. She took a quick shower and slipped on a comfortable yellow knit shift that dropped to her toes. She heard Malcolm rattling drinks in the parlor as she set the table in the kitchen for three and sliced a pound of fresh mushrooms.

She heard Shar clicking down the back stairs. Just as Malcolm entered the kitchen with the tray of drinks, Shar burst through the doorway in a slate blue long-sleeved sweater and matching gabardine pants that fell forever to the tops of her shoes. Her only decorations were her gold thistle earrings and smoky eyes. Her face glowed with love when she saw Malcolm.

Tears welled in Laney's eyes. She wasn't envious of Shar's happiness, only sorry that she and Gray seemed to have lost the same joyousness in only one week.

"Excuse me," she said, and hurried down the hall to the library. Kudzu was curled up asleep on the hearth rug. The kitten's explorations at Tina's farm must have exhausted him, Laney mused. She sat at her desk and dialed the phone. Gray's phone rang and rang and she was about to hang up when she heard the click. Gray's voice was husky with sleep.

"Gray, have you eaten? Malcolm is here. How about having dinner with us?" she asked.

"Laney, I ate a late lunch about three," he said groggily.

"Fast food, I bet. Then how about dessert around eight?"

Laney heard him sigh. There was a long pause before he responded. "All right, but one thing, Laney, please let's not discuss Derek's murder. I want to forget about it for a night, okay?"

She heard the heavy fatigue in his voice as though his mouth lacked the energy to form the words. She could only agree to his wish.

In the kitchen, Laney sipped on her drink at the breakfast table, and Shar chattered away to Malcolm about their adventures during the time he was in Ocala. They hardly touched their drinks, they were so full of each other.

"So, we think the person who wrote the blackmail note and the kitten note are the same person." Malcolm listened patiently while Shar continued with the information gained on their trip to Washington. When she showed him the black eight track tape they had found that afternoon at Tina's farm, he studied it carefully.

" 'Tongue Twisters.' What does that mean?" he asked. "How do you know that this is a copy of the tape that the police were looking for?"

"We don't," Shar answered.

Laney, who was putting the finishing touches on three tomato, cucumber, and Bermuda onion salads suddenly dropped her paring knife with a clatter onto counter. "Shazam!"

"That means that our reknowned sleuthhound has unraveled another clue," Shar explained to Malcolm wryly.

"Shar, the ruined cassette that the police found in the creek had the word 'Tong' written in ink on it. Tong! . . . the first four letters of Tongue Twisters! The rest had been washed away by the creek water! It has to be the original tape!" Laney thought she would burst with joy.

"Laney, you just revealed to Malcolm that the police recovered the cassette and that the tape was lost," Shar said.

"I did, didn't I?" Laney said with dismay. "Oh Malcolm, you won't tell a soul, will you? I promised Cutty and here I've blabbed to two people."

"Your secret stops with me, Laney. But tell me, how will you ever hear what the tape contains without an eight track player? I doubt they make them anymore."

"That does present a problem, but maybe an antique shop would have one."

"Hold your tongue, woman," Shar retorted. "I had one of those players in high school. What are you implying?"

"You're far from an antiquity, my dear," Malcolm reassured her.

"I'll find one, somehow," Laney said, dropping four tablespoons of fresh butter into a large sauté pan on the range top. When the butter began to bubble, she dropped in the mushrooms and stirred with a wooden spoon while Shar made toast from thin slices of Maddy's homemade white bread. Laney seasoned the mushrooms with salt and pepper and added a little flour and a cup of light cream. Malcolm stirred while she scooped up the soaking asparagus and placed it into a microwave dish. She covered it, scooted it into the microwave and set the time for five minutes. Just before she served the creamed mushrooms over the buttered toast, she laced the sauce with a dash of sherry. She topped the bright green asparagus with lemon butter.

They were so ravenous, that hardly a word passed among them while they ate. When only four asparagus stalks remained in the bowl, and the plates were so clean that Shar debated about whether or not to place them in the dishwasher, Laney fixed a pot of hot tea to go with their dessert.

Laney had just sliced the casaba melon when she heard Blackberry barking on the front porch. With a quick warning not to discuss the murder, she hurried down the hall. When she opened the door, Gray stepped into the hallway, dropped Puccini to the Persian runner and locked his strong arms around her. He only held her—no kisses, no words—but she could feel his tenseness ease off where her fingers pressed his back. When he finally released her and stared into her eyes, he murmured, "I love you, you know."

"I know," she said, the way she always answered his favorite expression of love to her. His eyes were a little too bright and she smelled bourbon on his breath.

She held his hand and led him to the kitchen.

"Good to see you again, Gray," Malcolm said, extending his hand. They shook and Shar poured the tea from Cara's favorite blue and white China teapot into the matching cups. Laney scooped vanilla ice cream onto the slices of chilled melon. She handed Gray a napkin as he sat down next to her.

"How long will you be here this visit, Malcolm?" Gray asked.

"About three days. My farm manager wanted to see the farm and the manager's house. He brought his wife."

Gray seemed withdrawn and played with the ice cream on his melon.

"They should be pleased with the house. It's quite quaint, as I remember it," Malcolm said. "They have two children and it will be adequate."

Without warning, Gray staggered to his feet, his face deathly pale. "I . . . I'm sorry . . . would you excuse me? I . . . I don't feel well." He rushed from the table and grabbed Puccini, who was licking milk from Kudzu's dish, and flew down the hall. They heard the door slam.

The three of them looked at each other in amazement. Alarmed, Laney followed but Gray was too quick. Before she could reopen the heavy front door, she heard the sound of the Jeep's engine and for the second time in a week, he screeched out the lane.

While Shar and Malcolm took over the parlor, Laney retreated to the library where she called Gray's number over and over. She finally gave up, deciding he either had gone to bed or just didn't want to talk to her.

She booted up her computer, and again resisting the urge to begin revising her manuscript, she reopened the St. Clair High

School reunion document once more. She finished the "In Memoriam" page and began copying all the graduates' current addresses and phone numbers from the file that Amanda had given her. In a special section called "What are we doing now?" she began listing each graduate and filling in his or her occupation, marital status, number of children and hobbies from a questionnaire each graduate had filled out and sent to Amanda. There were three of the alumni that hadn't sent their forms in and she phoned them and got the information over the phone. She was about a third of the way through the forms when Shar exploded through the doorway. Kudzu scrambled under the tan leather sofa.

"Do I have seaweed between my teeth or what?" Shar asked, practically in tears.

"Uh-oh . . . let me guess. Malcolm refused to bed you again."

"You're damn straight."

"Shar, when are you going to learn that sex is not the way to a man's heart."

"His heart isn't the organ I'm thinking of."

"He welcomed you with open arms today, didn't he?"

"If that's a beginning, the end will probably be a chastity belt with a dead bolt lock."

"Shar, he's nuts for you. When you broke out of the forest playing the pipes in that kilt, I thought he was going to break into a Highland fling on the spot. Take my word for it. It will mean more when it comes. Give it time."

Shar shrugged. "I know you're right. But why do I always think I have to do it to be loved?"

"You've got me there, Shar. You have so many wonderful qualities. Why do *I* love you? You make me laugh, you're unpredictable, you're loyal, you're smart, you're outlandish—"

"Stop, woman. I don't need a house to fall on me—one brick will do." She bellied part way under the sofa and retrieved Kudzu. Sitting cross-legged on the rug, she petted the kitten absent-mindedly. Laney could hear the kitten's motor from the desk chair. "What do you think got into Gray tonight? Do you think he's really sick?"

"I just don't know. I tried calling him," Laney said, while she leafed through the high school yearbook.

"All of a sudden, the color just drained from his face," Shar said. Laney recalled Gray listening politely to Malcolm just before his outburst. "Maybe . . . just maybe . . ." Laney thought out loud as she clambered to her feet. She charged out the door and raced to the kitchen.

There it was, just where Malcolm had placed it before dinner. The eight track tape—the label facing upward on the table next to his place mat. Gray had only to glance across the table and he would have seen it.

She picked it up and walked slowly back to the library.

"Laney . . . the look on your face. You're scaring me." Shar said, as Laney entered the room.

Laney held out the tape to Shar.

Realization hit Shar. "You think he saw the tape."

"It was lying on the table right next to Malcolm's place—label up. He must have seen it."

"Do you know what you're saying, woman? The name on the label—it means something to him."

Laney's heart flailed in her chest. When she spoke again, her words echoed in her ears as though she were in a cavern. "How would Gray know what 'Tongue Twisters' meant? Only Peter and Derek knew what was on the tape. Peter, because this was his tape— Derek, because we think he was blackmailing Chris with a stolen copy of it." She sat back in her chair shakily. "Then Chris must know what's on this tape too or he wouldn't be paying the blackmail to keep it quiet."

"Laney, Derek is dead and Chris is still receiving the notes. Someone else must know what's on the tape."

"I know. That's what I'm afraid of," Laney said, trying hard not to believe what she was thinking. "What if Gray were the one blackmailing Chris?"

Shar looked up at her. "Laney, I know you. You're starting on one of those head trips of yours. Gray can't be the one blackmailing Chris. There has to be another explanation for Gray's reaction on seeing the tape."

"You're right, Shar." Laney took a huge breath and shook her head like she could shake away all the bad thoughts she was suddenly having. "The only way we are going to get to the root of this is to play the damn tape." She picked up the tape again and focused on the name. " 'Tongue Twisters.' What does that mean to you, Shar?"

"Besides the obvious, it sounds like the name of some rock group. You know, like 'The Sex Pistols' or 'The Rolling Stones' from our era."

Laney flipped the tape onto the desk and picked up her yearbook. Like a magnet, she was drawn to the page with Chris, Derek, Pete and Bart at the tree. "Were you ever in some kind of secret club when you were a kid?"

Shar giggled. "I remember belonging to a club with some other girls when I was about eleven or twelve, before I started to think about boys." She giggled again.

"What's so funny?"

"We called ourselves the Sulumarsha. Su for Sue, Lu for Lucy, Mar for Marlene, and Sha for Sharlene. Original, huh? God, I almost forgot about that. It all started over some gigantic black oak tree we adopted in the woods in Pittsburgh. It was one of those terrific climbing trees. We each claimed a section of the tree and named it after ourselves. For a couple of summers we did everything but sleep in that tree. We'd pack our lunches and haul them up in a basket. We carved our initials in the bark. We hung a bull rope and made a swing. We swore we would never tell anyone about the tree. Pricked our fingers on a cactus needle at Marlene's house and sealed our pledge in blood."

"Is the tree still there?"

"Are you kidding? The woods were slowly taken over by urban sprawl. For a while it was still standing in front of some low cost housing project but I think the concrete finally smothered it and it was cut down."

"What if these four guys were in a secret club of some sort?" Laney speculated.

"And called themselves the 'Tongue Twisters?' " Shar made a face.

"Why not? You did it."

"Good Lord, woman, I wasn't a senior in high school."

"Maybe they formed it when they were younger and it just continued . . . one of those rites of passage things. . . and you know how immature guys were." Laney could tell Shar wasn't convinced.

"Where would the name, Tongue Twisters, come in?"

"Maybe they all had a name starting with a letter in common in a tongue twister . . . say, like the S in: She sells seashells down by the seashore."

Shar stared at the picture of the four guys for a moment. Okay . . . give me paper and pencil."

Laney obliged with a tablet from the bottom drawer of the desk.

"Give me the names," Shar said, replacing Kudzu on her lap with the tablet. "Woman, I can't believe I'm doing this."

"Peter Sands, Bart Prescott, Chris Taylor, Derek Beale." Shar wrote the names down. Kudzu sparred with the pencil as she wrote. "Let's see, we've got two B's—Beale and Bart, and two P's—Prescott and Peter. She circled the letters. Won't work, Laney."

"Not so fast," Laney said. Let's see if they have any middle names. She thumbed to the section of the yearbook with the graduates' photos and full names.

"Let's see, Peter didn't have a middle name." She turned back two pages. "And . . . Bart's middle name is James. Nothing in common yet." She turned to Chris Taylor's picture. "Christopher Perry Taylor! That's three P's, Shar!"

Getting interested, Shar climbed onto her knees and waited for Laney to get to Derek Beale's picture. His middle name jumped out at them and Shar beat Laney to the punch, "Purvis!"

They looked at each other and both crossed their eyes at the same time and repeated, "Purvis?"

"And the most common tongue twister there is uses words beginning with P," Laney said.

"Peter Piper," Shar exclaimed. "Peter's name is even in it."

Laney became pensive. She flipped back to the photo of the guys. "Shar, do you think we're overstating this? Couldn't this just be a coincidence?"

"Sure. But why the name 'Tongue Twisters' on the tape?" Shar said, suddenly a believer. She gathered up her kitten and snuggled him close to her face. "One thing is certain, though."

"What?"

"When we play the tape, we'll know for sure."

19

Gordon hung his head out his office door. "Tell Rudd to get the hell in here, pronto!" Closing the door behind him, he crossed behind his desk and sat facing Gray and Marshall Knight who were sitting in gray tubular chairs that were meant to be uncomfortable.

Marshall sat rigidly, a crackled leather briefcase across his knees, his legendary open galoshes on his feet even though the early morning shower had lasted less than fifteen minutes.

Doc looks like shit, Gordon thought, as they waited for Freddie. But he wondered how he would look if he were a suspect in a murder case.

Freddie rushed into the room with a Styrofoam cup of hot coffee in one hand and a greasy paper wrapper exuding the unappetizing odor of a sausage and egg biscuit in the other.

"Sorry, I'm late," he said, laying his breakfast on the corner of Gordon's desk and pushing the record button on the tape recorder centered in front of Gray and his attorney. He whipped out a dog-eared pocket notebook from his khaki shirt pocket and snatched the pencil from behind his right ear.

"Are you ready?" Gordon sneered at his deputy. Freddie nodded, a quick blush washing over his chubby features.

"Now Doc, what's all this about?" Gordon asked.

"Want to report a theft of a restricted drug."

"Is this related to the break-in Thursday night?" Gordon asked.

"Yes."

"What's the drug?"

"Thanatol . . . a phenobarbital drug used for putting down animals."

Gordon's gut did a toss. "When did you discover it missing?"

Gray looked at Marshall. The attorney nodded his head.

"Right after you left Friday morning. Evidently, during the break-in, someone borrowed my keys and lifted the bottle from the locked drawer in my vet bed."

"Damn it, Doc, that was three days ago. Why did you wait so long to report it?"

"Scared, I guess. With everyone thinking I killed Derek, reporting this drug missing wouldn't help my case much, now would it?"

Gordon felt a bit of sympathy for the guy. "How's the drug delivered?"

"By injection."

"Are there any syringes missing?"

"Hard to say . . . have three open boxes in different sizes in my pharmacy. I just grab handfuls as I need them."

"This Thanatol . . . what's the antidote?"

"Is none."

Gordon felt sweat tickling along his hairline and he ran his fingers through his crewcut. He bounced a pencil on its eraser a couple of times, catching it in mid-air. Suddenly he turned to his deputy. "How about a cup of coffee, Freddie?"

"Sure, Sheriff." He jumped to his feet, grabbed his biscuit and shot out the door.

When the door clicked behind him, Gordon leaned over the desk and pushed the stop button on the tape recorder. "Doc, you called here the other morning to say that you had found your keys . . . that you had just mislaid them. Off the record, now . . . was that before or after you found the drug missing?"

In a quick move, Marshall laid his hand on Gray's arm.

Gray patted his attorney's hand, his eyes never leaving Gordon's face. "After," he answered.

Laney shifted the Whooptie into reverse and gave the parallel parking between two pickups a second shot. She knew that Benzie Bender and another retired gentleman sitting on the bench in front of the courthouse had a wager going on how many "licks" it would take. The back tire scraped the high curb and she released the clutch too quickly and stalled.

"It's times like this when I'd consider trading the Whooptie in for a new car," an exasperated Laney said. She started the car and pulled out again.

"I'm for that," Shar said in a monotone.

This time Laney managed to wedge into the spot.

Shar shouldered her door open and visually measured the distance to the curb. "Not bad if you have cab fare."

As the two of them approached Second Hand Rose, they passed one of the windows flanking the entrance. Laney gawked at the antiques and collectibles that were jammed into the cramped area. A propeller from an early airplane was propped diagonally from corner to corner. Mounted to a bare area on the wall, a motley boar's head gaped downward into a claw foot tub painted iris green. On a wire soap dish hanging from the tub edge, a hand carved Pinocchio puppet with a chipped nose sat wide eyed. Between collectibles and scattered into every available inch of space were scores of movie and circus posters, vintage photographs and postcards. The owner, an antiquity herself, loomed in the doorway—a colossus dressed in a yellow caftan, the hem decorated with bumblebees collecting pollen from red roses.

"Well, well, well . . . where have y'all been keeping yourself, rusty gal?" Rose asked, reaching out and springing a frizzy coil of Laney's hair.

Laney gave the large woman a hug and turned to introduce Shar. "Shar, meet Rose Cohen. She's a Yankee like you. Lived in the Bronx until last year."

"Glad to meet you, Rose," Shar said, grimacing with the handshake.

"Oy, you're a long drink of water, aren't you?" Rose said, lifting her bushy white brows. Her hand slipped into a shallow pocket and Laney saw her finger a silver flask. "Can I help y'all with anything?"

"I'm looking for an eight track player that will play one of these things," Laney said as she retrieved the tape from her shoulder bag. Shar wandered off into the gloom of the shop.

"Where'd you get that old tape, already?"

"It's a long story, Rose, but it's imperative that I find a player right away."

"To be honest, I have no idea if I have one. I still haven't gone through all the dreck Herb left me. Y'all welcome to look around, though."

"Can you give me some idea where . . . which direction to look?" Laney was beginning to get antsy and her voice had an edge. Rose lifted her twenties flask and unscrewed the lid. The top swung down from a chain.

"Have a swig, rusty gal," Rose offered. When Laney shook her head, Rose took a deep one herself, wiping her painted mouth with the back of her hand. "By the looks of you, I'd say something's noshing you. It couldn't be the hoo-ha around town about that boy-chick of yours, could it?" Taking a quick look around to see if anyone had seen her nipping out on the sidewalk, Rose sauntered into the shop, eyed her sunken spot on the third cushion of the horse-hair davenport, backed up and sank with a swoosh. Flipping off her yellow sandals, she propped her puffy feet onto the couch, one painful hike at a time.

Suddenly, Shar rushed from the back of the shop. "I think I found one under an end table full of LPs," she yelped.

Laney scrambled after her through an archway under a sweeping staircase that led to Jessica Mill's second floor apartment.

They stepped perilously over stacks of sheet music from the thirties, boxes of forty-five rpm records, a clarinet case and a set of bongo drums until they came to a table balancing several metronomes. Shar doubled her body, reached under the table and dragged a dusty two by one foot plastic wood grained box into view. Laney recognized the player immediately as like the one she'd had as a teen.

"If only it works," Laney said at the same moment she spotted the frayed cord and missing plug.

"I can fix that if you buy a new plug," Shar announced. "In seventh grade, the girls and the boys switched Home Ec and Shop for six weeks at Sterrett School. I learned how to change a plug and fix a leaky faucet. I even made a small bookcase in wood shop. The guys learned how to eat the cookies they didn't burn."

They found Rose where Laney had left her, on the davenport nursing her flask. Laney crawled out into the window bay and retrieved a poster advertising a nineteen thirty-eight movie starring Loretta Young and Richard Greene called *Kentucky*. When she glanced out the window toward the courthouse, she was startled to see Gray and his lawyer walking down the steep concrete stairs. Laney's heart dropped to her toes. More questioning, she determined. Has something else happened? She was tempted to run out and call to him but he seemed to be in deep conversation with Marshall.

"Look what else I found," Shar grinned as she held up a wooden love spoon with a thistle carved in the handle. She explained to Rose that the thistle was the national flower of Scotland.

"Oy vey, already. The national bird must be the housefly," Rose retorted with a snort. Laney was surprised when Shar chuckled.

Laney paid for the player and the poster. When Shar asked for the price of the spoon, Rose replied, "For a meshuggener, I only charge a fin." Shar handed her a five dollar bill.

As they walked out the entrance, Laney whispered to Shar, "What's a meshuggener?

Shar, who had lived in a Jewish neighborhood all her life, giggled, "A crazy person."

20

Laney and Shar met up with Malcolm and the Smiths at the Finish Line for lunch. Malcolm had invited Shar to accompany them to Taylor Ridge afterwards to inspect the farm and manager's residence. As soon as Laney finished her chili, cornbread and iced tea, she excused herself so she could stock up at the grocery and run by the hardware to buy a plug for the tape player.

The sky was still overcast as she drove into the parking lot at Hickory Dock. Her mother was drying off the picnic tables and chairs from the shower earlier. Two black garbage bags bulged with the trash her mother had collected from the trash cans near each table.

"Several of the girl scout troops are having a father-daughter cookout here this evening, if the rain holds off," Maddy said. She blew at a couple wisps of her hair that hung over her eyes. Laney reached over and tucked the strands under her sailor hat. Impulsively, she hugged her mother to her, and for some reason, a shaky exhalation preceded an urge to cry.

"Laney, honey, I know things are worryin you about Gray. What can I do?"

"Mother, everyday you help me with the bed and breakfast meals. You can't know how much that helps. Gray's problem will work itself out. We know he didn't do anything wrong."

"Speakin of Gray, I think I know whose kitten that was that got left on his doorstep."

Laney, who had just scooted a picnic bench back under the table, snapped around to face her mother. "Who?"

"You remember Walker Scott don't you?"

Laney felt a flush come over her with the mention of the teenager. "Dory Beale's son by her first marriage? . . . sure, what about him?"

"Well, he and a couple of his friends were here to rent some canoes yesterday. I was surprised to see him. I thought he had gone back to school after Derek's funeral but he said he was on his spring break this week."

"Mother, what about the kitten?"

"Well, the kid who was drivin—Jamie, the Harris boy. His father owns Harris Fertilizer."

"Mother!"

"Oh, all right. Anyway, Jamie asked me if I wanted a kitten. He said he had orders from his mom to ask everyone he met, so they could get rid of four kittens born five weeks ago. Walker told him he should do what his mom did, just drop them off on someone's doorstep some night. He said that's how she got rid of Calley's kitten last week. He said it was a male tabby."

"I'll be . . . Mother! . . . you didn't tell him that you knew where she dropped it, did you?"

"Of course not."

Laney grabbed her mother about the waist and swung her around in a dizzying spin. "Mother, you wanted to know how you could help me? You just helped me more than you could ever know."

By the time Laney arrived home, the sky had darkened and it threatened rain. Laney thought of the scout cookout and hoped her mother hadn't prepared the picnic site in vain. Her main thoughts were of what her mother had told her about the kitten. She couldn't wait until Shar got home to tell her. If Dory was the one who had typed the kitten note, she also was the person who had used the same typewriter with the old ribbon to type the blackmail note sent to Chris. As she put the groceries away, she glanced at the calendar on the inside of the cabinet door above the kitchen desk. Today was Monday. She wondered if Chris had made another payment that morning at ten o'clock. Where was he dropping the money? How much longer could he continue?

She wiped down the eight track player and placed the tape and the new plug on the kitchen counter. Kudzu was under her feet every minute. When the sky suddenly brightened a bit, she walked outside and played fetch with Blackberry in the yard. Since the sun was peaking out from behind a gold edged gray cloud, she mounted her bicycle and raced down the blacktop to the mailbox and back. She rounded the yard and started for the lower barn, Blackberry a galloping smudge ahead of her. No one was in sight as they sped by the foaling stall, office and horse barn.

When she got to the crossing, Laney dismounted and rested her rubbery legs. The undisputed winner of every race waded up to her hips in the water, lapped until full, then swam a wide circle before shaking on the rocks.

Blackberry, exploring the stepping stones along the riffle, found a rotting fish that was fetid enough to initiate a roll among the pebbles and tiny shells. Laney was sure she would need a bath before she could allow her into the house.

Noticing the time, Laney hopped her bike and backtracked, giving the teaser, Applejack, a yell as she swung by his paddock. He tossed his great black head and paced the fencing. She stopped when she reached the office, seeing a note tacked to the foaling stall door. She straddled the bike as she read:

> *Dr. Prescott:*
> *The mare and foal are in the foaling stall. Like I told Natine, it's a little early for foal heat scours, so I thought you might want to take a look at him. I had appointment in Lexington. If any treatment needed, leave medication or call me.*
> *Aaron*

Laney kicked the stand with her foot and settled the bike. Blackberry dropped in the grass and shut her eyes. Laney hadn't seen the foal in a couple of days and she snapped the latch on the stall door and cracked it slowly so that Unreasonable wouldn't startle or try to escape.

She heard Thistle's whinny and expected the gray mare to nose the stall door as she opened it. Instead, she only heard the week old foal whinny and then cry again. She reached around and flipped the light switch on the outside of the building and looked into the stall.

Unreasonable lay on her side in the straw—her legs outstretched, stiff and still. Her eyes were open and unseeing. Laney knew instinctively that she was dead. Thistle stood by her body, her bleak and desperate cries becoming stronger as Laney beheld the tragic scene.

"Unreasonable." The single name was all she could muster—the emotions flowing through her so deep and painful. When she finally collected her thoughts, she concluded that the mare must have reached the end of her long life after the difficult delivery only a week ago. The gray mare was twenty—old for a mare with a new foal. Tears tracked her cheeks when she finally wrenched her eyes away from the lifeless horse.

She was leaving the stall to call Gray when she saw it. The syringe lay on a wooden sill near the door. There, for anyone to see. There, where she knew no syringe had ever been left. Her hand froze, fingers recoiling. With her heart hammering, she latched the door and rode her bike in a reckless flight to the house.

21

Laney spied Gray's Jeep long before she whipped between the pilasters. She skidded and dropped her bike next to the Cherokee. The front wheel of the bicycle continued on a nowhere trip as she jumped into the truck and in breathless fragments of sentences told Gray about finding Unreasonable dead in her stall.

The furrow between his eyes that she couldn't remember being there a week ago deepened. He took her hand and squeezed lightly. "This must really be tough on you, but the mare was old, Laney. Maybe she had an aneurysm as a result of the difficult birth. Happens sometimes."

"But I read the note that Aaron left asking you to look at the foal. Didn't you see Unreasonable?"

"Laney, I swear. I haven't been to the farm until now. Natine gave me Aaron's message to stop by to see the foal hours ago but I had other calls and just now finished them up." Gray's Jeep jerked to a stop in front of the foaling stall.

They could hear the pitiful cries of the foal as they climbed out of the Jeep. Gray paused to read the note on the stall door before he unlatched it. He drew in his breath when he saw the gray mare lying there in the straw. He knelt next to her. Thistle butted her head against his shoulder as though Gray could provide the nourishment he wanted.

Another vehicle stopped in front of the stall. "Laney, is that Aaron?" Gray asked, but before Laney could answer, Aaron was standing in the doorway.

"What happened?" Aaron said, his face blanching when he saw Unreasonable. His arm thrust out in front of him as though warding off evil. His green eyes were large and bright in the artificial light.

Gray ran his hand down the mare's neck and stopped at a small bulge at the jugular.

"She's had a recent injection. Have you medicated her today, Aaron? Maybe given her a flu vac?"

"No way, Dr. Prescott. I always call you for any vaccines or medications. The only injection I sometimes give is HCG to make a mare ovulate after breeding."

"Then what's this, Aaron?" Laney said.

Aaron swung around and stared at the syringe on the window ledge. He ran a nervous hand through his short blond hair. "I have no idea. I never leave a syringe about," he said. He reached for the syringe.

"Don't touch that, Aaron!" Gray's voice cracked like a firecracker. The foal leaped into a corner.

"Gray, what is it?. . . why? . . . you're afraid of something," Laney said, searching his face.

Gray crossed over to the sill and the three of them stared at the syringe. A pink substance had dried in a teardrop shape at the end of the needle.

"Laney, could I use the office phone?" Gray asked. She nodded and he left the stall.

"Miss Laney, we're going to have to make arrangements for a nurse mare for the colt. I'll get in touch with Tom Thatcher. I hope he has one available," Aaron said.

Laney saw the light click on in the office through the observation window. Gray lifted the phone and punched three digits. My God, he's calling the police. She ran out of the stall and stood in the doorway of the office. She heard Gray tell someone he would wait until they arrived. When he hung up the phone, he turned slowly and saw her standing there, his face a study in consternation.

"Know I should have told you but you've been through so much

in this past year, I just wanted to spare you . . . but now . . . with this
. . . you have to know."

"Quit sparing me, Gray. What is it?" Laney steeled herself.

"Think the mare was injected with a lethal substance." His jaw
muscles twitched, then clinched.

"The syringe?"

"Yes."

"But why would you suspect—"

"The clinic break-in," he interrupted. "My euthanasia drug was
stolen."

"God, Gray! . . . the police . . . do they know?"

"Yes. Told Gordon this morning."

"Just today?"

"I know, Laney. Gordon already gave me hell for waiting so
long."

"Why did you?"

"Afraid. Afraid of one more thing against me. First the fight and
no alibi for the time of Derek's murder. The missing tape at the
scene. The police finding my dehorners. The clinic break-in that
Marshall believes the cops think I may have staged to make them
believe someone was looking for the tape." His hands frantically
combed through his unkempt brown hair. "The evidence is mount-
ing, Laney. And now Unreasonable may have been put down with
my own drug."

"But what purpose would killing the mare have?"

"Don't know. Maybe someone just wants me to look as bad as
possible . . . is setting me up."

The two of them watched silently as Aaron hooked a shank to
Thistle's halter and stretched the rope around the foal's rump to
guide him out of the stall. The colt resisted, whinnying pathetical-
ly.

Laney heard another vehicle pull up at the office. She knew it was
the sheriff. "We need to talk, Gray. Stop by before you leave, will
you?" Laney asked, watching his face darken like an umbra with her
request. He's remembering the reason for his bolting exit last night,
Laney thought.

She had finished speaking to Gordon and was on her way back to
the house before she realized that he hadn't answered her.

She really wasn't surprised that Gray hadn't stopped by after talking with Gordon, but she was growing angry by his continuing remoteness. When she chased the fishy smelling Blackberry out the front door, her face glowed hot when she saw the two vehicles leave together. Shortly after, as Laney, Shar and Malcolm were sitting on the screen porch while Shar worked on the player plug, she thought she heard a truck drive down the lane.

"I think that's the truck to take the mare away. The diagnostic lab will do an autopsy," Laney said.

"Thank God, I just couldn't go down there and see Thistle until I was sure Unreasonable was gone," Shar said.

"When's Gray coming?" Malcolm said. "I'm sure he'll want to hear the tape. It appears our crack electrician has just about finished her project."

"He's not. I saw him leave right behind Gordon," Laney said as she poured tea from the teapot. She squeezed lemon, sprinkled a sweetener and sat rigidly in one of the wrought iron chairs at the round table. Malcolm settled in the wicker rocker within reach of his cup of tea on the table. Kudzu lay in his lap.

The sky had gradually darkened with approaching dusk and Laney had lit candles in hurricane globes instead of turning on the porch lights.

"*Finis.* Let's see if it works," Shar said, setting the player on a wicker end table and lifting the cover to the outdoor receptacle. "Well, here goes," she said, and plugged it in. "Lights in the kitchen didn't dim. That's good. Where's the tape? That's the real test." Shar sat cross-legged on the floor in front of the eight track player.

Laney fetched the tape from the kitchen counter and handed it to Shar who slipped it through a hinged door in the front panel.

Nothing happened.

"Push the program selector," Laney said.

Shar did and track "A" glowed red.

22

For a few breath-holding moments, Laney heard only squeaks and groans coming out of the eight track player, then abruptly she heard the boisterous voice of a young man.

"*Let's go on. He'll find us when he gets here,*" said a voice with slurred words.

Shar turned up the volume.

"*Aw shut up, Chris. You'd be the first one to bitch, if we left you,*" another voice said.

"*I say we wait. Man, put another log on that fire. It's cold as hell in here . . . Peter?*" the same voice yelled. "*That's the last log. Anymore out back?*"

"*Derek, I'm bringin them,*" a barely audible Peter said.

A bunch of thuds and clanks.

"*You sure you wanna do this? Jeez, that water will be freezin,*" Peter said.

"*You chic-ken, Petey?*" Chris said in a sing-song voice. His words were garbled.

"*Yeah, you chicken? Cluck, cluck, cluck,*" Derek said.

Lots of drunken laughter.

"*Quit your cluckin, Derek, you son of a cluck. You're hoggin the sauce. Pass it over,*" Chris said.

"*Bart's here,*" a voice in the distance yelled.

"*Yea-a-a, Bart. Let's go swimmin,*" Derek said.

Scrambling noises, then a click.

"Is that it?" Laney said, as nothing but tape hiss met their ears. Then the player clicked a second time.

More tape hiss, then moans and cries.

"*Get the goddamn fire goin. I'm gonna freeze,*" *Derek said. Lots of banging, thuds.*

Laney figured someone was throwing logs on the fire.

"*I'm gonna puke,*" *Peter said.*

"*Get in the bathroom, you stupid ass,*" *Derek said.*

More noise. Someone was crying in the background—great heaving sobs. Shar looked at Laney with open mouth. She shrugged.

"*Who taught you to drive, you son of a bitch,*" *Derek shouted.*

"*I don't know what happened . . . happened too fast.*" *Chris said between sobs.*

"*Quit your blubberin,*" *Derek said.*

"*I killed him,*" *Chris said.*

Laney's eyes shot to Shar—Shar's to Malcolm.

"*We were smashed,*" *Peter said.*

Instantly sober, Laney thought.

"*Bart . . . Bart,*" *Chris screamed.* "*He was floatin inside the car.*"

Laney's hand flew to her mouth.

"*We all got out through the windows. Why couldn't he? I tried to pull him out . . . pulled on his arm but he wouldn't budge . . . he was floatin but he wouldn't come,*" *Peter moaned.*

"*Clothes must have been caught on somethin,*" *Chris said, beginning to cry again.*

"*Think he was already dead? Maybe hit his head or somethin?*" *Derek murmured.*

"*He was out cold when we climbed in his car to go swimmin. Don't know how the hell he ever got here from the party,*" *Derek said.*

"*I had to shove him over into the passenger seat to get behind the wheel, remember?" Chris said.*

"God, I can't get warm. Got to get out of these trunks and get dressed," Derek said.

Laney could hear his teeth chattering as he spoke.

"Yeah," somebody said. Lots of scrambling around.

Still someone sobbed in the background.

"Gotta call the police," Peter said.

"No phone," Derek said.

"I was driving. They'll arrest me," Chris said.

"No they won't. We're all minors," Derek said.

"I just turned eighteen," Chris said.

"God, that's right," Peter said.

"Peter, we'll all get the shit for this . . . drinkin and all. Sneakin into your dad's cabin," Derek said.

"It'll be all over town . . . that we took Bart's car and ran it into the creek . . . killed him," Chris said.

There were more cries from Chris and Peter. Slowly, they dwindled to whimpers and then stopped. A moment of silence followed.

"Doesn't have to be like that," Derek said tentatively.

"Whatta you mean?" Chris said, beginning to cry again.

"We could . . . you know . . . just go home like we didn't know it happened," Derek said. His voice was stony.

"We can't do that," Peter said.

"Why not?" Derek said. "No one knows we're here . . . that we went for that joyride."

"You mean we could just pretend we didn't know nothin about Bart coming out here?" Chris asked.

"Yeah. He was just another teen drivin drunk after a grad party. He decided to take a spin through the Sands' farm and ended up in the creek."

Laney's and Shar's eyes locked as they listened to Derek's emotionless proposition.

"What about us? We were right here. No one will believe we didn't know nothin—" Chris began.

"Who said we were here all night?" Derek interrupted. "It's just one o'clock. We'd already hit a few parties before we came here, anyway. We just clean up the joint . . . get rid of the wet suits and go home. Our dry clothes are right here where we dropped them." Derek's voice was getting more excited by the

moment.

"It's not right," Peter said. "We have to own up to it . . . take our knocks."

"Damn it, Peter, you can be such a prig!" Derek answered. "If this gets out, it'll follow us the rest of our lives. Shit . . . Chris has been accepted at Harvard in the fall . . . and let's not forget whose going to MIT. How would an accomplice to manslaughter look on your first résumé, Peter?"

"I can't . . . it's not right," Peter said.

Derek spoke again, calculatingly gentle. "Peter, listen . . . what about our pledge as the Tongue Twisters? Always stick together . . . ever since we were snot-nosed kids . . . five years now. Bart was one of us. I know what he would do. We can't bring him back, Peter. God knows if we could. . . ."

Chris began to cry again.

"I'm not the only one you have to convince," Pete said.

"I know," said Derek.

"I heard everything," a hollow voice said far away. The voice broke down into the agonizing sobs that had been in the background ever since the teens had returned to the cabin.

Who is that, Laney wondered?

His weeping became more audible as the unidentified individual approached the vicinity of the other young men and wherever the microphones were planted.

"You heard?" Chris asked.

"He was my twin," a familiar but younger voice said.

Laney shot to her feet. Gray! He couldn't have been there, but he was and speaking to Chris, Derek, and Peter.

"God . . . my Bart . . . I couldn't save him. The doors . . . they wouldn't open. He was trapped! . . . I couldn't get him through the windows! I dived over and over!"

Gray's weeping seemed to go on and on until Laney and Shar were crying too. Malcolm dabbed at his eyes with his handkerchief.

Gray! Oh my God, Laney thought. Gray Prescott—the fifth Tongue Twister.

"Gray, Derek wants us to—" Peter began.

"I know . . . God, I know," Gray said, finally sobbing to exhaustion, becoming silent.

The tape growled. Then Gray spoke again. He sounded used

up. "But he's gone, Peter. My brother's gone. A stupid accident.
Any one of us could have been behind that wheel." Whimpers
came from the dregs of some emotional residue left in him.

"It's a mistake," Peter protested. "But if his own brother . . ."

"You agree, Gray?" Derek asked.

"Yes," Gray whispered.

"Peter?" Derek prodded.

"Yes."

"Chris?"

"Yes."

"Say the watchword," Derek commanded.

"Tongue Twisters," they chorused.

23

The tape ended with a veiled whisper of Laney's name. Only when Shar turned off the player, did Laney realize the plaintive broken sounds weren't coming from the tape.

"Laney . . . Laney," Gray breathed, as though it were his last. He stood wearily in the opening of the French doors, his pale face shining wet in the flickering light of the candles. His arms dangled listlessly at his side and his broad shoulders sagged in emotional exhaustion.

Knowing this was a time only for Laney and Gray, Shar grabbed Malcolm's hand and they escaped with Kudzu out the screen door.

So wrapped in Gray's pain, Laney didn't know that they had gone. She took both his hands in hers and lifted them to her own wet cheeks and to her lips and to her heart.

"I heard it all with you," Gray said. "Every painful damning minute of it. Oh my God, last night when I saw the eight track tape here—"

"So you knew what the tape was?" Laney interrupted softly.

"All I needed to see was the name Tongue Twisters in Pete's handwriting on that eight track. You see, that was one of the rules of our club. Never to repeat the name to anyone. We swore on our lives when we were only twelve years old. All these years I kept the secret, Laney."

"But Pete didn't. He broke the vow with his suicide," Laney said.

"What do you mean?"

"Tina showed Peter's suicide note to me. He wrote: 'Forgive me. I can't take it anymore. After this, you will understand.' "

"After what?"

"That's what I asked Tina. Then she told me that Derek was the one who discovered Pete hanging from the rafter. He had called Derek to come to the cabin."

"Derek?"

"I think Pete couldn't stand the guilt anymore and planned to leave the tape for Derek to do the right thing after his death."

"I . . . always thought he killed himself because he had lost his job."

"Surely that was a contributing factor, but now that I've heard the tape, I believe the cover-up of Bart's death was Pete's primary reason for killing himself. To Peter, personal integrity was the most important quality anyone could have."

"And against his conscience, he made the ultimate compromise because I agreed." Gray dropped his chin to his chest. His lashes, clusters of tiny points from the tears, fluttered against his cheeks. Laney led him to the wicker rocker and guided him until he was seated. His head flopped backwards to the headrest and his eyes closed. She sat on the floor, her head resting against his knees, her arms about his legs.

For a long time, the only sounds were the sounds of the night, so when Gray spoke again, it startled her. His legs stiffened. "The eight track tape! Where did it come from?"

"This tape is the original that Shar and I found at the cabin on Sunday. Peter must have made a copy at some point when he updated his equipment. And the cassette copy was the one that fell into the creek when Derek fell . . . the cassette that the police found in the creek." Laney felt that she could not hide anything from Gray, now.

Gray leaned forward in the rocker and lifted her head from his knee. She saw the candlelight reflecting in his eyes, wide with shock.

"Are you saying the police found the tape?" he asked.

In a few sentences, she related what Cutty had told her and her theory that the police had withheld the information from the public to fool Derek's murderer into making a mistake.

"The tape was ruined?" he asked eagerly.

"Only the four letters, T-O-N-G, remained on the label."

"Tongue Twisters," Gray said.

"Yes, and I'm sure Derek was blackmailing Chris with it." Laney spent the next half hour explaining everything else she had discovered since Derek's death. She showed him the blackmail note that she had witnessed Chris receiving after the funeral and Gray compared it to the kitten note typed on the same paper and typewriter. She explained that her mother had discovered that Dory Beale had left the kitten and the note at his clinic. And finally, that according to Aaron, Mary Wakefield and Derek had had an affair.

"Are you saying that Dory may be continuing the blackmail?" Gray asked.

Again, Laney dropped to her knees in front of him and wrapped her arms around his legs. "What do you think? And I just thought of something else. The kitten note said, 'I hate deadbeat dads.' Walker's father left them high and dry years ago. Don't you remember Derek bitching about the absence of child support?"

"I do, but—"

"Dory and Derek must have blackmailed Chris, then Dory decided to continue it after Derek's death."

"But why blackmail Chris? Why not me? Chris and Amanda were their dear friends."

"I've thought about that too. Only you and Chris had something to lose by the tape becoming known. I think he chose Chris because of his impending promotion to Chairman of the Chemistry Department at the university. He knew how protective Chris was of his reputation. It's even evident on the tape."

"Laney, Chris's attitude toward me lately . . . do you think he believes I'm the one who is blackmailing him?"

"I wouldn't be surprised. When the police announced they were looking for a tape that might be connected to Derek's murder, Chris probably thought it was the tape that he was being blackmailed with. Maybe Chris thought that Derek had found out about you blackmailing him and you killed Derek to shut him up. "Gray! The break-in! Could Chris have been looking for the tape?" Laney was hesitant to imply that Gray's good friend could do that to him.

"Laney, if it was Chris, then he stole the euthanasia drug too." His fingers dug into Laney's shoulders and he pulled her up to his chest. "Laney, if the police discover that Unreasonable was killed by a lethal injection, that means Chris was here on the farm today." He buried his face in her hair and his arms crushed her like a vice.

"Gray, you're hurting—"

"Aw, Laney, forgive—"

She interrupted his apology with her mouth and all their repressed thoughts and fears and passions combined in that kiss. His tense lips slowly yielded and softened as she kneaded hers against them until they parted and his breath mingled with hers.

"Laney," he murmured, as their lips separated, his mouth moving over her face and down her throat until, through her blouse, she felt his hot breath upon the swelling of her breasts. She didn't know how he loosened the buttons, only that quickly she felt his tongue and lips upon her skin. With a groan, she lifted herself and led him to her bedroom behind the stairs. Leaving a trail of scattered garments, their urgency pressed them toward the bed where it exploded into an emotional release of all the pain of past events.

Although Gray had transported her to these heights of passion before, tonight, every touch seemed a new exploration. When the room settled back into night shadows and sounds, Laney lay in his arms, consumed and satiated by his love for the first time in a long time.

24

"Honey, I have to go," Gray whispered in her hair. Her eyes shot open and a shadow crossed her eyes when she saw that he was dressed to leave. He straightened and his hand lightly brushed her lush hair, a dark cinnamon cloud spread across the pillow in the gray light of morning. She grasped his hand and he hated that he was going to have to wrench it away.

"I have calls, Laney, and things to think about. I have to make some decisions about all that I learned last night." He was struck with the impact his own words had on his body. The knot returned to his gut and his heart played a fast rhythm inside his chest.

He stooped until his face was level with Laney's. "No more secrets, though. When I sort everything out, I'll come to you and tell you. But I have to think it out on my own. Understand?"

She didn't answer, only smiled that uncertain smile of hers and nodded. He kissed his favorite cluster of freckles on her nose and slipped his hand from hers.

Gray had just finished palpating a mare at Gary Overland's farm when what he had to do struck him full force. He stripped the manure covered plastic sleeve from his arm, told Gary to breed the mare the following day and rushed to the Jeep before Gary even removed the twitch from Mera May's nose.

Leo Nucci sang "Largo al factotum" from *The Barber of Seville*, while Gray drove through Hickory and he was aware that this was the first time in days he had listened to opera. On the dash, Puccini yawned and stretched.

Taylor Ridge Farm lay along a ridge above Squire Road. It was located along the same ridge as Tina Sands' farm except that the land was farther from town—seven miles farther. For years, the farm had been used for the production of hemp. Soon after hemp production in the United States was outlawed, Chris's father had begun a Hereford cattle operation. When Chris inherited the farm, Chris had asked Gray to do the cattle work. Then, just a week ago, Chris had called the office and had told Natine that his services would no longer be needed. Gray didn't know who was doing his vet work now.

Gray turned the Jeep onto the concrete driveway that led to the house. He rumbled over an iron bar cattle gate that separated the long span of white plank fencing that badly needed a coat of paint. He could barely see the federally styled two-story house through the tall pines surrounding the pale yellow structure. He pulled up in front of a second neglected white fence, this one a straight rail picket and gate that enclosed the yard preventing livestock from wandering too close to the house. As he stood on the stoop, after twisting the door knob bell, he noted that the house paint was also peeling badly. Malcolm will have some maintenance to do, Gray thought as he waited for someone to answer the door.

Suddenly, the door swung violently open. Chris stood in the opening and by his high color, Gray realized that he must have observed his arrival.

"What are you doing here?" Chris demanded, his face a study in fury. Gray almost didn't recognize his friend. Always stocky in build, he had shriveled down to the skeletal form of an ill man and he squinted from eye sockets that seemed pressed deep by sculptor's thumbs.

"My God, Chris. Are you ill?" Gray's concern was spontaneous and sincere.

"What in the hell do you care, you son of a bitch! Get off this farm before I call the police!"

Gray was taken unawares by Chris's anger. He shoved his foot in the opening of the door as Chris moved to slam it in his face. He had to find a way to get him to listen to him.

"Chris . . . I haven't been the one . . . let me talk to you. I know who is doing this to you," Gray pleaded.

"What are you going to do?" Chris spat, his eyes suddenly bulging in their bony hollows. "Hit me? Kill me like you did Derek?"

"I didn't! . . . you've got to believe . . . give me fifteen minutes, Chris. That's all. I swear I'll leave . . . just fifteen minutes." Gray felt Chris's pressure on the door relax a bit with his words.

"Chris, who's there?" a voice from upstairs called.

Chris's head jerked toward the stairs, "It's no one, Amanda . . . a salesman. I'll be up in a few minutes with your breakfast."

My God, he's keeping all this from her, Gray thought. He remembered how Chris always protected her.

"I'll tell Amanda, I swear I will," Gray said in a quiet tone. It was worth a try to get Chris to listen to him. He pushed against the door.

"More blackmail, Dr. Prescott?" Chris retorted. But he released the door and motioned for Gray to follow him to the den.

Gray followed his shuffling form past the staircase to a door off the center hall. Chris opened the paneled door and held onto the knob as Gray passed into the room, closing the door behind him softly. Gray noticed that the packing had already begun. Several cardboard cartons of books were stacked against a unit of bare shelves and a couple of empty boxes lay in the middle of the floor.

Chris turned the lock and spun to face Gray. His hands were balled into fists and his chest heaved. Gray saw that he wasn't dressed for work. Instead, he wore a pair of worn jeans that hung low on his slight hips and a blue chambray shirt with long sleeves rolled to the elbow. Gray assumed he had taken the day off to pack or to care for Amanda who perhaps was ill in bed.

"What could you possibly have to say to me? Make it quick," Chris demanded.

Gray took a sucking breath and exhaled. "I am not the one blackmailing you," he began. Chris's face was expressionless. "I think I know who is," he went on. The only sound in the room was Chris's heavy breathing. Gray plunged ahead. "Dory's the one."

Another extreme wave of emotion flashed over Chris's depressed features and his eyes sucked inward to tiny black pits.

"Dory? You callous bastard! . . . how dare you?" The words erupted from Chris's curled lips and he took a step towards him.

Gray stood his ground. "It's true, Chris. I have proof. I have one of the blackmail instructions to you and it matches the type, paper, and ribbon condition of a note that she left anonymously on my doorstep with a kitten she dropped off."

Chris blinked. "The note . . . how—"

"Laney found it at your office the day of the funeral," Gray said quickly. He pulled the folded sheets from his jacket pocket. He had taken them from the back porch before he had left Laney's that morning, not really knowing what he would do with them. He spread them out on the desk. Unmoved, Chris was unwilling to give them a look.

"Look at them, Chris. The wrinkled one came from your own trash can in your office," Gray said.

Chris glanced quickly at the notes, then stepped away.

"Compare them, damn it!"

With Gray's outburst, Chris glanced over to the door as though Amanda might hear it and come downstairs to investigate. Chris stepped over to the desk. He lifted the two sheets of paper. His eyes shifted from one to the other several times.

"See the red tape on the edges and the watermark when you hold it up to the light?" Gray asked.

Chris took them to the window and studied them. He laid them back on the desk and Gray could see that he still wasn't persuaded. "You could have typed both of those yourself," Chris said.

Gray told him of the conversation Maddy had with Dory's son, Walker. "Dory left the kitten and the note in a box at my clinic. Call Maddy if you don't believe me," Gray said pointing to the phone on the desk.

Chris scrutinized the notes again. He lifted the phone book, looked up a number and dialed. Maddy answered, and Chris asked her about her conversation with Walker. Chris murmured, "So you actually pulled the note from the box the cat came in?" He kept glancing at the notes while he listened. When he finally hung up, his face had turned ashen.

"Where's the tape?" he asked abruptly, his words thick with emotion. He cleared his throat.

"Dory never had the tape," Gray said, not really knowing for sure if that was true. "The cassette dropped in the creek when Derek fell . . . and when the police recovered it, the tape inside was missing."

"You mean the tape was destroyed?" Chris's eyes blinked with fatigue. Then in a flat, detached voice he muttered, "Derek died because of that tape."

"You killed him?" Gray asked bluntly.

Gray's question jerked Chris to attention. "God no! . . . you—"

"I didn't like what Derek had become, but I didn't kill him, Chris. I believe he was the one who began the blackmail and when he died, Dory continued it."

"No . . . no," Chris whined, fighting the truth with all his might. Pain flooded his features. "He was my friend. When I told him about the blackmail, he promised to find out who was doing it."

"You told him?" Gray was incredulous.

"Yes, and the day before he was murdered, he told me that you were the one blackmailing me."

"Me?"

"When I read that the police were looking for a tape that might be connected to Derek's murder, I thought that maybe Derek had confronted you about the blackmail and you had killed him to keep him from exposing you."

"Aw, Chris . . . it's time to rewrite the script," Gray said.

Chris settled stiffly in his leather desk chair while Gray pulled up a Windsor chair. He had to follow Chris's head movements with his own before he finally managed to make eye contact with him.

Gray began with Laney's visit to Tina's after realizing that Chris was being blackmailed. He went through what Laney had told him the night before.

"So you think Derek took the tape from the cabin the day Pete killed himself?"

"He had to be the one. He was the one who found Peter's body and I told you the wording in the suicide note. There had to have been something more with the note."

"That was in November, about a month before I received the first blackmail note," Chris said.

"Do you still have it?" Gray asked.

Chris gazed at Gray for a long time before he bent and pulled out the bottom drawer of his desk. When the drawer was on the floor, he reached far inside the opening and pulled out four envelopes. He extracted a sheet of paper from each envelope. There were several sentences on one of the sheets and on the other three, triple numbers and an M like the one Laney had recovered. Chris spread them out on the desk with the two Gray had brought.

After studying them for a minute, Gray was certain. "They match," he said. Chris nodded. Gray pointed to the original note. "May I read it?"

Chris nodded a second time.

"I have the tape of the Tongue Twisters' last meeting. I will send the tape to the police if you do not leave fifty-thousand dollars in Locker 20 at the Fayette Mall on Monday at ten o'clock. Leave the mall immediately."

"My God, Chris," Gray said.

"I thought the fifty would take care of it, but it was just the beginning. The notes just kept coming . . . and coming. Asking for smaller amounts . . . but every week. The farm already had a hefty mortgage and now I have two. I've borrowed from my credit union . . . against my insurance policies . . . I've even hit my friends. It broke me, Gray." He dropped his head in his hands and his shoulders shook.

"Where are the rest of the notes?"

Chris raised his head. His red eyes were even more sunken than before. "I threw them away. The first four were the only ones I kept. They always come to the university."

"Chris, this has to stop . . . even if it means the truth coming out about that night."

Chris sprang to his feet. "No! . . . No! If the university finds out about what we did that night, my chairmanship is gone."

Gray spoke gently. "There's more than a chairmanship at stake.

Someone killed Derek over this tape. Maybe even Dory."

"But why? It's hard enough to believe that she could blackmail me, but murder?"

"There's another possibility. Perhaps Derek's death didn't have anything to do with the tape. What if Dory killed her husband because he was having an affair with Mary Wakefield?"

Chris's jaw dropped. "They were having an affair?"

"It's from a reliable source."

Chris gathered up the four notes and placed them back into the envelopes.

"There's another problem, Chris. My clinic was broken into last Thursday night and my euthanasia drug was taken from my Jeep. Then yesterday, a pet mare of Laney's died suddenly. Police think there's a strong possibility that the mare was put down by that drug."

Chris crashed down in his chair.

"Someone has it in for me . . . someone that believes I have that tape." Gray gazed deep into Chris's eyes.

"Gray, no! . . . you don't think I—"

Gray said nothing.

"I didn't. I swear." Chris's face displayed total repudiation.

"Don't want to believe it but to be perfectly honest, that's one of the reasons I came here today. To ask you if you were the one who broke into my clinic."

"Thursday night." Chris thought hard. He brightened. "I worked! . . . I worked late at the university. Call John Farris. He's one of my post docs. We're working on a research project together. I didn't leave the lab until midnight."

"Your word is enough," Gray said.

Chris combed his fingers through his unruly hair. "You're much more generous than I've been with you, Gray. I thought you were the one doing this to me. How can I make it up to you?" Gray thought he was going to cry again.

"By going to see Marshall Knight with me."

"The attorney?"

"Yes, it's time the last two Tongue Twisters got some legal advice."

25

At eight, the odor of dead fish awakened her. Laney groaned, sleepy eyes searching the room. She discovered the offending dog spread out on the hearth rug. She could almost see the stench curling above the collie like wavy lines in a cartoon. Spotting the door to her room ajar, she surmised that Shar had let Blackberry in and had fed her before going to bed. She crawled out of bed and shooed the animal into the hallway and opened the windows to air out the room. She had just stepped into the bathroom when she heard a light tap at her door. Reaching behind the open bathroom door, she grabbed her robe and slipped it on.

"Laney, may I come in?" Shar called from the hallway and swept inside. Shar scrutinized the tangled bedclothes and the wake of garments on the floor. "Tsk, tsk, tsk," she said, with a sagacious smirk and a slow wag of her head. "I'd say this is an irrefutable case of debauchery."

Laney felt the blush travel into her hairline. "Is nothing sacred, my cheeky friend?" Laney said, as she darted back into the bathroom.

When Laney emerged, Shar was gone but she could hear her banging around in the kitchen and talking with Malcolm. She dressed hurriedly in a pair of beige chinos, white blouse and a blue vest with faces of Kentucky Wildcats peering through UK initials.

This will tear Gray up she smiled to herself, recalling their long history of playful rivalry over his favorite team, the Louisville Cardinals.

A shading of makeup to contain the freckles and a quick touch of mascara was all she had time for. She remembered that Jesse was coming to clean today so she stripped the bed and piled the sheets and yesterday's clothing in the middle of the floor. Deciding in a reckless moment to allow her hair to dry naturally, she scrunched the red ringlets with her fingers and left the room.

As she entered the kitchen, the smells emanating from the oven drew at her jaws.

"What is that?" she asked, knowing that it had to be something from the freezer. Shar was as inept as Gray in the kitchen.

"Apricot turnovers a la Maddy," Shar piped. "The directions for heating were on the wrapper. Mal made the coffee."

The aromas were driving Laney mad with hunger. She peeked into the oven and withdrew the pastry triangles just in time. She dusted them with confectioner's sugar and passed them under the broiler flame until glazed.

When they all sat down at the table on the screen porch, Laney saw the eight track player on the end table and was immediately reminded of the tape they had heard the night before. The black plastic cartridge jutted from the player opening. They were about to dig in when Gray and Jesse opened one of the French doors.

"Gray let me in. I can't find my key," Jesse said.

They stepped onto the porch. "What's going on?" Gray said, his hands tucked under his arms.

"We're in a feeding frenzy," Shar said, sighing with her first mouthful of turnover.

"Would you like one before you start on the house?" Laney asked Jesse.

"I'll take a rain check for lunch," she said and passed back into the kitchen.

"Is that invitation open to me?" Gray said, lifting Laney's mass of hair and nuzzling her neck as he passed.

Laney felt a tingle all the way to her toes and noted Gray's ready smile.

Gray lifted Kudzu from a chair, dumped him in Shar's lap and pulled the chair up to the table. Laney jumped up to get him a plate and coffee but he was already into a turnover before she returned.

"Talked to Chris. Convinced him I'm not responsible for his blackmail. We're going to see Marshall this afternoon." Gray told them everything that had transpired at Taylor Ridge.

"So what do you think Marshall will advise you and Chris to do?" Shar asked.

Gray shrugged, washed the last of his turnover down with coffee, and stood. "I have a couple more calls before our appointment this afternoon. Talk at you later." He sneaked in a second neck nibble on his way out the screen door. "Wrong critter on that vest," he called as he passed from view.

Laney had just concluded Blackberry's bath when Malcolm and Shar returned from the lower barn after checking out Thistle and her new mother.

"You may have won the war, but Blackberry won the battle." Shar quipped when she saw Laney. Even with plastic apron and gloves, Laney's hair sparkled with spray from the hose and she dripped water from her nose and chin.

Laney stood with her hands on her hips watching the collie streak around the yard between rolls in the grass. "Don't know why I bother," she said. "Look at her."

Laney dumped the water, squirted out the number two galvanized tub and lugged it to the carriage house where she hung it on a nail on the wall. Malcolm and Shar carried the shampoo and towels into the house.

Jesse was eating her lunch on the screen porch when Laney collapsed into the rocker.

Shar fixed tea and brought it out to the porch, and she and Malcolm sat down at the table with Jesse.

"Say, is that the eight track player you bought yesterday?" Jesse asked.

"How did you know about it?" Laney asked.

"Rose told me. She said you had some eight track tape you wanted to play on it," Jesse said, taking a bite of a turnover left over from breakfast.

Good grief, Laney thought. She had forgotten that Jesse lived in the second floor apartment over Second Hand Rose's. Nothing in Hickory got by Rose or Jesse. Laney was glad she had put the tape up after breakfast. Jesse would probably have wanted to hear it.

"Well, I have an old Sex Pistols eight track tape that I wanted to hear," Laney lied. She observed Shar's brows lift and her mouth twitch.

"That reminds me. What in the world is wrong with Amanda Taylor? She looks like death warmed over," Jesse said.

"When did you see Amanda?" Laney asked.

"Yesterday morning . . . at Rose's. I was on my way over to Sarah Winter's to clean when Amanda brought in some stuff for Rose to sell."

"Well . . . she's just been running ragged getting ready for this move," Laney said.

"Yeah, I heard they sold their place and are moving to Lexington. But I guess you know all that, being friends and all," Jesse said, finishing the pastry. Laney wondered just how good a friend she was, since she hadn't seen Amanda since their lunch at the club. I've truly neglected her, she thought. I'll call her later today.

Blackberry nosed the screen and Shar let her in. The collie reestablished residence by finding a corner. Kudzu tried in vain to get her to play but the dog shut her eyes to the kitten's pirouettes.

Jesse carried her plate into the kitchen. After Malcolm peeked around the door to make sure Jesse was out of earshot, he said, "You know, Laney, if Dory finds out you have the tape, she may try to acquire it."

"Dory hasn't had the tape since Derek died and that sure hasn't stopped her from continuing the blackmail," Shar said. "As long as Chris believed the blackmailer had it, those little notes were all that were needed to keep the money coming."

"If I may make a suggestion, Laney? Put the tape in a safe place until Gray and Chris talk to their attorney and he decides what they should do with it," Malcolm said.

"Good advice, Malcolm. I'll put it in my safety deposit box today," Laney said.

26

"Hm . . ." Marshall said, as he read the six notes that were spread over his desk—the four that Chris possessed, the wrinkled note that Laney had recovered, and the note that had been enclosed with the kitten. Marshall's mumbles were the only sounds in the room besides the creaking of his desk chair as he rocked. His face above the wall of papers and law books that rimmed his desk appeared troubled. Gray glanced at Chris who sat stiffly to his left. His gaunt friend clutched the grimy blond wooden arms of his chair which was the ugly match to the one Gray squirmed in.

"Well," Marshall finally said, lifting a rubber gloved hand to scratch his nose. "In my opinion, if the police match these notes to the typewriter and the person who owns it, they should have a strong case for blackmail. Also, it's a federal offense to use the mails for the purpose of extortion. The postmarked envelopes that the notes came in will do nicely in establishing that offense, if the same typewriter was also used for addressing them. At first look, the type seems to match. Unfortunately, that several people have handled the notes may have destroyed any prints."

Gray was relieved that he hadn't touched the four notes that Chris had showed him. They should only have Chris's and Dory's prints on them if she hadn't worn gloves when she typed them and slipped them into the envelopes.

"Marshall, since the tape that is referred to in the note was destroyed, will that make the case of blackmail harder to prove?" Chris asked. Gray held his breath. He had not disclosed to either Chris or Marshall that Laney and Shar had found a copy of the tape.

"Chris, as a rule, even if the person who is being blackmailed actually committed a criminal or dishonorable act, it does not matter in the eyes of the court. The perpetrator can still be charged with blackmail," Marshall said.

"Even if I paid him the money?" Chris asked.

"Even if you didn't pay him a red cent. But in that case, the charge would be more like attempted blackmail."

Chris sat forward in his chair. "What do I do next, Marshall?"

"Go to the police," Marshall said. "These notes must be turned over so that if any prints remain, they can be traced."

Marshall paused, then asked softly, "Chris . . . you wouldn't want to tell me what was so incriminating on the tape that you felt you had to pay hush money, would you?"

Chris swallowed, his sallow skin rippling over his gaunt face like a waxy wave. His crepey lids dropped in answer. Nothing but the rasp of Marshall's chair could be heard.

Marshall reached under the papers and extracted a manila folder and carefully placed the notes and envelopes inside and closed it. He removed his rubber gloves. "Anything else you need to tell me?" he asked them both.

"A couple things," Gray said. "Remember the drug I told you about the other night?" Marshall nodded. "Yesterday a mare on Laney's farm died suddenly. We found a syringe near her body. Gordon is getting the drug analyzed. Could be that drug that was stolen from my Jeep."

"Do you have any idea who did it?" Marshall asked, glancing at Chris.

"Wasn't Chris," Gray said. "Anyway, he has an alibi for the night someone broke into the clinic. I think Dory broke in looking for the tape and took the drug. Now, for some reason, she is doing some deadly mischief with it . . . to make me look bad."

"We'll tell Gordon your suspicions when we turn over the black-mail notes," Marshall said. "While they search Mrs. Beale's house for the typewriter, they can also look for the drug. Now, what's the other thing you wanted to tell me?"

Gray opened his mouth, then closed it. He just wasn't ready to tell anyone about the eight track tape.

"Slipped my mind," Gray said.

27

"When will Malcolm get back?" Laney asked Shar who was pulling a T-shirt the color of lemons over her head. Malcolm was driving his farm manager and his wife to Blue Grass Airport to catch a flight back to Ocala. He was staying on a couple more days, much to Shar's delight.

"Smitty's plane leaves around six. He should be back by seven-thirty," Shar said as she smoothed the oversized shirt down over her thighs and turned around to face Laney.

Laney read the message spread across the front of the shirt: "I'm not forty. I'm eighteen with twenty-two years experience."

Laney, who was stretched out on Shar's bed, doubled up in laughter. "Where do you find those things?"

"A little hole in the wall in the Strip District. The guy who owns it really appreciates women. I'd marry him if he weren't gay." She plopped down beside Laney and pulled on her slip-on canvas sneakers.

"Nice of Malcolm to hang on here a couple more days," Laney said. "Bet you'll miss him when he leaves."

Shar didn't reply. Instead, she jumped up and announced, "I'm ready." Laney could barely see the bottom edge of Shar's denim shorts below the shirt and her smooth slim legs made Laney sigh enviously.

The two of them hit the front staircase running. Shar beat her, hands down, with her posterior banister glide. Kudzu, asleep on the first step, scampered down the hallway toward the kitchen.

Laney could hear Jesse finishing up her vacuuming in the dining room as they dashed out the door. Anticipating the fun when Laney and Shar grabbed the bikes from the stand, Blackberry took off across the yard. She was well ahead of them as they turned toward the lower barn. Afternoon shadows from the wild cherry and the still mostly bare black walnut trees lengthened across the blacktop, and filtered sun dappled their faces as they raced. The day was an unusually warm eighty-five degrees and Laney realized Shar hadn't pushed the season at all by wearing her shorts.

By the time they reached the lower crossing, the Border collie was already swimming out into the creek.

"I dare you to roll in dead fish," Laney called to the dog.

Not giving her the chance, they started back up the grade and headed toward the office. Blackberry followed after a quick body shake. Aaron was nowhere in sight when they dropped their bikes. The office door was open and they drank great gulps of water from the small sink. Through the glass window, Thistle and the nurse mare—a rather aloof older mare of dubious pedigree—stood eyeing Laney and Shar. Thistle lowered his head and nudged the swollen bag of the scruffy brown and white pinto mare and began to suck thirstily, putting an end to any doubts Laney may have had whether the foal and her new mother were compatible.

"When Mal and I were down here last night, Aaron and Tom Thatcher hooded the mare and rigged a fostering gate in the stall so that Maria couldn't kick the foal until she got used to him," Shar said.

"I wish I could have been here," Laney said as she remembered her evening of discovery and passion and wondered how Gray's and Chris's appointment with Marshall had gone. She was anxious to get back to the house to retrieve any messages.

They watched Thistle and Maria for a few more minutes, then headed back. Jesse's gray station wagon was gone when they arrived. Laney unlocked the door and dashed into the library. The light was blinking on her answering machine and there were two messages. The first was from Gray. He said the meeting with Marshall had gone as expected and the three of them were headed for the sheriff's office. He ended with his usual "I'll talk at you later." The last message was a hang-up.

Shar stepped into the library, her eyes searching. "Laney, did you see Kudzu?"

"Sure didn't. Did you check the screened porch?"

"Yes. I hope Jesse didn't let him slip outside," Shar said.

"I'll help you look," Laney said, leaving the library. "I'll check the upstairs. He's managing the steps pretty well these days."

Laney covered all six of the bedrooms and the four baths. She couldn't help noticing how pleasant the rooms were. Everything was spotless and ready for the first wave of guests on Friday. Outside each room, Jesse had placed a lined basket ready to be filled with homemade cookies and fresh fruit to be placed in each room as a welcoming gift. On the dresser in each room would be a vase of fresh flowers.

"Did you find him?" Shar called from the back stairs.

Laney skipped down the steps where Shar was waiting with a frown clouding her face.

"No. You look around the back of the house and I'll check the front in case he got out and is hiding in the bushes. She rushed out the front door onto the porch and called the kitten. Blackberry lay in a corner asleep. After Laney had checked behind every bush and tree in the front of the house, she returned to the porch and met Shar dashing out the door.

"He's gone," Shar cried. Tears welled in her gray eyes. "You don't think that Jesse would take Kudzu, do you?"

"Absolutely not." Laney replied. Shar paced back and forth in the kitchen while Laney dialed the Finish Line.

"Jewel? This is Laney McVey. Fine. Jewel, would it be possible to speak with Jesse?" Laney paced along with Shar while she held the portable phone to her ear. It seemed the longest time before Laney heard Jesse's soft hello.

"Jesse, did you lock the door when you left to go home?"

"Yeah, Laney."

"Was Kudzu in the house when you left?"

"Oh yes. Can't you find the little dickens? I put him in the pantry and shut the door so he wouldn't try to skip outside when I left. I gave him plenty of water an—"

"He's not there, Jesse. You're sure you locked the door when you left?"

"Of course. I turned the latch like I always do. I really need to go. Call me back when you find him or I'll worry all night. Just leave a message with anyone." She hung up the phone.

"You don't think someone took him?" Shar whimpered.

"Jesse said she locked the door when she left. You have to have a key to open these dead bolts." Then like receiving a well placed thrust to the solar plexus, she gasped when she remembered Jesse saying that morning that she had lost her key. She searched her memory for the rest of the conversation but it wouldn't come to her.

Laney lifted the phone from its cradle and dialed the Finish Line for the second time. Jewell seemed a little peeved when Laney asked to speak to Jesse. Laney waited for several minutes until the owner, Maury, got on the line.

"Could Jesse call you back?" he asked. "She's taking an order for a party of eight."

Laney apologized and said she would get with her later.

"C'mon, Shar," Laney said. "Let's run into town. There's a quick way we can talk to her. I have several things I want to drill her about."

"I better leave Mal a note," Shar said. She scribbled a couple of sentences on a scratch pad and ran down the hall to tape it to the front door. Laney had just checked to make sure the French doors were locked when she halted and doubled back. She stared through the pane at the wicker end table where Shar had placed the eight track player the night before. The table was bare.

"Oh God, no!"

She rushed through the house into the library, holding her breath as she yanked open the middle drawer of the desk.

She knew the result of her negligence before she even scanned the contents. The tape was gone.

28

"Woman, let down the flaps on this aircraft!" Shar shouted, as they careened down the final hill leading into Hickory.

"Someone was in my house, Shar. In! . . . my! . . . house!" Laney said, her white knuckles throttling the steering wheel as though she were on a motorcycle. She sat forward in her seat, every muscle a coil ready to spring.

Shar tightened the seat belt across her lap. "It must have been while we were biking and after Jesse left. That's only about a window of forty-five minutes. Someone must have known we were out."

Laney slapped her forehead. "I had a hang-up on the answering machine after Gray's call. Someone with a cell phone could have been lurking nearby, waiting for the answering machine to pickup, indicating no one was at home."

"You think that someone is Dory, don't you?"

Laney slapped her left turn signal and turned into the Finish Line parking lot. "I'm not so sure anymore."

After a wait of about five minutes, they were seated at a small table near the bar.

"I'm really not dressed for dinner," Shar said, glancing down at her yellow shirt with the blaring message.

"Anything goes here," Laney said, waving at Jewel working the cash register.

"Laney, I'm too upset to eat anything. Let's just order a drink and as soon as you get a chance to talk to Jesse, we'll beat it out of here. I can't wait to get my hands on whoever took my Kudzu."

A harried looking Jesse staggered out of the kitchen door balancing a gigantic round tray. She kicked open a portable tray table and settled the tray next to a table with four diners that Laney didn't recognize. Tourists, she thought, remembering that it was just a few days before derby week festivities began, culminating with the big race on the first Saturday in May. She had noticed as they drove through town that the city had already mounted the derby banners on every lamp pole down Main Street. The Stoney Creek Bed & Breakfast's first derby guests would arrive in three days.

"What can I get you guys?" Jesse asked, suddenly appearing between their two chairs with a pencil poised above her order tablet. Her bobbed hair had lost some of its bounce and there were marinara stains on the front of her turquoise jockey shirt.

"Just a cup of tea and some of your derby wings for me," Laney said.

"Ditto, but no wings for me, thanks," Shar said.

"Found Kudzu, I gather?" Jesse said, as she wrote.

"That's why we're here, Jesse. We didn't," Laney replied.

Jesse gasped, her face blanching. "Jeez, Laney, I put him—"

"Someone got into the house and took him," Laney said, concealing the fact that the tape was also missing.

"I'll be right back," Jesse said, and disappeared into the kitchen. In no time she returned carrying a small tray with two brown glazed inverted cups acting as lids for the two matching individual teapots, and a heaping plate of Maury's specialty—chicken wings dripping with his hickory smoked barbecue sauce. Jesse served them and then pulled over a chair from an adjacent table and squeezed in next to Shar.

"Jewel's covering my tables while I take a break," she said. "When I told Maury you had a problem, he said to take as long as I needed."

"This will only take a few minutes," Laney said. "Did the phone ring while you were at the house today?"

"Once as I was leaving, but the answering machine picked up before I could answer it."

"Only once? I had two messages when we got back. Well . . . one from Gray and a hang-up," Laney said.

"I don't know about that. Maybe someone called while I was vac-uuming and I didn't hear the phone and the answering machine picked that one up too."

"Didn't you tell me this morning that you couldn't find the key to my house and Gray had to let you in with his?" Laney asked.

"Yeah, I hang all my cleaning clients' keys on a key rack just inside my apartment door. This morning, when I looked for yours, it was gone. I have tags on them with each client's name."

That's just hunky-dory, Laney thought. "You also told me this morning that Rose told you about me buying that eight track play-er yesterday."

"Yeah, she told both of us about the player you bought to play some kind of tape."

"Both of you?" Shar asked, her eyes fusing with Laney's.

"Yeah, me and Amanda Taylor. Laney, remember me telling you Amanda was at Rose's to consign some of her stuff yesterday?"

"I didn't realize that Amanda was present when Rose told you about my purchase of the tape player," Laney said, getting more unsettled by the moment.

"I was just leaving to clean at Sarah Winter's and I stopped down stairs at Rose's when I saw Amanda. While we chatted, Rose told us about the player you bought."

"Did you notice any reaction from Amanda when Rose men-tioned the player or tape?" Shar asked.

"No . . . well . . . that's a toughie. She already looked God-awful. Uptight like . . . like if I said boo, she would have a go-to-pieces."

"Did you leave then?" Laney asked.

"Yeah, I was running late. I'm supposed to be at Sarah's by one o'clock."

Laney had a sudden thought. "Jesse, do you lock your apartment door when you leave?"

"Only the outside entrance above the alley. Inside, the apartment opens into Rose's shop and she's always there except at night when she goes home. Then she locks up and sets the alarm. It's as safe as can . . . oh my . . . I see what you're driving at—that maybe Amanda took the key from my apartment some time while she was bringing in her junk. Would Amanda do that?" Jesse's eyes widened. "And take Kudzu? What in heavens for? I could get her a half a dozen kitties with a single phone call."

Laney pulled some bills from her wallet and tossed them on the table. "Thanks, Jesse. You've been terrific. We're outta here," she said, and without as much as a sip of their tea or a bite of Maury's wings, the two of them dashed out the door.

"Let me guess, woman. We're on a flight path to Amanda's house," Shar said, tightening her seat belt once more.

"Right you are," Laney said, her eyes set tight on the road ahead—her foot practically to the floor boards of the Whooptie. Darkness had fallen while they were in the restaurant and Laney, who hated driving at night, squinted at the headlights of the occasional oncoming car.

"Laney, you must know what all this means. If Amanda discovered via Rose that you needed the player to play a tape and she broke into your house to get them, she must know about the blackmail."

"Right. And Chris thought he had kept her in the dark about it all this time."

"This opens all kinds of possibilities, not the least of these is that she could have been the one that broke into Gray's clinic, looking for the tape."

"Right again, but if she was the one, then she must have stolen the euthanasia drug," Laney said.

"Good God, woman! Unreasonable went to her eternal rest from an unhealthy pop of Thanatol . . . and now . . . the grim reaper has her sights on my Kudzu!" Shar shrieked.

"Stifle, Shar! I can't have an hysterical wench on my hands when

I talk to her," Laney said.

"Talk to her? Not on your life! This is something for the police!"

"I just can't do that to her without trying to reason with her first
. . . after all that she's been through. Chris will probably be there
and can help."

Laney pulled off Squire Road into the entrance to Taylor Ridge.
The car lights flashed on the peeling fences as they rolled over the
cattle gate and drove toward the house. When Laney stopped the car
and turned off the engine, the yellow house appeared weathered and
ghostly in the bright light of the moon. The windows reflected black
as though the house were uninhabited.

"Let's go, Laney," Shar said. "No one's home."

"Wait," she said, and got out of the car. The picket gate creaked
as it swung open and banged shut behind her. Laney rang the bell
knob. She waved at Shar in the car, her friend's face white in the
moonlight.

The door opened slowly. Chris stood in the opening, his face
barely visible in the darkened hall. He turned on the porch light.
His cadaverous face lit up, then collapsed into disappointment.
"Oh Laney. I'd hoped it was Amanda. You haven't seen her, have
you?"

"That's why I came, Chris," Laney said, truly dismayed at his
condition. "I wanted to speak with her."

"I don't know where she's gone . . . we had words . . . she left."

"I . . . I'm sorry." Laney saw that he was ready for bed. His navy
robe hung open over pale blue pajamas. His feet were bare.

"I had a late meeting with the Dean of Arts and Sciences today. I
got the chairmanship. I told Amanda when she got home. I thought
she would be happy. Instead, she cried and ran out the door. I don't
understand."

Laney couldn't tell him about any of it. She didn't have the heart.
Instead, she barely croaked congratulations and turned away. She
heard the door close softly behind her.

"She's not there," Laney said as she climbed back into the
Whooptie. "Chris said she came home, then left again when he told
her he had gotten the chairmanship of the department. She cried
when he told her. . . . Why would she cry?" Laney thought out loud.
"That's what they both wanted."

"Maybe they were tears of relief."

"Or guilt," Laney said, starting the Whooptie.

Laney pulled out on the highway and they traveled toward Hickory in silence.

"Where could she be?" Shar asked.

"I haven't a clue. But we'd better get back before Malcolm sends out the troops."

"Laney, the gate's open," Shar said.

"What?"

"The gate we just passed . . . the gate to the cabin."

Laney pulled over onto the shoulder. "Maybe the people who live in the house opened it. I have Tina's keys on my ring." She shut off the engine and pulled the ignition key out. The ring of keys jangled as she turned on the dome light. "Shar, they're gone . . . the two keys with the red tag that reads 'Sands' cabin' aren't here. Amanda must have taken them too."

"They were in plain sight on the hall table . . . in the bowl," Shar said. "But why would she take them?"

Laney jammed the ignition key back, started the engine and did a U-turn in the highway. "I don't know, but I'm sure as hell going to find out," she said, and swung through the gateway.

29

"What are you doing sitting out here all by your lonesome?" Gray asked Malcolm as he walked toward the porch. The yellow porch lights cast a golden glow over Malcolm's face.

"Waiting for the girls. I don't have a key to get into the house," he said. He jumped from the swing and met Gray halfway and handed Shar's note to Gray. "I'm beginning to get concerned. See the time Sharlene wrote on the note?"

Gray read it under the porch light and saw the time noted was six-forty. Shar had written that Kudzu was missing and they were going to the Finish Line to see Jesse. That they had been gone several hours was not what concerned Gray the most. It was Shar's rushed scrawl at the bottom of the note that the tape and the player had also been taken.

"What do you make of this?" Malcolm asked, a furrow appearing above his glasses and his hand stroking his goatee nervously.

Poor guy, Gray thought. He's not used to all this intrigue. "I'm sure they are all right," Gray reassured him, but didn't really feel assured himself.

Malcolm read his thoughts. "If the girls are pursuing the person who abducted Kudzu and stole the tape and player, they may be in danger."

"I'm hoping that person will be placed under arrest tonight."

Gray sat on the edge of a wicker stool and looked up at the worried little man. "I need to update you, Malcolm. Chris and I turned over the kitten note and the blackmail letters this afternoon and Gordon is probably serving Dory a search warrant as we speak."

"What about the syringe? Have the police identified the drug?"

"Yes, it's Thanatol, the euthanasia drug used to put down animals. They plan to search Dory's house for the drug also. Results of the autopsy on Unreasonable aren't in yet."

"What should we do? . . . remain here until the girls arrive?" Malcolm said, stooping to pet Blackberry who rolled onto her back to have her belly scratched.

"I'm going to trace them down. You're welcome to go with me or I can let you in the house with my key," Gray said.

"I'd like to accompany you."

The two of them climbed into Gray's Buick. Puccini acknowledged Malcolm by a jump into his lap and a tail swipe across his mouth. As the engine roared to life, the tabby jumped back into his lair of choice under the windshield. Accompanied by Luciano Pavarotti's tender aria, "Parmi veder le lagrime" from Verdi's *Rigoletto*, the two men in the chrome-finned monstrosity sped through the moonlight like a celestial pink shooting star.

The last diners were just leaving as Gray and Malcolm entered the Finish Line. Jewel and another waitress were carrying food from the salad bar into the kitchen. Gray found Jesse clearing a table near the front window. She looked up as Gray and Malcolm approached.

"We're just about to close, Gray, but I can get you a carry-out," Jesse said. Jewel stepped to the door, produced a key from her pant pocket and locked the door.

"We're not here to eat, Jesse. We just want to ask you some questions," Gray said.

"You and the other two. They didn't eat either," Jesse said.

"That's who we want to ask about," Gray said. He and Malcolm sat down in two chairs and watched Jesse while she dumped dishes and glassware into a plastic busboy tub on a chair. She looked beat.

"Do you know where they were headed?" Gray asked.

"They didn't say so I couldn't tell you for sure, but by their questions, I'd say they're at Amanda Taylor's."

"Taylor Ridge?" Malcolm asked. "Why on earth . . . ?"

Jesse related her conversation with Laney and Shar.

"You mean Amanda took Laney's key from your apartment and stole Kudzu from Laney's house?" Malcolm asked.

And the tape and player, Gray thought to himself.

"That's what they think," Jesse panted. She wiped crumbs into a pile, swooped them and the dishcloth on top of the dirty dishes and placed her hands on her hips. With her head bobbing side to side and gray eyes smoking, she retorted, "Listen, you two, if you see Amanda Taylor, will you give her a message for me? That if I ever catch up with her, I'm going to knock the tar outta her."

Gray hammered on Chris's door.

"It looks as though no one is at home," Malcolm said, just as the door swung open with a jerk.

"Gray," Chris said, his face haggard under the porch light.

"Have Laney and Shar been here?" Gray asked.

"They were here looking for Amanda about a half hour ago," Chris said. He had changed into a pair of jeans and a black polo shirt, his skeletal frame blueprinted by the clinging knit fabric.

"Where's Amanda?" Gray asked.

"I wish I knew. I told Laney that when I told Amanda that I'd been appointed Chairman of the Chemistry Department, she began to cry and she ran out. I haven't seen her since."

Gray reached in and pumped his hand. "Congratulations, you son of a gun," he said, but was afraid he knew why Amanda had reacted so. God, how was he going to explain?

Chris smiled wanly, held the door open and the two of them stepped into the foyer. He flipped on the light and the antique chandelier lit up the handsome entrance hall. Gray put his arm around Chris's thin shoulders and led him into the den. Malcolm remained in the foyer.

"Have to talk to you, friend," Gray said, guiding Chris toward a chair. Gray turned on the desk lamp. Chris looked frightened.

"Amanda knows about the blackmail," Gray began.

"You told her?" Chris sputtered, leaping to his feet.

Gray gently pushed him back into his chair. "Of course not, but by her behavior today, we have reason to believe she knows." Gray related Jesse's story and the contents of Shar's note, indicating all that was missing from Laney's house. Chris began to shiver uncontrollably.

"S-so there's another tape? . . . and . . . Amanda has it and the player?"

"And the kitten," Gray added.

"Why the kitten?"

"Have no idea but I think she has gone somewhere to play the tape," Gray said. "Think, man. Where would she go?"

Chris was pensive. "Maybe Dory's? . . . Amanda thinks she's her friend."

"Let's go," Gray said, hoping that Laney hadn't come up with the same conclusion. Dory, Amanda, Laney, and Shar—a combination made in hell.

30

"Laney, I don't like this. Please let's go back and call the police," Shar said.

"Look at the positive side. At least you didn't have to open the gate," Laney said, as she drove slowly over the dirt road, her left wheels riding on the elevated grassy center to prevent it from scraping the undercarriage of the Whooptie. "I just hope the cattle don't get out." Even if the moon hadn't been full, she could have made out the large white animals. Their luminous opal eyes moved slowly down the fence line toward them. She could hear the Charolais' intermittent mooing through the closed windows.

"Why would Amanda come here anyway?" Shar asked.

"Got me, but since she took the keys, she must have had something in mind."

"Poor Mal. He's probably starving to death on the front porch. He doesn't have a key to the house, you know."

"Look Shar! This gate is open too. Amanda *must* be here. The people renting the house wouldn't leave the gates open."

"Neither would someone who owns a cattle farm like Taylor Ridge . . . unless Amanda is so out of control, she doesn't care about moo cows any more," Shar said nervously. She fidgeted in her seat. "Why in hell don't you at least have a cell phone? Or don't they have them down here in the boonies?"

"I'll make a note to get one tomorrow."

"If we live until tomorrow."

Laney began the twisting drive through the woods—so dense that barely a glimmer of moonlight penetrated the blackness. The beams of the headlights lurched from one side of the road to the other, ricocheting off the evergreens like runaway bullets as the car maneuvered the sharp curves.

"God, woman, please slow down," Shar cried during the contorting descent. Without warning, Laney braked hard, the rear-end of the Whooptie fishtailing and spinning out inches from a pine tree. Shar let out a squeal.

"Shush!" Laney whispered. "Look!" She flipped off the headlights.

Through the trees, as though a delayed playback of their own descent, headlights of another vehicle careened down the opposite spiraling road leading to the concrete bridge crossing the north fork of Stoney Creek.

"Someone is coming from the cabin! It must be Amanda. We have to stop her!" Laney whispered, backing up and turning so that they were facing downhill once more.

"Oh-h-h, woman," Shar moaned, covering her eyes. "I'm going to wet my pa—"

With only a faint filtering of the moonlight through the tall evergreens for guidance, they pitched down the remaining curves, tilted around the final sharp turn onto the bridge and jerked to rest cattycorner across the lipless span where the Whooptie promptly sputtered and stalled. Without trees to obscure it, the moon beamed full faced upon the white Nissan and the pale concrete bridge.

The other vehicle continued lurching down the opposite bank. The lights blinked like fireflies between the black trees as it plunged down the steep grade.

"I'm going to wave her down," Laney breathed, and was out of the Whooptie before Shar had the chance to protest. Laney knew how terrified Shar was of bridges from the last time they had paused here, but she had to stop Amanda's flight.

"Laney, please don't—" Shar croaked, but Laney cut off her protest with the slam of the car door, and began waving her arms at the fast approaching car. As the car swung onto the bridge, Laney recognized it as Amanda's Saab. As the headlights hit her eyes in a blinding blast of light, Laney realized instantly that she had made a dreadful miscalculation. Amanda didn't see her until the last moment. She applied her brakes, but her move was too late and too slow. In a desperate effort to miss hitting Laney, Amanda jerked the steering wheel to her left. At the same instant, Laney dived to her left and met the concrete in a full body forward slide. Laney felt skin scraping from her forearms and heels of her hands as she slid, her hands skidding off the left side of the bridge so that she was looking down into the dark water when she came to a stop. She grasped the edge of the concrete and as she lifted herself with bleeding palms, she heard the crunch of metal against metal as the Saab hit the Whooptie. While scrabbling to sit up, she caught the Saab rolling backwards to a stop, and then watched horrified as the Whooptie bounced toward the far edge of the bridge.

"No!" she screamed, scrambling to her feet and running after the Whooptie as though she could will the car to stop. But with a clank, the front wheels dropped off the edge and the undercarriage gnashed the concrete like a giant rasp. Sparks flew as the Whooptie chewed the surface, slowed, then stopped, teetering—its rear wheels barely spinning a couple of inches above the pavement—the front half of the car hovering over the black water. With a final shiver, the car groaned, creaked, and was still. No sound reached her ears but the sounds of the night—the croaking of a frog, a faraway screech of an owl, and now, the thrashing of her own heart.

"God no! . . . Shar!" she screamed, tears spewing from her eyes as she rushed around to the passenger side of the Whooptie, straining to see inside the car.

"Laney!" Shar's muted scream came from within. "I'm going into the water." The car moaned and creaked as though Shar's cry alone was enough to shift the balance.

Laney stepped back from the car, fighting the urge to reach out over the water and open the car door. Quickly, she recalled how Shar always had to shoulder her door to open it. That kind of motion now would surely cause the car's plunge into the creek. She realized that the concrete edge of the bridge was the fulcrum holding the car suspended in a perfect balance.

Laney ran around to the other side of the car. She was astounded

at the damage the Saab had ravaged upon the driver's side. The front
fender and door were crushed inward and upward into the window
of mosaic glass. No way out that side of the car, Laney determined.

Behind her, she detected the hiss of steam and smelled the stench
of hot rubber. Spinning about, she discovered water vapor pouring
from the twisted hood of Amanda's Saab. Amanda's car had
bounced backward after the collision and had come to rest almost
perpendicular and only a few feet from the Nissan. Peering around
the folded metal, she saw that the driver's side door was open and
Amanda was gone.

Laney rushed back around the rear of the Whooptie to the passenger side.

Shar's face appeared at the window, distorted and white as she
pressed it against the glass. The moon lit her frightened features as
though it were day. Her eyes protruded wildly and she mouthed the
words, "Help me, Laney."

Laney abruptly recalled Bart's death at this very spot. Nausea
gripped her as she imagined the Whooptie plunging into the water
and Shar scratching at the window as the water rose higher and
higher inside the car.

But what could she do? The Saab wasn't driveable and it would
take ages to walk to get help. With Shar's hope and composure fading fast, Laney concluded that any help would have to come from
Shar herself.

"Shar, can you open the window?" she called. It was a moment
before Shar responded by looking downward. The window dropped
about two inches.

"Keep rolling it down, Shar," Laney called.

The window was about half way down when the Whooptie began
to creak and sway up and down.

"Stop, Shar! . . . God . . . stop whatever you're doing!" Laney
called. The tilting movement leveled off and ceased.

"Slowly now. No more movement than is necessary," Laney guided Shar.

The window dropped lower, inch by creeping inch until it disappeared into the door frame.

A motion out of the corner of her eye drew Laney's fixation away
from Shar. Over the trunk of the Whooptie, she saw the trunk of

the Saab suddenly open. Amanda raced to her left carrying a large can and laid it on the concrete about two feet from the edge of the bridge. She hadn't a clue that she had just rammed the Whooptie.

Rushing behind the trunk to the passenger door of the Saab, Amanda opened it and retrieved a small square item from the seat. The steam had ceased spewing from the radiator and the hissing had almost stopped.

"The tape!" Laney gasped.

"Who cares about the damn tape!" Shar retorted from the Whooptie's open window. "I've got to get out of here."

Amanda ran back and laid the tape on the bridge and unscrewed the lid of the can. She poured liquid over the tape and set the can down a few feet away.

"She's going to burn up the tape," Laney told Shar through the open window.

Just then, Laney heard a meow and her eyes shot to Shar who tensed in her seat. The Whooptie shuddered.

"Kudzu," Shar gasped, gently turning the rear view mirror so she could see behind her.

Laney saw Kudzu drop to the pavement in front of the open passenger's side door of the Saab and begin to creep toward the back of the Whooptie. The sound of metal grinding against pavement penetrated the night and the front end of the Whooptie dipped.

"Laney!" Shar screamed.

Shar held her breath as though any extra weight of air in her lungs would pitch the Whooptie into the creek.

"Laney . . . get . . . Kudzu," Shar gasped, letting her breath out in little puffs.

Willing to do anything to keep Shar calm, Laney ran around to the rear of the Whooptie but evidently Amanda had also heard Kudzu and beat Laney to the kitten. In one fluid motion, Amanda scooped up Kudzu and reached into her pant pocket at the same time. The moon illuminated a slender object. A syringe! Amanda lifted it to her mouth, pulled off the protective cap and spat it out.

"Don't take another step or the cat dies," Amanda sputtered, the fingers of her right hand poised over the plunger, her other hand clutching Kudzu in a vise grip.

Laney froze. My God, she *was* the one who broke into Gray's clinic and stole the euthanasia drug. Then she remembered. Unreasonable! She killed her!

"Please, don't . . . ," Laney began.

"No one is going to stop me from destroying the tape," Amanda wailed.

"No one will . . . I promise you," Laney said. "Let me hold the kitten, then you can do it."

"No! . . . stay away!" Amanda screamed.

The hand holding the deadly substance trembled and tears streaked Amanda's cheeks in the blue-white light of the full moon phase.

"Do it, Amanda. Didn't you hear the tape? It's evil. Destroy it," Laney said.

"I tried . . .the electric was off at the cabin." Suddenly realizing that Laney was only trying to distract her, Amanda turned and ran behind the Saab to the spot on the bridge where the tape lay.

Suddenly, the Nissan rocked violently. Fiery sparks flew from the undercarriage and the screech of metal mingled with Laney's own scream of horror as the Whooptie pitched forward.

31

The three of them sat in the wide front seat of the Buick staring straight ahead. Three men on a mission to find their women, Gray thought. It would almost be funny, if he weren't truly terrified that Laney had somehow gotten herself involved over her head again. Damn it, anyway. You'd think she would be extra cautious after her close encounter with death just a year ago. But just maybe Gordon had arrested Dory before Amanda got there with the tape—if indeed, that was where she was heading. And Shar and Laney probably decided to call it a night when they didn't find Amanda at home. When pigs fly, Gray thought grimly. He knew only too well just how persistent Laney could be. Gray's foot pressed down on the accelerator and the V8 two hundred fifty horsepower engine ate up the miles toward Hickory.

"Look out!" Malcolm yelled. Gray braked hard and swerved into the opposite lane to avoid hitting two cows wandering into the road. Puccini flipped off the dash onto Mal's knees and dug in with his claws. Mal grappled with the cat while Gray slowed and came to a stop on the shoulder.

"What the—" Gray began.

Chris turned his head and scrutinized the side of the road. "Looks like some of the Sands' cattle. Let's try to get them back through the fence where they got out."

Gray set his emergency blinkers and the three of them spilled out of the Buick. Chris herded the two Charolais onto the shoulder while Gray and Malcolm searched in opposite directions for the break in the wire fencing.

"Gray," Malcolm called. "I found the problem."

Gray hurried to where Malcolm stood in front of an open gate shooing several cows back from the opening.

"Rather irresponsible, wouldn't you say?" Mal said.

Gray joined Chris and herded the two cows back into the pasture and closed and latched the gate. He was about to snap the padlock when he hesitated.

"You know, Laney had Tina's key to this gate and the cabin. You don't think they may have come here, do you?" Gray said, not really asking—just talking to himself out loud.

"What the devil for?" Malcolm asked, scratching at his beard.

"I can't think of a reason either . . . unless . . . ," Chris said.

"What?" Gray said.

"I hate to think this of Amanda, but if she took the tape and player from Laney's, couldn't she have also taken the keys?" Chris said.

Gray's thoughts exactly, but he was glad that Chris had been the one to voice them. "Laney always keeps her keys in the bowl on the hall table. I saw them there just this morning. They were attached to a ring with a red tag clearly marked 'Sands' cabin.' "

"And if Amanda wanted to play the tape in private, what better place than the cabin practically next door," Chris said.

"I say we check it out," Malcolm said, grabbing hold of Gray's arm and pulling him toward the car.

"I'll open the gate and watch that the cattle don't get out," Chris said.

Gray and Malcolm climbed into the car and Gray started the engine. Before he turned the car around, he plugged in his cell phone and dialed Laney's number. The answering machine picked up. "Damn, still not home." He next tried Gordon's home phone. The sheriff answered on the second ring.

"Yeah?" Gordon said.

"What happened at Dory's?" Gray was blunt.

"Doc? . . . where in the hell have you been?"

"Long story, but at the moment Chris, Malcolm and I are on

Squire Road. Just got through herding some of Tina Sands' cattle off the highway. Someone left the gate open. We're going back on the farm to make sure everything is in order."

"I'll call the tenant and let them know you're on the farm," Gordon said. "Back to Dory Beale. Judge Nelson issued the search warrant and we found the typewriter, tablets, envelopes, Chris's chemistry building address—the works—in a neat little pile in Dory's library. She was very cooperative. She came in for questioning without a hassle. At first she said Derek had been the one blackmailing Chris, but when I said fingerprints found on the notes postmarked after Derek's death will tell the tale, she clammed up and wouldn't say anything else until she saw her lawyer."

"Damn, we were right! Did you find my drug?"

"Now that has me worried, Doc. Not a sign of it and Dory has a tight alibi for yesterday when Laney's mare was snuffed. Seems she met a friend in Lexington at ten-thirty, shopped, had lunch and took in a movie. Should be easy enough to check out. If it does, we're back to ground zero."

"We'd better get going. Chris is holding back a herd of Charolais at the gate. Thanks a lot, Gordon." Gray clicked off.

"We've got trouble," Gray said as he backed down the shoulder and turned into the opening to Sands' farm.

Chris swung his body into the Buick after closing the gate. "What took you two so long?" he asked.

"I called Gordon. He found the typewriter and all the other evidence he'll probably need to indict Dory. She blamed it on Derek, of course, but if her fingerprints are on any notes postmarked after Derek's death, that should do it." Gray banged the steering wheel with his palm. "If only Laney had grabbed the envelope when she rifled through your trash can the day of the funeral."

"No problem, Gray. Another note was waiting for me today when I met with the Dean. This time, I didn't open it."

"Splendid, Chris," Malcolm said.

Gray stopped the Buick after going through the second gate and Chris jumped out to close it.

"There is something you should know, Chris," Gray said when he hopped back into the car. "The police didn't find my drug."

"I . . . I think I know who might have it," Chris said, his voice barely audible. "Amanda."

Gray didn't speak, knowing how hard this was for Chris to admit.

Turning left, Gray began the winding ride down to the place where his brother had died twenty years before. "I don't know whether I can do this," he said as he felt the perspiration breaking out on his forehead. He hadn't been back here since that fateful Tongue Twisters' night in the cabin. Over and over in his dreams through the years, he had dived into the black water trying to save Bart. Not only had he borne the grief of losing his twin, he had kept the secret of what really happened here that night. Twenty years. He had kept the secret for twenty years. He rolled down his window and gulped the fresh air. Unable to go on, he slowed the car and came to a stop on the steep road.

Chris spoke, "I know what you're feeling, Gray. This is the first time I have been back, also." He reached behind Malcolm and laid his hand on Gray's shoulder. Gray felt the tears begin to flow from his eyes—silent, hot, and mitigating—and he was grateful that his friend was there with him and understood.

Suddenly, a ghastly cry rose from the darkness below and reverberated through the forest of evergreens. And because Gray was reliving his brother's death, for a moment he envisioned that Bart had cried out for help. Chris's gentle hand recoiled and Malcolm clutched at the dash. Gray opened the door and the dome light lit up their startled faces. A deep hiss came from Puccini on the dash and his fur bristled.

"We're only a hundred yards from the bridge. I say we go on foot," Gray said as he wound the window up, exited the car with the others and closed his door quietly.

They hurried along the road. No one spoke. The only sounds were their light footsteps and heavy respirations.

As they loped around the final curve in the road and escaped the darkness of the forest, the three of them drew up at the bridge at the same time. Gray's arm shot out and knocked the other two men backward.

"God help them!" he gasped.

32

The inhuman scream came from some unknown place deep inside Laney. And when her breath was spent, the sound still echoed over the water. With her fingers clutching at her eyes, she waited to hear the other sound—the concussion of the car as it impacted with the black water and began its sucking dive to the bottom of the creek.

It never came. Instead, it was still. Whipping her hands from her face, Laney opened her eyes and saw that the Whooptie was still there. But something was different. As though the center of gravity had shifted somehow, the car's rear wheels were resting on the concrete—and Shar was gone.

Laney knew immediately what had happened. Shar had overheard her conversation with Amanda behind the Whooptie, realized that Kudzu was in danger and had taken her chances. The car's violent rocking was caused by Shar going out the window and the screeching and grating had disguised her dive into the water.

"Shar," Laney gasped, running to the edge of the bridge. Her eyes scanned the water for some sign of her friend, but she could only see surface ripples fanned by a soft breeze.

Then something grasped at her foot. She leaped backwards. Like a ghastly apparition, a corpse-like hand with long nails clasped the edge of the bridge—and then a second hand. Laney dropped to her knees. "Shar . . . oh thank God . . . how . . . ?"

A wet face appeared and rested its dimpled chin on the back of the hands. Shar lifted a skinny forefinger to her lips.

"Shu-s-sh," she said, her teeth chattering. The water lapped at her shoulders.

"Let me help you," Laney began, grasping at Shar's hands.

"No . . . listen . . . I'm going to get Kudzu," Shar whispered, her teeth chattering.

"You can't. She'll kill him if you get near her."

"That's where you come in. You keep Amanda talking while I inch my way down the bridge to where she is."

"Yeah . . . sure . . . like she'll listen to me."

"You know how to do it . . . remember last year . . . I'm outta here." Shar dropped silently down into the water and began to tread alongside the bridge.

Laney could only comply. She walked around the rear of the Whooptie and saw Amanda walking to the open passenger door of the Saab. She held Kudzu under her right arm and the syringe in that hand. Amanda sat down in the passenger seat and with her left hand, rummaged inside the glove compartment of the Saab.

She must be looking for matches, Laney surmised. Standing a respectful distance away so as not to startle her, Laney said softly, "I have some matches in my car. I would gladly give them to you if I could."

Standing up, Amanda said, shortly, "I found some." She held the match book up to show Laney and backed away from her. "Don't get so close. I meant what I said. Nothing will stop me from destroying the tape!" She transferred the kitten to her other arm and brandished the syringe, taking a step towards Laney.

Laney retreated two steps. "I have no intention of stopping you. I will even help you, if you like."

"I don't need your help," Amanda said, her voice quivering.

Amanda kept backing along the side of the Saab. Laney followed her step by step until Amanda was at the trunk.

Amanda glanced to her left and stepped closer to the tape that Laney could now see lying near the edge of the bridge. Laney heard a sound behind her. Turning her head quickly while Amanda was focused on the tape lying in the moonlight, she thought she saw a man with a beard and glasses scoot behind the rear end of the Whooptie. Was that Malcolm? How did he get here? He must be with Gray. Thank God.

"Why did you do it, Amanda?" Laney asked bravely while her heart flailed inside her rib cage.

"Do it? . . . do what, Laney?"

"Kill Derek." Laney really didn't expect Amanda to answer.

Amanda drew in her breath. Her mouth opened and closed. The needle in her hand flashed silver in the blue-white light of the moon.

"He was blackmailing Christopher, while all the time pretending to be our friend. He would have gone to the police. He would have destroyed Christopher's dream."

Laney thought she heard an outcry from behind the Whooptie. Amanda didn't seem to have noticed. She continued backing toward the tape.

"How . . . how did you find out Chris was being blackmailed?" Laney asked.

"It was that night . . . the night we got home from the Blue Grass Stakes." Laney saw the anger in Amanda's face.

"You didn't know until then?"

It was though Amanda hadn't heard Laney. "I went to bed early. I awakened about eleven and Christopher hadn't been to bed. He hadn't been sleeping well for months and whenever I asked him what was wrong, he would only tell me that some of our investments had gone bad and that we would have to tighten up for awhile. Then, when he told me he had put the farm up for sale, I couldn't believe it." Amanda used the back of her wrist to wipe a tear away. She tossed her curls, frosted in the strange dawn-like light and swallowed.

"I knew he was keeping something from me but he wouldn't talk about it. That night I climbed out of bed and saw the light under the door to the den. It seemed the light was always on in the den at night." Amanda gazed at the tape and breathed a bottomless sigh. She wiped another tear. "But this time he left the door cracked and I peeked in. He had a drawer out on the floor and was putting envelopes in the opening. Later, after Christopher went to bed, I slipped back downstairs and read the blackmail notes . . . and I knew Derek was doing it."

Laney was astounded. "But how . . . how did you know?"

Amanda was sobbing now. "I'll tell you. Just let me do it first," she pleaded. Holding Kudzu under her arm, she placed the syringe in her teeth and without taking her eyes off Laney, she knelt and ripped a match from the book and struck it. She dropped it on the tape and with a swoosh, a giant flame shot into the night. Kudzu leaped in fright, her claws burrowing into Amanda's arm but she grasped the kitten ever tighter, removed the syringe from her mouth and held it in her right hand. Lowering her head, she placed her lips on Kudzu's head and cooed to calm it.

The flames got brighter and brighter and the Tongue Twister label curled and disappeared. Amanda smiled as the case began to melt around the edges and the acrid black smoke changed to pearly gray above the flames. She sat down on the concrete in front of the small fire and crossed her short legs, as though she didn't want to miss a second of the burning.

Since Laney had last seen her at the country club, Amanda's muscular body seemed to have shrunk a couple of sizes and her shapeless dirty sweats hung loosely. The light from the burning tape flickered over her tearstained swollen face and cast dark smudges under her eyes.

Laney stooped and sat across the fire from her. The plastic cartridge fed the fire like a long-burning candle and the eight track slowly turned into a bubbling liquid. But still it burned.

Laney knew that poor Chris's hard times were just beginning and wondered if Malcolm and Gray could hear what Amanda was saying. She didn't envy the person who had to tell him that his wife was the one who had murdered Derek.

"Go on, Amanda," Laney urged.

As the fire lapped at the shiny puddle, Amanda relaxed and continued, staring into the flames. "One morning, long before I ever knew about the blackmail, I was coming from the restroom at the Fayette Mall when, by accident, I saw Derek at one of the lockers removing a duffel bag. It was about ten-fifteen on a Monday morning in January. When I caught up to him, he said he was at the mall to buy a birthday gift for Dory. He even asked for my advice on what to purchase. He seemed a bit nervous as I remember, but he never mentioned the duffel. And I never gave it another thought either . . . until that night in the den when I read the blackmail notes, the night of the Blue Grass Stakes."

The fire was dying out and a breeze licked at what flame was left. Laney thought of Shar in the water all this time and worried that she would be ill. She glanced over at the edge and saw Shar's white hand grasping the bridge behind Amanda. Two shining eyes popped up.

"How did you make the connection?" Laney asked.

"The postmark on the first blackmail envelope was January thirteenth, meaning that Christopher probably had received it Tuesday, the fourteenth. The note said to leave the fifty-thousand on Monday, at ten o'clock in locker 20 at the Fayette Mall. That Monday was the twentieth, the day I was at the mall. I remembered because I had my annual check-up at Doctor Reese's at eight o'clock and I had decided to go to some of the white sales at the mall afterwards. I even checked it on my calendar later to make sure that my appointment was on the same day as I had seen Derek."

"Then what did you do?" Laney asked.

"All I could think of was that Derek had something on Christopher that he didn't want me to know and could cost him the chairmanship that he had waited so long for. The morning after the Blue Grass Stakes, I went to church like I always do and Mary Wakefield wasn't feeling well, so I offered to take her and the children home. When I stopped at her house, I saw Derek driving toward the back of the farm in his vet truck. After I fixed Mary a cup of hot tea and settled the children in front of the TV, I followed the road to the cliff. Derek already had his gear on and was getting ready to rappel. I confronted him right there and he laughed and told me there was nothing I could do about it. If I accused him, he would play the tape for the authorities. He grabbed the tape out of his shirt pocket and waved it at me. Then he shoved it back in his pocket and backed off the cliff. I lost control, Laney. I was so angry. I . . . I went crazy!" Amanda's eyes flashed and narrowed.

"The rope was anchored to a tree. I . . . I saw the dehorners lying in the bed of his truck and I cut it." Laney imagined those strong muscular hands snipping the rope like it was a piece of string. "I heard him cry out and saw him fall . . . and . . . and when he hit the ledge, I thought I saw something flip out of his pocket. There was a splash in the water. I was sure it was the tape, I threw the dehorners in the creek, thinking that any prints would be washed away." Amanda began to cry in relief with the thought, "Christopher was safe."

"But why did you break into Gray's clinic?"

"Thursday afternoon, the day after the funeral, I got a call from our insurance company that the loan against one of our policies that Christopher had applied for that morning would be ready Friday morning. I knew then that the blackmail continued and I thought that maybe the tape hadn't fallen into the creek after all . . . that maybe what I had seen was a fish jumping in the creek. Maybe Gray had found it the morning he discovered Derek's body and he was the one continuing it. I was beginning to believe that there was a conspiracy against Christopher."

Laney did a quick calculation. *That* insurance policy loan would be used to pay the blackmail asked for in the note she saw Chris receive at the university the day of Derek's funeral.

Amanda kept talking. "I broke in to look for the tape, but when I didn't find it, I remembered the drug he used to put animals down. I'd seen him lock it in his vet bed several times through the years when he had used it at Taylor Ridge Farm."

"You killed my horse, didn't you?"

"You know I did. I have the drug right here." She looked down at the syringe and the sleeping kitten. Streams of wetness poured down her cheeks. "I hated Gray. I wanted to pay Gray back for blackmailing Christopher. How else, than to make you think he killed your horse. So when I saw his keys . . ."

"But Gray didn't find any tape, Amanda. I was there with him when he discovered Derek's body. Later, the police fished an empty cassette out of the creek. The tape was probably carried away by a turtle . . . or who knows what? The police falsely claimed the tape was missing."

Amanda looked confused.

"Amanda . . . Gray didn't blackmail Chris. Derek did. And when Derek died, Dory took over the blackmail. She probably was involved in the scheme with her husband from the beginning."

"Dory? . . . my friend would do that?"

"Derek did it to his friend, Chris."

Amanda blinked and looked over at the smoldering glob of black on the pavement. "If the tape was ruined, what was that?" she said, pointing with the syringe.

Laney saw no need to tell her that the eight track had belonged to Peter Sands and had been hidden away all of these years. Since Amanda had never heard the tape or knew what was on it, Laney merely said, "It is destroyed, Amanda. No one can ever hear what might hurt Chris. It's all over now."

The words seemed to calm Amanda. Her shoulders dropped and her tight lips curled slightly.

At that moment and with hardly a sound, Shar swooped out of the water with one powerful surge of her sleek body and stood dripping on the bridge about six feet behind Amanda. Amanda's head jerked to her left.

"Amanda," a voice said softly from behind Laney. Amanda's head spun back with the sound of her name.

"Christopher," she said, slowly getting to her feet. Her arms dropped to her side and the kitten slipped to the surface of the bridge. The plunger of the syringe dangled from Amanda's slack fingers.

Shar covered the distance with two silent steps. Gently, she took the syringe from Amanda's limp hand. She didn't even know it was gone.

With a sob, Chris stepped forward and wrapped his arms around his wife.

33

"Would you look at this?" Shar squealed, twirling about the parlor while waving her left hand. As she spun, Kudzu's copper eyes stared wildly from a patch pocket in Shar's tunic. Shar fluttered her fingers in front of Laney's face. A gorgeous amethyst ring flashed on her third finger.

"That's beautiful, Shar," Laney said.

"Look at it, woman! . . . really look!" she demanded.

Gray grabbed her hand and saw the small thistle carved in the center of the stone. "Laney, you really should take another look," he said.

He passed Shar's hand over to Laney sitting next to him on the sofa.

"Shazam! Where in the world did you find it, Malcolm? Amethyst is Shar's birthstone."

Malcolm's face blushed red every place that wasn't covered with facial hair. "My little secret," he said, as he passed to the credenza and began to fix toddies.

"Is it wrong for me to be so happy just two days after that terrible night?" Shar asked.

"Of course not," Gray said. "You deserve a bit of happiness after that plunge into Stoney. Why you didn't develop hypothermia is beyond me. The water is still very cold the end of April." Gray jumped from the sofa to help Malcolm. "We all should be happy that this terrible ordeal is over, at least for the four of us. Malcolm, can't we convince you to stay another day or two?"

"I'm afraid not. I must leave in the morning, but I'll be back permanently next month," he said, handing Gray his bourbon and water and the Bloody for Laney. Shar swooped over and snatched her own Bloody from the bar. Malcolm, his arm around Shar, stood in front of the credenza sipping his Scotch and water. Gray couldn't help smiling at the two of them standing side by side. The top of Malcolm's head came just a hair above Shar's shoulder.

"You know," Malcolm said, "I can't help but feel guilty for purchasing Taylor Ridge."

"Enough of that," Gray said. "Talked with Chris this morning. The move is the last thing he is worrying about right now. He seems to be holding up pretty well, considering what he has to face with Amanda. But when he does think about giving up the farm, I think he'll realize that moving to Lexington will be a good change for him. He'll be near the university and the stress of farming will be behind him. And after he sells his herd and equipment and closes on the farm, he should be out of the red."

"Laney, since your derby week guests will begin to pile in tomorrow night, I've decided to fly to Florida with Mal in the morning for a few days before I have to be back at *Three Rivers*," Shar said.

"Aw, Shar," Laney sighed.

"Mal begged me, so I called Bernard this morning. When he heard my voice he said, 'I hear a giant sucking noise coming from Kentucky.' I believe he was afraid I might stay in the Bluegrass State like you did last year after spending your vacation here." I assured him I would be back on Monday.

"Stop by the clinic on the way to the airport to pick up a carrier for Kudzu," Gray said.

"Poor Nessie," Laney said, referring to Shar's dog back in Pittsburgh. The Westie had been boarded at a friend's while Shar was away.

"The rascal's getting spoiled. A little competition will do him good," said Shar.

Laney rose from the sofa and gave Shar a tearful embrace.

"I'm going to miss you . . . you wild, wicked woman," Laney said.

"Will you ever forgive me for your terrifying experience in the Whooptie?"

"It was worth it if it meant that piece of crap is finally scrap."

"Er . . . ah . . . I hate to tell you this, my fellow sleuth. Jay's Station called this morning and asked if I wanted to go to the expense of repairing it."

"You didn't . . . ," Shar began, her face darkening, her eyes daring Laney to affirm what she was thinking.

"You betcha."

After dinner, Shar, Malcolm, and Kudzu were off to the barn to see Thistle one last time. The night had turned cool, as Kentucky's weather often did in the spring and Gray had built a fire in the grate. Puccini curled up on the sofa. Gray settled in the green Morris chair, Laney sitting on the floor between his legs gazing into the fire. Her hair shimmered red and gold in the soft flickering light. He sprung a fiery curl and Laney turned and gazed back into his face with love. He stroked her freckled cheek, then ran his finger across her lips. She kissed it, and he felt his nose smart with a strong desire to cry.

"What are you thinking, Gray?" she asked, a tiny frown nudging her brows.

"How much I love you and how I worry about you."

"Just love me. The worrying is finally over."

"Yes. But what if Amanda had harmed you."

"You know, I don't think she would have unless I had prevented her from destroying the tape. Laney petted Blackberry, asleep with her head on her thigh. "What do you think will happen to her?"

"Marshall thinks there may be an emotional defense . . . like temporary insanity from extreme emotional disturbance."

"And if the court delivers that verdict, then what?"

"She'll be institutionalized and undergo psychological treatment."

"For a long time?"

"Maybe, it depends. But you should know, Laney, the state attorney is pushing for murder one. I only know one thing for sure. Chris will stand by her through it all, no matter what the outcome."

"I'm not going to press charges for Unreasonable's death."

"I'm glad."

"What about Dory?"

"Doesn't look very good for her. She could get up to five years and a stiff fine. According to Chris, her prints were found on several of the notes, even on two before Derek died. She had to have been in on it with Derek."

"Poor Walker, what will become of him if his mother goes to prison?"

"I imagine Dory's brother will take him in. I understand they've always been pretty close."

"What about the farm? Could Woody take care of it?" Laney asked.

"He has been since Derek died and I'm hoping he and Mary will settle their differences. Melinda and Terry don't need any more upsets in their lives."

Laney pulled her leg from under Blackberry's chin. She turned, hugged her knees, and stared up at him.

Gray was distracted by the cavorting yellow flashes in her brown irises. "God, what was Peter thinking of when he recorded that night at the cabin?"

"I think originally he just planned to record the Tongue Twisters' last night together. But when you all got back to the cabin after Bart drowned . . . I just don't know." She shook her head. "You know, Tina said he would lock himself in the cabin those last weeks and play something over and over. The girls thought it was a video. I think it was the tape and it drove him to suicide."

"That tape caused Derek's murder and me to be a suspect. And don't forget that the tape was the instrument that caused Derek and Dory to blackmail Chris."

"My break-in and ultimately, Unreasonable's death, too," Gray added.

"I wonder, since Derek and Dory were in the blackmail together, whether Derek ever played the tape for Dory."

"No way." Gray was emphatic. "Derek was a cynical man. He would never give Dory a sword to hold over his head. That he had the tape on his body when he went over that cliff tells me that he didn't let it out of his sight. He probably just made up some story about Chris's past and told Dory he had proof on the tape."

Laney reflected. "Five innocent boys forming a secret club called the Tongue Twisters. Could you ever have imagined that all this death, disloyalty, and hate could have resulted from such an innocuous rite of passage?"

"Not in a million years."

Laney's arms pressed her knees closer to her chest and Gray felt it coming. The question—the really big one. He had been waiting for it ever since she had heard the tape. He was ready for it. "All right, Laney. Go for it."

Her mouth twitched just a little—that he knew her so well. "What would have happened to you and Chris if the tape had been played to the police?" she asked, her eyes unusually bright.

He was surprised. It wasn't the big one. "I've asked myself that question a million times, Laney. I almost asked Marshall today when I saw him, but though anything said to your lawyer is confidential, I just didn't want anyone else to know what was on that tape."

"Well?"

"I spent a little time in the public library yesterday morning looking through the *Kentucky State Statutes*. The main thing I discovered was that there is no statute of limitations on a felony in this state. Chris, being the driver of the car and eighteen at the time Bart died, could have been charged with vehicular homicide, a Class D felony. I guess if it came out after all these years, he still could be charged with it. But let me tell you, he's already served his sentence as far as I'm concerned. And knowing Chris as I do, he will mentally serve any sentence Amanda gets."

"What about you, Gray?"

"It's not real clear. A lawyer would have to explain the law on this one. Maybe back then, if Derek, Pete, and I had gotten caught covering for Chris, we could have been charged with criminal conspiracy or facilitation. Being minors, the juvenile courts would have determined our fates. I really don't know if I could be charged today. And I'm sure as hell not going to try to find out."

"That leads me to one last question, Gray. That day we found

Derek's body . . . you discovered him first, remember? You sure were a long time coming back down the ledge after you found him." Her eyes danced, almost mischievously. "What if . . . ?" She took a breath before going on. "What if you *had* seen the tape lying on the ledge next to Derek's body with Tongue Twisters written on the label?" She bit her lip and rubbed her sore palms back and forward over her knees nervously. "Would you have? . . . or maybe even . . . did you perhaps? . . . toss that tape into the creek?"

Damn, it's the big one, Gray thought.